1
Kelly

Phuket, Thailand, December 2004

Settling on the poolside lounger, I opened my book and pretended to read. I knew there'd be four eyes on me so I'd have to make a good show of 'reading'. Later I will be questioned on the content, but I'm confident I'll be able to bore Carlos silly with minute details until he'll shout, 'Enough. Stop.'

Carlos, my possessive, controlling and violent so-called partner has no idea I've read this book. I'd read it piecemeal with care when he wasn't around in our apartment back in Melbourne. It looks 'new' and I replaced the book each time in exactly the same position on the 'to read' shelf of my bookcase.

For five and a half years I've been trapped in a relationship with Carlos. In the past twelve months I've made no attempt to escape – having almost resigned myself to this life sentence. But recently I've reached a breaking point. It can't go on. I have to work out an exit strategy. How did I get myself into this situation? It's a question I often ask myself but to figure that out I have to step back into the past.

In June 1989 I lived with my mother, father, two sisters and two brothers on a large rural property on the outskirts of Sydney. My father bred horses – it was in his blood, being an Irishman who grew up on a similar stud farm back in the old country. Until his father lost all their money to gambling debts, when, homeless and penniless, the family were re-housed by the council in a nearby city. My father escaped the bleakness of the council estate as soon as he turned twenty-one; emigrating from Ireland to Australia. He worked hard in the remote, outback mining area he was initially encouraged to settle in, saving enough to move back towards Sydney and put a down-payment on the property he bought after marrying my mother. The house I was born in.

In June 1989 I was having my first sleepover at my friend Kylie's house on a Friday night and all week I had been looking forward to this big event.

After dinner, Kylie and I pigged out on chocolates, ice cream and soft drinks while watching a couple of films. We talked and giggled into the early hours of the morning.

Late Saturday morning, after a sleep-in and a relaxing breakfast, Kylie's father drove me home. It was Saturday 24th June at 11.45am when we approached our house to discover fire engines and police cars parked outside. The date, day and time are forever seared into my memory. I'd checked Kylie's watch a moment before, worrying whether I'd be in trouble for being a bit later than I'd said I'd be.

'What's going on? Where's our house gone?' I shouted before opening the door and running towards the front gate. A policeman grabbed me, sweeping me off my feet before I could open it, saying, 'Whoa there girlie, where do you think you're going?'

I looked across to where the house had once stood and saw that it was a heap of smouldering ruins.

'NO!' I screamed, attempting to wriggle from his grasp. He held me in a firm grip though and I couldn't free myself. 'Mum! Dad!' I called out. 'Where's my family? Where are they? Are they alright? What happened?' I screeched at the policeman.

'And what's your name little girl?' he asked. I wanted to kick him and leap over the gate, desperate to find my parents. I didn't like him calling me 'little girl'.

'My name's Kelly … Kelly O'Brien and that's … my house,' I said almost choking on tears and pointing to the charred remains. He looked at me without speaking. Why wouldn't he tell me anything? Were they all in hospital suffering from burns? I had to know.

'Where are my family? What happened?' I screamed at him. Another policeman rushed over and pulled me away.

The one who had called me 'little girl' paled and turned to Mr. Mason, Kylie's father, who had followed me out of the car. He took Mr. Mason to have a quiet word with another man who was standing around with some firemen a few metres away. They'd all turned and stared at me when I started screeching. As I was held back by the other policeman, I watched, silent tears running down my face as Mr. Mason kept nodding or shaking his head. The man wrote down something that Mr. Mason told him then they shook hands. Mr. Mason walked back over to us saying, 'Come on girls we're going back to our house.'

Kylie, who I'd completely forgotten about, was standing behind me sobbing.

Mr. Mason said that apart from the house catching fire, he didn't know all the details of what had happened, but I knew he wasn't telling me the truth. He couldn't look me in the eye when he said it. I knew something bad had happened but it was even worse than I'd imagined.

Two women from the Department of Community Services (DoCS) turned up at Kylie's house. I fired a bunch of questions at them until they finally told me my whole family had died in the fire.

That shocked me into silence. They were all dead. Gone. How was that possible? I couldn't speak. I couldn't breathe.

They told me the fire started in the middle of the house. My brothers! They must have caused it were my first thoughts. I wanted to yell at them about it – but of course they weren't there to defend themselves. And maybe it wasn't them.

'The living room is in the middle of the house,' I said instead. 'Is that where the fire started? I don't understand. There's always a safety guard rail around the fire. In the winter months my parents bank it up when they go to bed so that it will still be going in the morning, but never with roaring flames. So, how could a fire have started?'

'We don't know. The fire service is still investigating,' one of the women answered.

'If I had been there I could've saved them all,' I said.

'You don't know that Kelly. There is no point in thinking like that,' the woman who blurted out the news said. 'If you had been there, you would've died as well.'

'No. I wouldn't've and I *do* know that. All my family, apart from me, are heavy sleepers. I also have a strong sense of smell. My father always says I have the nose of a bloodhound. I *would've* smelled the fire. I *would've* woken when the flames started to spread. I *could* have saved them all. I *should* have been there.'

Mrs. Mason, who was sitting beside me on the couch, then took me in her arms murmuring softly in my ear. I had no idea what she was saying as it was at that point something inside me snapped. I broke down, wailing and crying.

At the age of nine and three-quarter years old, I was now all alone.

The last time I saw my family was when I'd climbed into Kylie's father's car and turned to wave at them. My mother, father and two little sisters, aged five and three, were all standing on the front veranda frantically waving back. As though they knew it was the last time they'd see me. My older brothers had been playing French cricket on the lawn beside the house and didn't even notice me leaving.

All the time I was enjoying myself with Kylie, my

family had been dying. I couldn't understand why I hadn't known. Hadn't felt the agony of their last breaths. I've tortured myself imagining it many times since.

DoCS left me with Kylie's family until the Monday morning. The rest of Saturday and Sunday passed in a total blur. When DoCS collected me, I was placed in 'out of home care', miles from anyone or anything I had known.

I later learned from DoCS that the bank re-possessed our property. They advanced money from the 'estate' to pay for the cremation of my family and have plaques placed for them in the crematorium gardens about 20 minutes from our old home. I wasn't allowed to attend, and I've never been to see them. Maybe one day I hope to have the opportunity to do so.

The bank sold the land, all the livestock and supposedly found new homes for the rabbit, cats and dogs. Leaving me nothing but the clothes I had taken with me to Kylie's. I clung to those remnants from my old home long after they had become merely rags. Until a woman with a vicious mind discovered them hidden in my bedroom some years later and burnt them.

When I looked back on events as an adult, I realised that the bank's actions were suspect. Okay they paid for the cremations, but I'm sure some dodgy dealings occurred there. My parents had owned the stud farm for thirteen years. Not all years were successful. But a few weeks before the fire I'd overheard my father saying, 'just seven years to go and we will be debt free me darlin'.' At the time, I'd been in the kitchen, gathering cutlery to set the table for our evening meal and my father had his arms wrapped around my mother as he said it. They both seemed happy with my father's declaration. Surely that meant that my parents owned more in assets than the money they owed the bank? Since buying the farm my parents had built further stabling and the house, originally only a two bedroom, had an extra bedroom built at the back for the boys when my younger sister Megan was born.

Danny, Kane and I slipped into the world thirteen months apart. We'd been sharing one bedroom that we'd long outgrown. I was the youngest of us three and was so pleased when they moved to their own room. It meant I was rid of their wild hooligan ways. Our bedroom resembled a battleground more than a tranquil space for rest and I certainly didn't miss their smelly feet. Feet that were always dirty from running around outside without shoes. Mum would become so exasperated with them when, after bathing and going to bed, they would often sneak back outdoors. They'd slip into bed later, leaving tell-tale muddy marks or grit on the otherwise pristine white sheets. I'd give anything to smell their dirty feet again and would never complain (okay I might, but only in good humour).

Looking back on it now I wondered what had happened to the proceeds from the sale of the property, livestock and goods? With the house gone, the property would have dropped in value, but there were still lots of stables and other outbuildings that hadn't been damaged in the fire. We had a substantial amount of land and then there was the livestock. Who had received the money? And what about insurance? I'm sure my parents would have had the place insured – I'd heard them mention insurance a few times. Was a claim ever made, and if so, by whom? Had someone at the bank sold it grossly under value for a generous backhander? It was not something I'd thought about as a child but when I'd discussed it with Franco (one of the nicer bodyguards I have) a few years back he agreed that something was not quite right. He said there should have been a lawyer involved. If I ever have the opportunity I will follow it up one day. Not that I can see that happening anytime soon.

I had to stop 'reading' at this point. Recalling my family's deaths brought tears to my eyes. I fished my sunglasses out of my basket and pulled my hat down over my face as though I was going to nap. A short time later Benny, my bodyguard, disturbed my grief telling me Carlos wanted me back upstairs.

2
Kelly

Day 2 of 'pretend reading'

The following morning, I repeated the previous day's pattern and settled down to my 'reading' near the pool – one of the few places where I have peace and quiet to think.

The foster parents DoCS initially placed me with after collecting me from the Mason house, were nice enough. But their children – their *real* children, as they reminded me several times a day, were not. They whispered unpleasant jibes at me as soon as their parents were out of earshot. They kept asking me where I'd come from. With my long black hair, large brown eyes and quite olive skin they wanted to know if I was from India. Each time they asked me this question they, used sneering tones.

I am descended from quite a complex assortment of different backgrounds. My father was pure Irish, with pale skin, pitch black hair and startling blue eyes. My mother had deep olive skin, black hair and brown eyes. She told me that *her* grandmother was a dark-skinned Indian beauty from Malaya who'd married a Chinese Malayan man. My grandmother was their daughter and she'd married the son of an Englishman and a Chinese woman. Again, from a family who lived in Malaya. My mother and her two elder sisters were born in Malaya. My grandfather, the Chinese/Englishman was a mining engineer. He moved his family to Australia to live in the same outback mining town where my father had settled. My mother had gone to school there and by the time her father died, she was a recent bride, married to my father. From my mother's side of the family I'd inherited predominantly Chinese looking features, but had large brown eyes and darker skin which is why I think those kids thought I was Indian.

After my grandfather's death, my grandmother and her other two daughters decided to return to Malaysia. I knew my grandmother had remarried and that my aunts also had families, but I had no idea of their names or where they lived. All that information was lost in the fire. The authorities made no effort to trace my Malaysian relatives. They also made no effort to find my father's family in Ireland. I was so distressed at the time, it was a relief not to have to go off to a foreign country to live with complete strangers. But with what followed in my life, it might well have been the better option.

I hadn't lasted long with that first couple; with the fights their children and I became embroiled in. They said I was 'an uncontrollable bad influence'. I moved from one foster placement to another until a 'nice' couple, Mr. & Mrs. Hill, wanted to adopt me when I was 12. I had no say in the matter. DoCS said my angry outbursts in foster care meant that no-one else wanted me. What did they expect? That I would be a quiet little angel? That I would put up with the repeated bullying I'd experienced? Accept the hideous hand-me-down clothes I was made to wear in some placements? That I would compliantly eat the disgusting food one placement served? Never one to be quiet in those days, I spoke out. My family hadn't been wealthy, but my mother served nutritious tasty meals and clothed us with care. The foster families called me an 'ungrateful brat'.

With hindsight, I now know that I was a young girl full of rage with the world. Some days I was angry with my family for dying and leaving me all alone to live with strangers. I was angry with my brothers, who I suspected were to blame for the fire. I imagined them out of bed late that night on one of their nocturnal escapades, causing the fire guard to dislodge without them noticing. Mum was always telling them off for charging about the house knocking into things. Other days my conscience would get the better of me and I'd apologise to them all, talking to the one photograph I had of us. Blaming them was pointless because I didn't know what had caused the fire. The authorities, no doubt, considered me too young to furnish me with any details.

The 'nice' Hills turned my life into a living hell. She was sullen and distant and had no idea how to take care of, or show any affection to, a child. It was the husband who wanted me – in more ways than one. During the months of the adoption process, he was on his best behaviour. On completion, once I became 'theirs', the true agenda emerged. He visited my room with regularity, forcing himself on me. I lay in dreaded fear of him coming to me on the nights when he'd been drinking at his club. If I was lucky, he might be so tanked up with alcohol that he'd be unable to perform. Instead, he'd collapse in a drunken snoring heap on my bed, while I curled up on the chair in the corner of the room. I fought him as best I could and I sought Mrs. Hill's help but soon learned there would be no aid from that quarter. She became vindictive towards me. She was the woman who burnt the surviving rags of the clothes I'd been wearing back in 1989. I suspect that she wasn't really keen on his fumbling gropes either and was happy to be free of them. He was a particularly revolting man.

I finally told a teacher at the school what Hill was doing to me and asked her to call DoCS but she passed my revelations on to the Head who called my 'parents' into the school. I realised when the Hills came up to meet the Head, that they knew each other. Sitting outside his office I watched as the Head greeted them by their first names and shook hands. Snippets of their conversation drifted out to me through the closed door. I heard *"overactive imagination"*, *"very difficult"*, *"dreadful liar"* and *"you know what these kids in care are like,"* before the door opened and I was called into the Head's office.

'This statement you made to your teacher is just more of your lies, isn't it Kelly? Hmm?' the Head said.

I'd been in trouble before for not completing homework assignments the school had given me. Homework that necessitated handing in separate sheets, of either written work or artwork. Mrs. Hill refused to supply me with the necessary paper or equipment and my feeble excuse each time was, 'I had no paper to do the work on.' Of course, when the school contacted Mrs. Hill about this she'd told them I was a "dreadful liar". A phrase she repeated often about me.

In the Head's office that day, confronted by both the Hills and the Head, I knew there was no point in continuing with the truth. I sighed and said, 'Yes sir,' to his challenge.

We lived in a 'nice' middle-class northern Sydney suburb where things like that didn't happen of course. Only in a young girl's imagination. No one called DoCS and both the school and the Hills punished me. I gave up all hope of the school helping me, retreated into silence and bided my time – waiting for the right opportunity.

After enduring almost three years of his disgusting visits I'd reached a breaking point. I had to get away. I lay awake at night working out what to do – I just had to wait for the right opportunity when Mr. Hill was cashed up and fell into one of his drunken sleeps. It didn't take long and on that final evening, I edged my way out of the bed and showered quickly, dressing ready to leave. When I returned to my room he was still out for the count. I grabbed my metal lamp stand and whacked him hard over the head with it. Much as I wanted to kill him, self-preservation prevented me from going too far. He stirred momentarily when I hit him, and then lapsed into unconsciousness. I could see his chest rising and falling. Perfect. I searched his jacket, slung carelessly over a chair in my room, and retrieved his wallet. I knew it held a generous amount of cash as earlier he'd been boasting about his poker machine wins. All the cash went into a small bag I packed and downstairs I collected the copy of my birth certificate from the bureau in the lounge. DoCS had given the Hills my birth certificate so that they could change my name. Three years down the line I was pleased they still hadn't done it. I walked out of the house without a second thought.

I've no idea what happened to him or his wife, how he explained his injuries, or how they accounted for my absence. It was 10.15pm when I left the house and made my way to Central Station with no particular plan. I discovered I could catch an overnight train to Melbourne, so that was where I headed. I left Sydney without a backward glance to begin my career as a consummate liar, which I have to say, I accomplished with remarkable ease. No one believed me when I told the truth so why not lie? After a few nights in a guest house, I rented a room in a house share, lying of course about my age – saying I was eighteen. I lied my way into various jobs, waitressing or working in kitchens, for cash. When I actually turned eighteen, almost three years later, I applied for a tax number using my real name and the birth certificate which I'd brought with me. I half expected the police to turn up at my digs that night and arrest me, but none came.

Now I was legal I could find a decent paying job and a better place to live. The house I had been in for almost three years was shabby and occupied by a succession of drifting hippy types. I didn't mind Janna, a woman in her forties who owned the place, but some of the men who came to stay there were always stoned and thought I might be available for some free love. I wasn't. Once they got the message they left me alone. I wanted to move to an all-female house where I could sleep in peace at night, without worrying about some strange man entering my room seeking sex.

A range of night workers occupied my new, large house share. There was one strict house rule: men were not allowed in the house. Which suited me perfectly. We were a strange, mixed bunch, but I found the other women fascinating. I often watched Karen, who was a pole dancer, practise on a pole she'd installed in her spacious bedroom and wondered if I could do it. Karen seemed to earn *huge* amounts of money. I'd seen her take rolls of notes out of a drawer some weeks. She was able to save a hefty wedge of her earnings each month. She told me she was saving to start a business and for a deposit to buy her own house so that she could have her son living with her. He was in a country town with her parents for the time being. She sent money back home to cover the cost of his keep each month, and she visited as often as possible.

'Will you teach me how to pole dance, Karen?' I asked her one day, attracted by the idea of earning so much money. Waitressing was all very well, but I was never going to be able to save much money doing that. Like Karen, I liked the idea of having my own business one day. I'd even thought about enrolling in a college, studying for qualifications I'd never taken at school.

'You're a bit young Kelly. It's not an easy job. You have to put up with lots of unpleasant men leering at you.'

'I'm twenty-one,' I lied. 'And you seem to manage without any trouble from the customers.'

I would be 19 on my next birthday, but I'd told my housemates I was 21 when I applied for the room.

'That's because the boys at the club watch out for me. I share some of my earnings with them.'

'I could do that too.'

I nagged her about it at every opportunity. Eventually, she agreed and I spent the next six months practising under her guidance. I took to it like a duck to water once I learned how to gyrate and perform with more sensuality. That was the part I hated but if it meant I could move on to a better life, I decided it was worth sacrificing a little dignity. It was only acting after all. I'd always been good at gymnastics at school and the pole dancing seemed like a variation on that.

When one of the dancers at the club handed in her notice, Karen lent me one of her older outfits and arranged an audition for me.

The Club owner, Carlos Mosta, hired me on the spot. Under his penetrating gaze, I felt a little self-conscious. Determined to get the job however, I looked him in the eye and lied without compunction. Like Karen, I told him I wouldn't do lap dances. He gave me the stage name 'Lyla' and my dancing career commenced the following night.

The environment of the club with its leering men was quite distasteful but I was soon raking in the money and learned to shed my disquiet about everything. A year or two of doing this and I would have enough saved for my future. What I was going to do I wasn't sure. The trouble was I had no qualifications and, apart from the club, the only work I'd done was in cafes or restaurants. I thought I'd have plenty of time to consider my future but I hadn't bargained on Carlos. A few months into my work at the club, he regularly asked me to remain for drinks after closing time. At first, I resisted with politeness, citing tiredness and the need to share a taxi home with Honey. Honey was Karen's name at the club and I always had to call her by that name when we were there.

With a twelve-year age gap, I considered Carlos far too old for me. He was a very attractive man though and eventually he persuaded me to join him on a regular basis for drinks. One night after consuming a large quantity of alcohol – which I wasn't used to – I ended up back at his place. I wasn't aware of what his apartment was like on that first night, we were so engrossed with each other.

Carlos was the first man I'd ever been with by choice. I realised afterwards it was my only experience of someone being *with* me, rather than using me. In my naivety, I thought it was what people referred to as 'making love'. We 'made love' twice before crashing out, and once again in the morning.

While I showered he prepared breakfast and it was

only after coming out of the bathroom that I noticed how luxurious the bedroom was. I'd found the bathroom impressive, but this was something else. I moved around touching things and opening wardrobe doors. The whole room oozed money and I was keen to see the rest of the accommodation. Following the enticing smell of freshly ground coffee, I walked out into the open plan living-room and kitchen/diner, stopping in wonder. The apartment was the penthouse suite in a luxurious block. There were fantastic views across the city of Melbourne, of the Yarra River and out to Port Phillip Bay. There was also a large terrace where Carlos was setting out our breakfast.

'Madam's breakfast is served,' he said, putting on a posh English accent.

I moved out to the terrace and sat at his invitation. 'This is an amazing place,' I said looking around in wonder. 'It must cost a fortune to rent.'

'I own it,' he said, his chest sticking out proudly.

'Wow!' was all I could say in response.

'So, you like it?' he asked, with an eagerness to please apparent on his face.

'I looove it.'

'Do you think you could live here?' He moved closer to me with a serious expression on his face. I thought he was messing about at first.

'Live here? Me? With you?'

'Yes, of course with me, you silly girl,' he said taking me in his arms.

'But you hardly know me, Carlos.' I was feeling both excited and nervous at this point. He *was* serious.

'I've watched you closely over the past few months. We've spent time together and last night confirmed to me that you are the girl I want to be with.'

I should have picked up on his use of the word 'closely', and 'girl', but at the time it passed me by.

'I'm very flattered, but I imagine someone like you could have your pick of women,' I said, freeing myself from his embrace and moving back. I needed to see his face.

'I've had my pick of women. Lived with one or two over the years. They weren't for me. It's you I want, Miss Kelly O'Brien.'

I was seduced. Seduced by his charm, the sincerity in his eyes and of course, the luxurious apartment. I felt like a pauper girl receiving a proposal from a handsome prince. Excited, I said yes without really thinking it through or discussing it with anyone. I doubt it would have made a great deal of difference if I had. I was still so young, naïve and impressionable, despite fending for myself since I was 15.

Disappointed with my decision, Karen warned me that Carlos would make me stop dancing. I dismissed her warning with the arrogance of the young, thinking I could have my cake and eat it. Live in a luxurious apartment with a gorgeous man and still earn loads of money that I could salt away for my future. I even thought that my long-term future might *be* with Carlos. How young, ignorant and foolish I was!

I moved into the penthouse five days later. The next morning, over breakfast, Carlos announced I would no longer be dancing at the club.

'But I need to earn my own money,' I protested.

'What do you need your own money for when you'll be living with *me*?' he'd replied. 'I have all the money we'll need. Besides I don't want all those other men looking at your beautiful body.'

'I could go back to waitressing,' I suggested.

'No, I won't have you doing such a menial job. There's no need when I have loads of money.'

I noticed that he'd said *he* had money. Did that mean I wouldn't have any money? That I would have no independence? I'd saved quite a bit of money that was in a separate savings account. On instinct, I'd not mentioned the savings account to Carlos – in case things didn't work out. Before the new regime in my life kicked in, I'd returned to my shared digs and asked Karen to look after some of my things. My savings book, plus a few other precious things. I was worried that they might disappear if they went with me to Carlos's place. I'm not sure why. I had this vision of Carlos laughing at me about hanging on to things. He had no photos of his family anywhere in the apartment and he didn't seem interested in sentimental family nonsense.

I had one family photo of the seven of us. A few months before the fire, a customer purchasing a horse had snapped several shots of us all. Mum had given me one of the prints which I kept in my locker at school. DoCS had collected it for me and brought it across to my foster home. It was the only visual proof I had of my family's existence. I gave the picture to Karen for safekeeping as well as some silly cheap bangles my mother had bought for me. I'd been wearing them the night my family died. Karen gave me her parent's address in Shepparton, a country town, in case she moved back there as planned – and her brand new mobile phone number. I memorised both then destroyed the piece of paper which held the details. I was already hesitating about moving in with Carlos at this point and wanted to ensure I had a back-up plan if needed. Before becoming involved with Carlos, I had visited the house in Shepparton a couple of times with Karen. I was sure I'd remember how to find it again.

The first week with Carlos was like a honeymoon period – he never left my side. The following week when he announced he had to start going back into work, he wouldn't let me go with him. I waited until he'd set off one night, then dressed. I planned to turn up and surprise him. I opened the penthouse door to find a man there.

'Where do you think you're going?' he asked.

'I'm going to the club to join Carlos.'

'Sorry,' he said. 'My orders are that you are not to go anywhere.' He made me turn around and go back.

I was flabbergasted. He had a *guard* outside the door to make sure I didn't go anywhere. I should have paid more attention to the nagging doubts in my head. I realised in that moment that moving in with Carlos was a terrible mistake. But it was too late.

Almost six years later I'm still with Carlos. The first punch he inflicted on me was after what he considered was an *escape* attempt in that first year. It came as a shock. On that occasion I had only intended to run around a park. When he confronted me after my 'bodyguard' reported me, I said, 'I only wanted to take my shoes off and run barefoot in the park Carlos.'

'You were trying to escape,' he hissed.

'No, I wanted to be in the *fresh air*, not cooped up in air-conditioned buildings. I *love* feeling fresh grass under my feet.'

He shook his head as though he didn't believe me. 'There'll be no more park walks, unless one of my boys and I are with you – and no running – if you want to exercise you do it here in the penthouse or down at the pool.'

When I refused to say 'sorry' I received another punch.

Since then I have actually attempted to escape several times, but Carlos or my guards are always one step ahead of me. I paid a heavy price for those attempts. Carlos is a dangerous, violent man. If only I'd seen through his façade before becoming involved with him.

I live a life of luxury, but one where I am a virtual prisoner. I can go shopping, but always with a man in tow. I can 'lunch' with some of the wealthy women I have become acquainted with through Carlos and his friends, but always with a watchful eye on me. I have no real friends. *He* doesn't permit it. I live in his controlling, superficial world. His obsession with me is suffocating. In the early days, I'd wanted us to have a family. He wouldn't agree to it, insisting I had a coil fitted to ensure there'd be no unwanted pregnancies. He admitted he was too selfish to share our lives with children. It was the only sensible decision he made.

3
Kelly

Day three of 'pretend reading'

Phuket was my idea. Some of my acquaintances had mentioned it a few times. I'd looked it up on the net and showed Carlos one evening. He has to know about everything I do and he checks the internet history thoroughly. I thought a change of environment might be helpful. For both of us. We'd been to Queensland a few times and he was always more relaxed up there. He'd been so tense lately and I'd suffered as a result of it. To my surprise, Carlos agreed to a holiday in Phuket. He organised passports for us both (knowing my real age long before this) and announced we would be spending Christmas over there. He hated spending Christmas with his family. We'd visited them together *once* in all the years I've lived with him. Each year *he* pops in to see them but leaves me at home – under guard. I wondered if it was because he didn't want me to form any close bonds with any of his family members. The one time we were there together, his sisters had gone on about us marrying. Marriage was something that Carlos wouldn't consider the few times we'd discussed it back then.

'I've watched my brothers' marriages end in divorce and seen those mealy-mouthed ex-wives take them for a fortune. No bitch is getting their hands on my fortune,' he'd declared.

Not that I had the remotest interest in marrying him now. I didn't want to be with him at all. He'd made me sign an agreement that, if we parted – because *he* chose to, I'd have no claim on *his* fortune. I'm not sure whether that would have stood up in court. I'd managed to prise information from some of the women I often met for lunch. They were always happy to talk about their circumstances. It turned out de-facto wives were entitled to a share of their husband's estate in the same way as a true wife. It would have been handy to acquire some of his wealth if we parted. Providing me with an opportunity to start 'another life'. But I thought that it would be a foolish woman who would consider taking legal action against a man like Carlos.

I discovered that he not only owned the apartment that we lived in but co-owned the whole block with his two brothers. The whole family ran a large property empire. Carlos's club was just a lucrative sideline for him.

Unless I come up with something creative while we're here in Phuket, my chances of escaping Carlos are almost zero. We're spending two weeks here; flying back to Australia on 28th December. Carlos wants to be back in Melbourne for New Year's Eve, always a big night at the club.

Carlos isn't keen on swimming but he allows me to swim most mornings down at the hotel's pool under the watchful eye of one of his men. He also watches me from the balcony of our suite which overlooks the pool.

Once I've had my swim, I can sit on one of the sun-loungers, reading or chatting with other people. The only condition imposed is that I have to throw a dress, or top and shorts over my bikini to cover my breasts and bare stomach – and wear my floppy hat. It always surprised me that he agreed to let me wear a bikini for swimming.

I'd not long embarked on my morning 'reading' that day when a stranger's voice interrupted my thoughts.

'Do you mind if we sit here?' a woman with Eurasian features asked me.

'No, not at all,' I said. I recognised the woman who I'd passed on my way out of the ladies toilets near the entrance earlier. We'd exchanged smiles.

'I'm Lucy,' she said plonking herself on a sun lounger. 'This is my husband Tom.'

Tom nodded at me and smiled.

'Hello. I'm Kelly,' I said smiling back at both of them. It would make a pleasant change to have someone new to speak with. As long as I wasn't ordered back upstairs.

'You sound like an Aussie as well, are you?' Lucy asked me. I nodded.

'We flew in from Melbourne yesterday.' She spoke with the accent of the well-educated middle classes. Like my old school friends in Sydney when I lived with the Hills.

'Tom just sprung this holiday on me the day before we flew out. I'm so glad he did. Isn't Phuket beautiful? Have you seen much of it?'

'A little,' I said with caution. I wasn't about to reveal too much to this stranger. They might know Carlos. Although they didn't seem his type.

'Tom thought this holiday might help both of us. I suspect he was thinking more of me. I've not been very well for the past six months.'

She did look rather pale and I wondered what had been wrong with her. It wasn't long before I found out.

4
Lucy

Melbourne, Australia, December 2004

Tom returned home early from work today. Without speaking to me, he walked straight through into the bedroom area and a few minutes later re-emerged and disappeared with Clara. I suspected he was angry with me, fed up with the state of the place and my inability to cope. I assumed he was taking Clara out somewhere and felt a mixture of guilt and relief.

I'd had one of my panic attacks again today. I hadn't managed to do anything much so Clara had, once again, been neglected. It started when I approached the closed bedroom door. I struggle to go in there knowing there is no trace of Christopher. I'd kept some of Christopher's unwashed baby clothes and all his cuddly toys but when I spent hours in the room smelling them, Tom became angry. He removed all Christopher's things and gave them to a charity shop, saying we had lots of photographs to remember him by. I didn't speak to Tom for days while he redecorated the bedroom. The previous occupants of our flat had had a little boy and Tom insisted the boyish décor had to go.

This morning when I came out of the bathroom and turned to the closed door I started shaking violently. I retreated into the lounge, collapsing into a snivelling heap on the couch. A few pills later I was much calmer, but incapable of doing anything and dozed on and off for much of the day. Clara had periodically deposited small items on me while I was lying on the couch, in an attempt to gain my attention. But about all I could manage was, 'thank you, Clara.'

When Tom phoned at lunchtime and heard my slurred speech I could tell he was annoyed with me. I'd been better this afternoon and had been about to feed Clara when Tom arrived back home – earlier than expected.

I was in the process of tidying the lounge when Tom returned alone. Instead of the lecture I was expecting about neglecting Clara, he announced that we were going away to a place called Phuket. I'd never heard of it, but he told me it was a resort island in Thailand. He said he was in desperate need of a holiday.

'What about—,' I began to protest but he cut me off.

'It's all taken care of. We're leaving early in the morning so go and pack a bag. You will only need summer clothes, but throw in a couple of lightweight tops, just in case.'

The idea was appealing, but then guilty thoughts intruded. I sagged back onto the couch in despair. 'Tom, I don't think I can get on a plane and journey off to another country. What about Clara?'

'I've organised for Clara to stay with Laurie and Kim and left money with them. They will look after her.'

Better than you I knew he was thinking when he paused to look at me.

'I've already left her with them,' Tom insisted. 'Moving here was supposed to help you. You've spent *months* moping around our old house and then this place, grieving. Well, I've been grieving too. And I go to work each day. What's more, every night I return home and have *this mess* to deal with,' he said. He waved his arms around the chaos in our living room as though it spoke volumes. It did.

'I'm in desperate need of a break Lucy and it would do you the world of good to have a break as well. Things can't go on as they have been.'

'I know. I'm sorry,' I sobbed. 'But I can't help feeling riddled with guilt over Christopher's death.'

'The doctor's told you that it was nothing *you* did. The police have looked at it as well. We're not to blame. Sudden Infant Death is one of those things that happen on rare occasions to babies. His death has been examined with a fine-tooth comb. We are completely in the clear. So, it is about time you accepted that you weren't to blame and moved on. We have—'

'I *know*! Don't tell me what my responsibilities are,' I said standing and shouting at Tom. 'I just haven't been capable of dealing with anything. The tablets have helped in some respects but made things worse in other ways. I don't like taking them. They leave me feeling totally zonked out and incapable of doing *anything*.'

'I've noticed. Come on Lucy, it'll do us both the world of good. Just the two of us. And you could see if you could manage without the tablets. I don't think it's healthy for you to be taking anti-depressants every day.'

I knew I had to do something. Tom was clutching at straws, looking for ways to haul me back into the real world. I owed it to him and Clara to make an effort. A minute later, I said, 'Okay Tom, I will. I'd love to ditch the pills. So where is this place? Show me.'

Later that night I began to look forward to our trip to Phuket. We hadn't been abroad since our honeymoon to Bali almost three years ago now. I was pregnant the following year. The idea of a luxury hotel, where I wouldn't have to do anything, sounded wonderful. There would be nothing of Christopher there. No matter where we moved to in Melbourne, Christopher would be present. I didn't want to forget him – but I knew I needed to pick myself up for Tom and Clara's sake.

Christopher had died in our previous house and, after a few months, I could no longer bear being there. So we'd packed up and moved into our current rental. We hadn't owned the previous house so it was an easy move. We'd bought a large bush property where we planned to build our own house, but after Christopher died we put all our plans on hold.

Laurie, who Tom works with, mentioned that a vacancy was coming up in his block of flats. So, Tom and Laurie made all the arrangements and the ground floor flat became ours. For now. Until we're ready to face the house build.

My mental state didn't improve after moving into the flat as Tom had hoped. If anything, I seemed to sink into a deeper depression.

Kim, Laurie's wife, had been very good at helping out, but I'd rejected her overtures of friendship. Now I felt guilty knowing she would be looking after Clara for us for two weeks.

As we pulled up outside the luxury hotel in Phuket, I frowned. Guessing I was worrying about the cost, Tom turned to me and said, 'You only live once Lucy, so let's enjoy this holiday.'

It was the wrong thing for him to say as Christopher had died after such a short life. Things had been easier for him. He'd always had other things to think about while he was at work all day. I'd resigned from my job after Christopher's death while still on maternity leave. I was stuck in the flat, seldom venturing out because I was such a mess. There were many days when Kim took Clara out, along with her son Freddie. When we first moved into the flat she kept suggesting I clean myself up and go out with them for the day, but I'd refused. Some days Tom just dropped Clara off with Kim in the morning and didn't bring her home until the evening. Kim gave up calling around and I don't blame her. I have been very self-indulgent, allowing my all-consuming grief to take over my life. I frightened myself a few times when I bothered to look in the mirror. Hair all over the place, greasy, and straggling across my face. It's no wonder everyone avoided me. Tom complained that I frequently smelled. He once dragged me into the shower and turned it on with me fully dressed. I made a bit more of an effort after that.

If only my parents or grandparents had been around, I'm sure I would have coped better with their support. I still hadn't altogether recovered from their deaths, although it was seven years since they'd died. The four of them were wiped out in an instant one night on the freeway when they drove into the back of a large road train that had swung out into the next lane as my father had attempted to overtake it. The police said that my father had been driving too close to the road train.

My sister Eva seemed to make a speedy recovery from their deaths. Much like she had after our brother Noel's death. She persevered with her degree course, going on to eventually qualify as a lawyer. Unable to move on, I took a year out from my degree and spent that year in the country at my grandparents' property. There were plenty of things to sort out there and the wide-open spaces helped me grieve in private. While I was there I went over everything to do with my brother's death and tortured myself with the details until I felt I was going crazy.

I remained at the property until Eva, who was still living in our parents' house, said she wanted to sell both properties. With probate settled I couldn't defend a longer stay.

Eva bought a slick city apartment with her share. I put mine into the bank and returned to university, to complete my degree in Business Studies. With some reluctance I moved into Eva's spare bedroom, paying her a reduced rent (as she frequently reminded me). I'd only intended to stay with Eva until I found my own place. Even though I had money in the bank I couldn't decide what to do with it and just ended up remaining at Eva's. We muddled along – with difficulty at times.

Once I finished my degree I started working in a large company and was still living with Eva when *we* met Tom in a bar one night. We were both instantly attracted to him. But it was Eva who was quicker off the mark and he landed in her bed that night. Ten months later they talked about marriage, but Tom wanted a family. Eva didn't. I knew it was wrong, but it was then I saw my chance because *I* did want a family.

I'd dated a couple of other men while Tom and Eva were together but none of them matched up to my expectations; they weren't Tom, who I had fallen madly in love with. I tried not to feel resentful about him being with Eva. It was Tom who was the serious one and I didn't believe Eva really loved him. Being a narcissist, I wasn't sure she was capable of love. I was also suspicious that she was with him to spite me. I don't know what I would have done if Tom and Eva had married. I justified my subsequent actions on the basis that it would have never worked out long term for them. One night, when Tom and I were sharing a meal alone in the apartment, the spark between us led us into bed. We knew Eva was working late on a case and we weren't expecting her home. She walked in and caught us red-handed – just as we were about to take a shower (together). She screamed at us both to get out. Tom and I have been together ever since and married the following year.

Eva wouldn't take any of my calls after we left her flat. She either didn't answer her mobile or she'd hang up on me if I managed to make contact on the landline. I left her a message when I discovered I was pregnant – she might have thought it was cruel of me, rubbing salt into the wound. But I was naïve enough to hope my sister would congratulate me. After all, she didn't want children. Tom left her a message when Christopher died. She didn't respond to that either. Or the card we'd sent her months before with baby photographs.

We unpacked our cases that first day at the hotel in Phuket and then went off exploring. In the evening we ate at a small restaurant down on the beach front. That night Tom and I made love for the first time since Christopher's death and I drifted off into drug-free relaxing sleep.

5
Kelly

Tom and Lucy, the couple I met down at the pool today, lost their baby son in a tragic cot death. I didn't know what it was like to lose a living child, but I knew what it was like to lose your whole family.

Lucy told me how depressed she'd felt after her son's death and how she'd felt guilty, helpless and incapable of doing anything.

'And the way I've neglected Clara since Christopher's death is shameful,' she said. 'Not taking her out for walks or to run around in the park. Or even feeding her when I know she must be hungry. Tom usually takes her out after returning from work. She's been so good. She has the occasional whinge, but considering how neglectful I've been, she's been marvellous. She turned one a few months ago and was born a few minutes after Christopher. I didn't want to go away, but Tom said we really needed this time for ourselves.'

I didn't like to interrupt Lucy, but I felt tempted to ask her why she hadn't thought about finding a new home for the dog if she struggled to look after it. Perhaps

Lucy was emotionally attached to it because it was born on the same day as her son. Unusual name for a dog I thought. The only other time I'd ever heard this name was from the book 'Heidi' that I'd read as a child. From what I remembered, Clara was the invalid wheelchair-bound character they took to the mountains.

Lucy filled me on Tom's Welsh background and while he was in the pool, she confessed how she'd snatched Tom from her sister Eva, giving me the full details of what happened.

She and Eva no longer spoke as a consequence, which was a shame, Lucy said, as they were the only family each of them had. I thought it was such a sad story. The sisters falling out like that over one man. Then the baby dying. I conjured up images of Eva raining curses down on Tom and Lucy, which caused me to shiver.

Like me, Lucy came from a complex mix of different backgrounds, but with Australian, Vietnamese and Chinese heritage. She mentioned that she'd had a younger brother, who'd drowned when she was eleven. I wanted to ask her more about the brother but she raced on, talking nine to the dozen about the rest of her family. Lucy's parents and all her grandparents were dead, so, apart from Tom and an estranged sister, Lucy was quite alone. Like me.

When I told Carlos about them, he invited Tom and Lucy to join us for dinner. I knew Carlos had watched us from the balcony and would question me about them anyway.

At the meal Carlos was staring hard at Lucy. 'You and

Lucy look a lot like each other,' he said turning to me.

'I was thinking that when we were out at the pool this morning,' Tom said, nodding.

Lucy and I looked at each other and shrugged. I couldn't see it myself.

'No we don't,' Lucy said. 'Okay, we both have slim figures, long straight dark hair and brown eyes. But I think you mean we both have *Eurasian* features – or more likely *Asian*. Do you think we look the same as Thai women?'

Tom looked a bit embarrassed at Lucy's comment and tucked his head down, but Carlos wasn't fazed by it.

'No, neither of you look like the locals,' Carlos said shaking his head and with a look of disgust on his face. 'They're … anyway you're both around the same height.'

Lucy and I were both on the short side – about 5ft 3inches. My skin was darker than Lucy's, but she might have looked extremely pale from staying indoors for so many months.

Carlos enjoyed their company at the meal, despite some tense moments when Lucy asked questions. He suggested we dine together each evening which Lucy agreed to with enthusiasm. I wasn't sure that Tom was too happy with the idea, but he went along with it.

Since being in Phuket, Carlos has spent a lot of his time on the phone or on his laptop doing business. Some days we ventured out together for short periods in the afternoon, exploring other parts of the island. Most things I suggested he dismissed, claiming they would be boring. The only thing we did together, which he said he enjoyed, was to take a boat trip out from a place called Chalong.

Lucy suggested we meet at the pool every morning which I was happy to agree to. It at least gave me some respite from Carlos.

6
Lucy

I found myself pouring my life story to Kelly, the woman I met at the pool. I don't know why. She was just so easy to talk to. Her partner spent most of the morning sitting on their balcony watching us while wheeling and dealing. Kelly told me he's a bit of a business tycoon. If you ask me he seems a bit creepy – the way he watches her. She didn't say anything detrimental about him, but I can see she's not happy. An associate of his, one I'd noticed at the pool earlier, came to our room this afternoon with an invitation to join them for dinner.

I was buzzing with energy this morning, for the first time since Christopher's death. Talking to Kelly was far better therapy than any of the sessions we'd paid for.

'So, what do you do Kelly?' I asked her over dinner. 'I mean, do you work?' I'd been so busy talking about my life earlier today, that I hadn't asked Kelly much about hers.

'She doesn't have to, she has me,' Mr. Business Tycoon replied on her behalf.

Kelly smiled, but I could see the smile was false. I was shocked to see the difference in her appearance at the meal. As well as wearing loads of flashy jewellery, she was wearing *a lot* of make-up. I suspected *he* might be responsible for her appearance. Some men loved their women all made up like that. Thank goodness Tom wasn't one of them.

'I had been thinking about gaining some qualifications. Maybe studying for the HSC because I didn't do it at school. Then I thought about doing a business degree,' Kelly said, looking at me and ignoring *him*, 'and—'

'But Kelly and I have decided that she doesn't need to do that,' *he* butted in to finish her sentence.

I told her I had done a business degree. How it wasn't particularly exciting but could lead to many different types of employment. I also mentioned what a great social life I'd had at uni. It was obviously the wrong thing to say. Mr. Business Tycoon sat glaring at me. Carlos is his name and I don't like him one bit – but I'll make an effort for Kelly. Otherwise, he might say she can't associate with me. I think I'd put his nose out of joint earlier when he claimed Kelly and I looked like each other.

I kept quiet after that, watching how they interacted and let Tom and Carlos do most of the talking. It is clear *he* decides what Kelly can and can't do. Why is she with this man? She seems very intelligent. I don't understand why women let men walk all over them like that. Perhaps it's about money. Undoubtedly, from all he has said tonight, he is very wealthy. Is that what holds her to him or is it something more sinister?

'What did you think of Carlos?' I asked Tom when we returned to our room that night.

'I got the impression that he's a bit of a male chauvinist with regard to his wife. But otherwise, he seems okay. Why, what did you think of him?'

'I don't like him one bit. And they're not married. Kelly referred to him as her partner in our conversations, although I suppose it amounts to the same thing as a marriage.'

'I just assumed,' Tom said. 'I thought his laugh was a bit over the top when I told him my name was Tom Jones. That annoyed me. Although I felt better when he said he liked Tom Jones's music.'

'He seems to have an unhealthy control over Kelly, and it worries me a little... What Tom? What's wrong? Why are you grinning at me like that?'

He pulled me down onto the bed, still grinning madly. 'I think it's great that you're taking an interest in something. That's why I'm smiling. This is more like the old you, Lucy. Sticking up for others. Now how about we change the subject – I'd rather focus on you and me.'

At the pool several mornings later, I broached the subject of Kelly's relationship with Carlos. I thought I'd grab the opportunity while she seemed relaxed and Tom was taking one of his long swims. Our chats so far had mainly focused on me and Phuket sights. I had gleaned very little about Kelly's life or background, other than her Asian ancestry. That might have been because I gabbled on so much, but I detected a wariness in her and that remaining quiet was a deliberate choice.

'I used to work for Carlos,' she said, 'and we started seeing each other. Very soon after he asked me to move in with him. I was seduced by his charm, his luxurious apartment and wealth. I had no idea what I was stepping into. I'd never had a serious relationship before that or even what you might call a boyfriend.'

'How long have you been with him?'

'More than five years. Next June it will be six years,' she sighed.

'I've noticed he seems a bit controlling. Do you mind that?'

She turned and looked up at the terrace where Carlos was watching her and waved. When she turned back, she removed the false smile she'd put on for him and scowled.

'Yes. I mind. I mind very much.'

'Have you never thought of leaving him?' I felt stupid immediately after saying that. Of course she would have thought about leaving him. But why hadn't she?

She snorted. 'Every day. I've made several attempts, but the price is too high. He, or one of his men who watch me, always catch me.'

'What do you mean, the price is too high?' I asked. I imagined Carlos attacking Kelly and knocking her about. I thought he was the type to play the role of a wife beater with relish.

'It doesn't matter. Let's just say Carlos makes me regret that I'd even contemplated it, let alone tried to escape.'

I knew it. From what Kelly was intimating, Carlos

was violent. I'd sensed his aggression several times over meals when something he didn't like happened. Even over simple things like the waiter putting our food orders in front of the wrong person at the table.

'So he hurt you when you tried to leave him?'

'I don't really want to talk about it Lucy if you don't mind. It's not something I'm comfortable with.'

'I'm sorry. I can see I've made you angry,' I said.

'No, it's not *you* who has made me angry. I'm angry every day just thinking about my situation. But I have to let it go, otherwise my self-loathing and my hatred towards him would make life impossible. I just focus on surviving every day.'

Surviving! I knew what that was like – but Kelly's situation was entirely different to what mine had been.

'What's with the Barbie doll look you put on at night? Is that one of his demands?' I couldn't help but ask this. It seemed so out of character with the little I knew of Kelly. I was sure he was responsible.

She looked at me with surprise. Perhaps she wasn't used to someone talking so directly to her. 'Yes,' she said after a pause, 'and I hate it, but Carlos thinks I look ugly and naked without a lot of make-up.'

'What? You've got to be joking! You are beautiful in your natural state. It's that make-up that makes you look …'

'Yes, thanks, Lucy. I do know what it makes me look like.'

We sat in silence for a few minutes. I wasn't sure if I'd offended her with my blunt question. In the past, I'd had a habit of 'putting my foot in it'. Now I'd done it again.

Kelly needed to get away from this creep. 'What about this place?' I asked her. 'Could it provide an opportunity to escape?'

She looked at me for a moment – maybe deciding if she could trust me.

'I've considered it. I've been thinking about escape a lot recently. But I have no money. Nothing. He controls everything. I do have some money back in Melbourne, in an account Carlos knows nothing about, but I don't have access to it from here. So it would be impossible. Besides, there's always 'a guard' watching over me.'

She nodded her head in the direction of a man sitting at a table on the other side of the pool. He was sipping a drink and acting like he was reading a newspaper. It was the same man who'd delivered the dinner invitation to our room. I'd noticed that he was always around when she was down at the pool. I wasn't sure if it was coincidental that the same man stood up and followed her into the hotel each day. Now she'd confirmed it. Unbelievable, the lengths some men will go to keep that noose around a woman's neck. Now I was determined to find a way to help her. I'd worked with women who'd been on the receiving end of their partner's violence.

'Tom and I could help you. We could give you some money. And we could cause a distraction with the guard which would give you an opportunity to take off.'

Kelly looked at me with scepticism. 'Why would you do that? You hardly know me.'

What could I say to Kelly to convince her? I didn't want to frighten her off by showing her too much of the warmth I felt for her. She was such a lovely person and was becoming more like the close sister I'd always desired in Eva (but never had).

'I don't like to see women being treated the way Carlos treats you. I worked at a battered women's shelter one year during my university summer break. It was a harrowing four months. Some of the things I saw there broke my heart and I learned that two of the women who returned to their partners lost their lives. I ...'

'If, and when, I escape from Carlos, I plan to make damn sure he won't ever find me again. I certainly wouldn't go back to him.'

I nodded. That was good to hear – but I'd heard women in the shelter say the same.

'I would like to know you're safe Kelly. And I don't think you are in this relationship with Carlos. As I said, Tom and I could give you some money, and you could always pay us back when you can access your own money. If you couldn't afford it, it wouldn't matter all that much.'

'I doubt your husband would be willing to be involved. He and Carlos seem to get on very well.'

'I'm sure Tom would help. He doesn't like Carlos's attitude towards you either. Their 'getting on' is superficial. Tom's very easy-going and gets along with most people. I know he wouldn't choose Carlos as a friend though.'

I watched as the spark of hope in Kelly's face vanished.

'No.' she said shaking her head. 'It's hopeless. I'd need my passport and he keeps them in a safe in the suite. I don't know the code.'

'Right. Well, we'll think of something. I'll talk to Tom about it later and we'll see what we can come up with. I could do some research online and see what major exits there are out of Phuket.'

'Thanks Lucy, but you know, thinking about it, I'm pretty sure it wouldn't be safe for you and Tom to become involved. Carlos would work out that you helped me and he might ... actually I'm pretty sure he and his henchmen would *deal* with you and Tom in ways you couldn't begin to imagine. It's not worth it. Forget it.'

'I'm not afraid of him and I'm not going to forget it, Kelly. You have worked wonders in helping me. It's about time someone helped you.'

She looked at me with surprise.

'What do you mean I've helped you?'

'I had sessions with different grief counsellors and therapists after Christopher's death. None of them helped. Sitting here talking to you every day has helped me tremendously. You were willing to listen to me pour out my grief without making judgements or asking stupid questions like the therapists did. Also seeing your situation with Carlos has shifted my self-pitying attitude back into the real world again. Tom can't believe the change in me. In just a matter of five days! That's why I *know* he will help.'

I noticed tears sliding down Kelly's face.

'I've been alone since I was almost 10 years old,' she said. 'With no-one to help me.' It was then she poured out her story. The devastating loss of her family. The foster care. The adoption years including the verbal, sexual and emotional abuse she received from the couple who were supposed to be her 'parents'. Her escape to Melbourne and her years there until she met Carlos.

'No wonder you fell for Carlos's lifestyle and charm,' I said. 'He would have seemed like the answer to every young girl's prayers. Especially someone who had been through your experiences.'

'I really had no idea what I was getting into – although one of the other dancers warned me. Some days it seems like I will be living in my prison hell for the rest of my life. If I'd had children it might have alleviated the bitterness of my situation, but Carlos refused to have any. At first, it upset me. Now I know it's better that we never had children. *He* would have resented them. He would've been a terrible father and I would've been tied to him forever. At least there's only me, and there's always the hope that he will become tired of me and dump me.'

'That might not be for many years to come yet. Why should you lose the best years of your life tied down to such a controlling man?'

'I jumped into it of my own free will. It's my fault I'm in this situation,' she said.

'No,' I said shaking my head. 'That's too simplistic a view, Kelly. Did you tell him anything about your background? Like the loss of your family and your experiences following that?'

She nodded. 'Not at first. But when I started having drinks with him after work, he asked me lots of questions. Like a gullible fool, I answered them.'

'So, he exploited the fact that you were completely

alone. Vulnerable, with no one to turn to. And much younger than him.'

'I guess so, with hindsight. That's exactly what he did; knowing no one would be there to rescue me.'

Tom came out of the pool at that point so we ended our serious conversation and started talking about mundane matters instead. A short while later Carlos's man came over and told Kelly that Carlos wanted her to go back up to the room. We agreed to meet for dinner again that evening. It was Christmas Eve.

7
Lucy

Tom's eyes widened in surprise when I told him about my idea later in our room. He started shaking his head.

'I don't think Carlos would be too happy about us helping Kelly escape,' he said, his brows furrowing in concern.

'No he wouldn't, but we could make it seem innocent so that he had nothing to challenge us about. I'm *sure* we could do it Tom. Listen. You could chat with the 'guard' to distract him. Start talking to him tomorrow – wish him Happy Christmas or something. Then it would seem more natural for you to talk to him again the next day. It has to be soon as they're due to leave on the 28th. We'd have to get some money for her today. I'm not sure if the banks would be open Christmas Day or Boxing Day. If we leave it until 27th, it might be cutting things fine. Do they celebrate traditional Christmas holidays here?'

'I don't know Lucy. And you make it sound so simple – what if it doesn't work?'

'We won't know unless we try, will we? And I've

thought of a way around the passport issue.'

'What's that?'

I took a deep breath. I knew Tom was not going to like my suggestion, but it was the only idea I could come up. Kelly and I do have a *similar* appearance and people didn't really look too closely at those of us with 'foreign' looks. They think we all look the same.

'I could give Kelly my passport. I reckon she could pass for me – as you said, there are similarities between us. Then we could report it stolen a day or two later. Don't forget we're here until the New Year. If we report it stolen say on the twenty-eighth, Kelly would be back in Australia by then. Or somewhere else, depending on where she decides to go. The Australian Embassy in Bangkok would issue a new passport for me – or temporary papers for me to get home at least.'

Tom screwed his face up and shook his head. 'No. I can't see that working Lucy. It could mean there'd be a delay before we could return home. We're scheduled to fly out on Sunday the 2nd and I'm due back at work the day after.'

'It's the only way, Tom. If any problems arose, you could always leave me in Bangkok and I could travel back at a later date. We would have to leave the hotel a day or so earlier and go to Bangkok to obtain travel documents for me and change our flights.'

Tom kept shaking his head. 'No. I wouldn't be happy about leaving you alone in Bangkok.'

'Well we'll just have to hope that the embassy will sort things out quickly, or you'll be late back to work. I'm sure your boss would be understanding if you explained that my passport was stolen. Come on Tom. We have to do this.'

I could tell he wasn't convinced. I would have to work harder on my powers of persuasion. The more I saw and heard of Carlos, the more I wanted to help Kelly. He really was a first class creep. And I suspected a very dangerous one. I *had* to help Kelly get away from him. But I needed Tom's co-operation.

After making sure no-one else was in the 'ladies' that evening I outlined my proposals to Kelly. I imagined Carlos having spies everywhere. She looked at me with surprise and then went quiet.

'Kelly?' She hadn't said a thing. I didn't know if her silence was due to her thinking it couldn't possibly work or that she hadn't believed I would help her.

'You really want to do this?'

I spotted that spark of hope in her eyes again. 'Of course we do,' I said. 'I wouldn't suggest it otherwise.'

'It could work, but I'd worry about the difficult situation it could leave you in, plus the issue of the money. You'd have to give me your contact details.'

'I will and don't worry about our situation,' I said taking her hand. 'I'm sure everything will be fine. I can assure you the money is not a problem. We have quite a lot of savings put aside to build our house. And let us worry about the rest. It's a golden opportunity for you to take off. You'll need to have something with decent pockets that I can stuff the money and passport into. Say when I give you a hug or something, so Carlos won't see anything suspicious. Tom and I have been to the bank this afternoon and I already have the money for you.'

Kelly dropped her head, closed her eyes and stood in silence for a moment. As though she was praying. Then she raised her head, looked at me in the mirror and asked, 'Are you absolutely sure you and Tom want to do this?'

I nodded. 'One hundred percent.'

She heaved a big sigh. 'Okay, I'll think about what suitable clothing I can wear. Boxing Day you say we should go for it?'

'Yes, Tom can casually greet your 'guard' tomorrow and then on Boxing Day he will stop for a longer 'chat,' blocking his view of you. Once Tom stops to talk to your guard, you can make out like you are going to the loo or something and just take off.'

Kelly's nose screwed up and her eyes narrowed. Was she doubting it could work?

'We can practise some things tomorrow,' I said. 'You'll need to stand and give me a hug to wish me 'Merry Christmas'. When we part tonight stand and throw your arms around me and give me a kiss, so Carlos will have seen us being affectionate and not view it as something unusual. Wear something with pockets tomorrow and we'll see if Carlos notices anything. I won't actually put anything in your pocket tomorrow. We'll do that Boxing Day.'

Worry was etched on Kelly's face. She started taking deep breaths and withdrawing her hand from mine, she gripped the edge of the sink. After a few seconds she turned to me and said, 'Oh my God. Right. Let's do this.' She looked excited now. I'd convinced her!

Back in the privacy of our room, I told Tom we'd be doing a practise run on some things the following day. I went through what I was proposing. He frowned but nodded. In order to persuade Tom that my plan could work, I'd filled him in on some of Kelly's background, including all her years of abuse. Both in care and with Carlos.

'So you see Tom, Carlos had taken advantage of a vulnerable young girl who was alone without support. He keeps her as a virtual prisoner,' I'd said.

Tom had worked out that I was right about that.

'Kelly won't talk about it, but I'm convinced he has been violent towards her when she tried to escape in the past.'

I knew using the word 'violent' would be the final clincher. Tom loathes hearing about violence perpetrated on women.

'Okay Lucy, you've convinced me,' Tom had finally said. He smiled as I threw my arms around him.

We'd withdrawn a total of eighteen hundred American dollars that day for Kelly, using different debit and credit cards. We chose American dollars as we knew most people in Thailand took that currency. I'd put all the money and passport in a sealed plastic wallet that one of the banks gave me. We were all set.

8
Kelly

Carlos and I woke early on Christmas Day, exchanging Christmas wishes that evolved into a 'love-making' session. I inwardly cringed every time Carlos made sexual demands on me, but I had long managed to 'act' as a willing participant, rather like I imagined prostitutes did, and the truth is my body would often betray me. Carlos knew exactly how to make my body respond.

After showering we ate a light breakfast and exchanged small gifts. We'd agreed that, as we'd be abroad for Christmas, we'd limit our gifts to a few small items. He presented me with a gorgeous, sleek, red dress to wear for the Christmas lunch. Plus, a diamond necklace. This is what he considered small items! He hinted that my main present would be waiting for me in Melbourne. I hoped I'd never see it.

I gave him a beautiful blue shirt with a maroon tie, a pair of silver cufflinks and an expensive watch – one that he'd mentioned he liked. All courtesy of the credit card he supplied. He'd mentioned the watch so many times, I knew if I didn't buy it, he'd be furious. But I hadn't bought him anything else. Those items alone came to a small fortune.

Carlos seemed pleased with his gifts but I froze when he suggested that I refrain from my normal pool jaunt that morning. Did he have some sixth sense or something? Each time I'd planned an escape in the past, he seemed to be expecting it. I had to make sure my routine wasn't disrupted. *Stay calm. Stay calm.*

'Carlos, you know how much I love to swim. I need the exercise to work off all the food we've been consuming. And besides, I told Lucy I'd meet her down at the pool later this morning.'

'Okay, okay. It would have been a nice treat for Benny to not have to go down there this morning. It's Christmas Day after all.'

'You know he doesn't have to come down. I'm only going for a swim and a chat with my friend.'

He shook his head and gave me a look that told me I should know better than to suggest I go unescorted anywhere. No change there then. I could feel my body starting to tense up – at all costs I had to avoid reacting to him. I kept up the mantra in my head. *Stay calm. Stay calm.*

'You have become very pally with this Lucy,' he remarked quietly. A quiet voice was always a sign of disapproval from him. And sometimes a precursor to sudden violence. I wasn't going to be lured into his game. It was all about preventing me from going to the pool.

'I've told you what we talk about. Things are still very delicate for Lucy since the loss of her son.' I focused on keeping my tone serious, with a hint of indifference. If Carlos believed going to meet Lucy was of paramount importance to me, he would make damn sure it didn't happen. *Stay calm.*

'So you say, but she seems fine to me. Although when you two went to the ladies last night, Tom mentioned that he couldn't believe the transformation in Lucy since she's met you.'

'Lucy just needed someone to take an interest in her and listen,' I said shrugging.

'There's therapists for that kind of thing.'

'She tried grief counselling and therapy. It didn't work for her. No doubt because her grief was too raw.' *Stay calm.*

'Hmm. Okay, but don't stay down there too long this morning. It's Christmas Day after all.'

'You've got a lot of calls to make Carlos – to your family remember? I'd be sitting around twiddling my thumbs while you do that. I'd rather be exercising.'

Carlos liked me to exercise, to keep my body trim. For him of course. He'd bought me various exercise machines that were in the penthouse back in Melbourne and encouraged me to use them and the pool in the basement daily.

'Yes, I know,' he sighed, 'I'd better get these calls out of the way then. You go on down to the pool.'

I'd won the battle this time.

I swam my usual twenty lengths and then, after towelling off, I threw some clothes over my costume. My bikini bottoms immediately drenched the shorts I'd put on, looking like I'd wet myself. But the baggy t-shirt seemed fine, with a few odd wet patches showing. I knew everything would soon dry out.

When Lucy arrived she rushed over, and I stood up to give her a hug. I felt her hand slide into my right pocket. Tom greeted me with a quick peck and Christmas wishes as well, then turned and dived into the pool.

Lucy and I both agreed that the shorts had the perfect size pocket to hold the passport and money. I would need to stand like I had today for her to be able to slip the plastic wallet in.

Tom stopped to wish Benny a 'Happy Christmas' as he passed by him on the way back to our loungers. That went well with Benny standing to shake hands. I didn't look, but Lucy told me that Benny only took his eyes off me for a few seconds to acknowledge Tom. That's what he's paid for I guess, but it didn't look too promising for tomorrow.

Lucy said Tom planned to stand in front of him tomorrow and attempt to engage Benny in conversation, while she and I walked off together to go the toilets in the foyer. We'd done that before, but Benny had followed us of course. Standing in front of him would block his view of me momentarily. Would it give me enough time to escape? I knew there were always taxis around the front entrance of the hotel. If I could make it there I could jump in one and take off. Hopefully. The whole thought of tomorrow was nerve-racking but exciting. Could we do this? It might represent my only real chance of escape. Oh, how I wished it would succeed. I hadn't decided whether to head straight for the airport or travel by other means to mainland Thailand and then find another route out of the country. I thought the latter would be the safest option. Carlos was bound to head straight to the airport in search of me.

It was going to be difficult for me to remain calm for the next 24 hours. When I thought about it though, I'd been acting a part with large measures of success for some years now. I was confident I could perform well for one more day.

Christmas dinner was relaxing and enjoyable. A little different to what we were all used to back at home. Carlos even relaxed enough for Benny to join us for the meal. Normally Benny would be standing on sentry duty nearby and have to wait for his meal until Carlos had me imprisoned back in our suite.

We slept for a few hours in the afternoon and then Carlos and I went for a walk down to the beach, trailed by Benny as usual. It was surprising how many people were out and about. I seldom spoke on these forays, but listened as Carlos prattled on about this or that. If any moments of silence occurred I'd drop in comments about the scenery. Anything to keep his mind wandering on to *us* as a topic.

We had a light meal later that night in our suite, rather than in the restaurant. Carlos gave Benny the evening off. At 10 pm I declared I had a splitting headache and needed to go to bed. I did have a headache, no doubt caused by nervous worry, but it wasn't splitting. I would have been nominated for an academy award for my performance though. Carlos wasn't the least bit suspicious and was all concern. He clearly hadn't noticed anything untoward down at the pool this morning or he would have raised it. So far so good.

Violent rumbling woke us early the next morning. 'What the bloody hell was that?' Carlos asked sitting upright in bed.

'I suspect it was an earthquake. An article I read in a magazine down in the hotel lounge said they were commonplace around here. I asked a woman on reception and she reassured me that the hotel was built to withstand them and that they were nothing to worry about.'

When I looked at Carlos, his usual olive-skinned face was deathly white. So there is something you're afraid of, I thought. He was unable to relax so he took a shower while I ordered a light breakfast and sat out on the terrace. I couldn't eat through nerves and only drank some orange juice.

After a suitable interval, I stretched and stood. 'I'm going to change for my swim,' I announced.

'Righto,' Carlos replied with indifference. He was engrossed in his laptop. No doubt looking up 'earthquakes.' There'd been a second one while he was in the shower.

I dressed with care, choosing a casual dress with large zip pockets that I threw over the bikini I was wearing that day. I grabbed my book, placing it together with my towel and swimming cap into my basket. Lastly I put on my floppy hat and sunglasses

Carlos was on the phone when I re-emerged from the bedroom, no doubt organising Benny. He stood and took the basket from my hands. He flicked the towel up and, satisfied that I had nothing else in there, apart from the book and swimming cap, passed it back to me. I couldn't help bristling a little at this inspection, although I should have been used to it by now.

'Benny will be here in a minute,' he said. Sure enough, there was a knock on the door and Benny was there waiting for me. He led the way down the corridor to the lift and, as I watched his back, I wished he would disappear so we didn't have to go through this. So I could meet Lucy in the foyer, hop in a taxi and take off.

When we arrived at the pool no-one else was there yet. Benny sat at his usual table and I walked over to my normal spot. After placing my basket beside the lounger I turned and looked up at the balcony of our suite. Carlos was there looking down at me, although I could see that he had his laptop with him. I hoped he would become distracted with that later. On the floor below I saw Lucy waving before she disappeared. I didn't really want to swim this morning knowing I would feel uncomfortable taking off with a wet costume, so I stalled for time by discarding one of my sandals and dipping my toe in the water before walking back to the lounger hoping Lucy and Tom would arrive soon. Just as I sat down, they appeared.

I stood up and gave Lucy a hug, feeling her place the plastic wallet in my pocket. While she was still hugging me I surreptitiously closed the zip. I looked at Lucy and couldn't help but laugh. Nerves I supposed. Tom had paused at the other end of the pool dipping his foot in as though to test the temperature of the water. He then started walking towards Benny. The moment was now approaching. Any second now and I would calmly walk off. I turned and looked up at Carlos. He was still on the balcony, looking down at us. I waved at him and smiled and as I turned back to talk to Lucy I saw a large dark shape out of the corner of my eye. Others around the pool stood, stunned, silent, frozen. People who had just come out to the pool started screaming. A wall of water hurtled at us with a force so violent, there was no hope of escape.

I watched momentarily mesmerised, as a launch crashed down on Benny and Tom. They didn't stand a chance of surviving that. Lucy screamed and threw one arm around me, her other hand clutching mine. I thought I could hear Carlos calling my name. The water swept us up like flotsam and hurtled on taking chairs and tables, which swirled, bobbed and crashed around us. We were submerged for a time and I thought *this is it, we're going to drown*, when suddenly we rose to the surface, still being swept along. I could see we were heading straight towards a palm tree. After spitting out the sea water that had found its way into my mouth, I managed to yell to Lucy to try and grab hold of it. We smashed into the tree, stunned by the impact. I managed to grab it with one arm, using the other to drag Lucy closer to me. She quickly let go of my hand and embraced the tree and me. Our legs were kicking around in water that was trying to pull us back into its depths. The palm's trunk was very slim and I wasn't confident it would hold us.

When I looked up I could see it was bending. The force of the water was too fierce for its flimsy frame.

I could see that ramshackle buildings were collapsing. Chairs, tables and other items were being thrown around, crashing into other obstacles. We could hear people screaming in the distance and saw bodies tumbling past us. A car swept passed me, the edge of it knocking into my left hip. I cried out and the pain of it almost caused me to relinquish my precious hold on the tree, but I clung tight.

'What the bloody hell happened?' Lucy shouted at me.

'I'm not sure. I think we just experienced a tsunami.'

'Did you see what happened to Tom?' she panted. Lucy had obviously missed the launch landing on him and Benny. I shook my head indicating no, but I couldn't look at her. Now wasn't the time to tell her.

'Kelly look, if Tom and I don't make it out of this, will you promise that you'll go to our place and get Clara? Look after her or take her across to Tom's parents in Wales?' Lucy was shaking as though she was freezing cold and her eyes were wild.

I couldn't understand why she was talking like this right now. If I wasn't so terrified myself I would have laughed at her ludicrous request.

'I mean it, Kelly. I don't want Eva, my sister, to have her. I would rather she was with you than Eva. I'm sure Eva would get rid of her or send her to a home.'

'I don't even know where you live Lucy, except that you're in Yarraville, not far from the river.'

She rattled off the address – as if in our present

circumstances I was going to remember it!

'Promise me, Kelly. Please say you'll do it.' She seemed desperate and babbled on. 'Collect Clara from our neighbours, Kim and Laurie. They're in the flat right above us. You can stay in our place if we don't make it back, looking after Clara until you decide what to do. You've got my passport. Pretend you're me or something like we planned for your escape.'

'Lucy, I .... I don't even know if I am going to make it out of here either.'

'You stand a much better chance than me. You're a strong swimmer. I'm not.'

'But Lucy ...'

'*Just promise me, Kelly. Promise me!*' she screeched. She was quite hysterical.

'Yes alright. I promise.' I couldn't help but worry about her state of mind. Worrying about a bloody dog! I looked around and saw that the water was no longer sweeping inshore. In fact, it now seemed to be flowing back towards the sea, dragging bodies with it.

'We need to hold on tight Lucy,' I shouted, 'the water seems to be heading back out to sea. If we're not careful it will drag us with it.'

Just then something large and heavy loomed up out of the water's depths knocking into both of us. It seemed to come from beneath us, jerking upright, scraping past our bodies and bashing my face hard before disappearing off again. I heard us both scream and felt Lucy lose her hold of the tree. I tried to grab her, with the one hand that had been knocked off my hold on the tree. But the water was moving too fast and she was swiftly swept away. As I tightened my grip on the tree I screamed at her to grab something. Anything she could. I don't know if she heard me. The water pulled her under and she disappeared from my sight.

I clung to the tree sobbing, worried about Lucy. It seemed like hours that I was there. My arms were aching and there was a searing pain in my left hip. It felt like flesh had been torn from my legs and my face was pouring with blood. My hair was matted with sand and god knows what else. All around me was chaos and I didn't know what to do. I considered climbing down from the tree and heading inland towards higher ground and safety. But at that moment I heard a commotion coming from the direction of the sea. People were running, slipping and sliding in my direction. And behind them another huge wall of water. It was happening again! This wave seemed taller than the first. In desperation, I tried to climb higher, but the wall of water hit with such violence it ripped me free from my fragile hold on the tree before I could. The water swept me further inland and I noticed people sweeping past me clinging to items. One of them, a woman with blood dripping from her everywhere, looked like Lucy. I tried to call out to her, but at that moment some debris battered my body. My face took another impact and I thought my left arm was going to be ripped off. The pain was agonising. I stopped fighting the power of the water. It was clear I was going to drown, why not just let it happen? I surrendered to it and felt the water drag me along under its surface. It wouldn't be long now. I knew I couldn't hold my breath for many more seconds. Then

I felt myself rising and was washed up onto some kind of roof terrace hitting some railings and being flung clear of the water.

I gasped and spat out some of the disgusting water, hooking my right hand around a railing. My left arm was dangling uselessly. I looked up and could see further floors to the building I had landed on, all with terraces. There were some people peering in fear over the railings. Locals by the look of them.

'Hang on Miss, we get help,' one of the men said.

I doubted I'd be able to hold on to the railing long enough before help came and I wasn't sure if the surface I was laying on would hold me if I let go. I coughed and choked spitting more water out of my mouth which left me unable to speak. My body went into a spasm and I felt my arm slip from the railing as I drifted into unconsciousness.

9
Franco

Phuket, December 2004

Nico and I arrived in Phuket on 28th December. Nico, Carlos's older brother, who had been my friend since school days, had turned up at my place early that morning saying, 'Pack a bag, we're flying out to Phuket in a couple of hours.'

'Is it Carlos?' I asked him. 'Are we going to collect a body?'

'No, he finally got through to me late last night. He's okay, but Benny is dead and Kelly is missing. He wants us to go over and help him look for her.'

I'd been at Nico's place with my family on Boxing Day when we saw events unfold with the Tsunami that hit multiple countries. My first thoughts were that I hoped Carlos had been one of those who'd lost his life in Phuket – although I didn't wish the same to happen to Kelly. So I was disappointed to hear what Nico had to say.

At the hotel Carlos filled us in on his search so far. He'd found Benny's body and that of a young man called Tom Jones, the husband of a woman called Lucy who'd been swept away with Kelly. Carlos had watched it all happening from the safety of his hotel balcony. He'd looked at several bodies, but Kelly wasn't among them.

'What about the hospitals?' Nico asked.

'I've been to both hospitals in Phuket – there's a public one and a private one. They claim they have no-one by the name of Kelly O'Brien who has been admitted. But the bastards wouldn't let me look through all the wards and so she could be there – still unconscious. They wouldn't know who she is because she didn't have any identity on her. Some of the people I saw had horrific injuries.'

'Well if she's there, she'll let them know her name when she comes around,' Nico said. 'But perhaps we should be looking elsewhere. What would you like us to do?'

'I think we should split up. One person needs to go around the beaches. They're still recovering bodies there. They've set up an emergency morgue and plan to dig mass graves, so someone needs to go there and check the bodies coming in. I went there yesterday and they let me look at the women who'd come in. Kelly wasn't among them – thank goodness. I'll walk around the streets and check out some of the hotels. Apparently some of the hotels have taken in people with minor injuries.'

I ended up at the makeshift morgue. It wasn't a pleasant

experience. Body after body came in, and although many of them were almost unidentifiable, I could tell none of them were Kelly. The skin on the women I looked at was too dark and they were wearing cheap clothes. Apparently hordes of cheap labour had come over from Indonesia to work in Phuket. Officials told me the families of these people would be too poor to collect the bodies which is one of the reasons they were digging the mass graves.

Two mornings later as I entered the reception area, I came across Carlos raising his voice to a man who was shaking his head.

'Why are you being such a prick about it?' Carlos said challenging the guy.

Without saying another word the man walked off in disgust.

'What was that all about?' I asked him.

'That was Tom Jones' father. You know, the one who died with Benny. He's flown out here from the UK to collect his son's body. I asked him if he had any news of Lucy and he told me she was rescued and taken to a hospital. He's been to see her, but he claims her injuries are so bad, only family is allowed in to see her. I only wanted to question Lucy to find out what happened to Kelly, but he said no.'

'Well calling him a prick isn't going to help your case.'

'He is being a prick. I only need to talk to her for a few minutes. He wouldn't even tell me which hospital she's in. But don't worry I'll find out where she is and get to speak to her.'

I didn't like the sound of that. Carlos is a determined bugger. Once he makes a decision, he's like a terrier with a bone and won't let go of things. He was pretty desperate to find Kelly and I wouldn't put it past him to cause more trouble at the hospitals.

On New Year's Eve, Nico and I decided we needed a break. He managed to persuade Carlos to take a night off and go out on the booze. There were still plenty of clubs, bars and restaurants open.

Carlos had bullied his way into the ward where Lucy Jones was and learnt from her that she and Kelly had been separated after the first wave. The hope of finding Kelly alive was diminishing. He was in a pretty bad state about the news and Nico thought we should take him out and get him drunk.

After plying Carlos with drinks until almost 5 in the morning, he was sick as a dog when he woke up on New Year's Day and stayed in bed.

When we spotted Tom Jones' father in the bar that night, Nico and I approached him, and Nico apologised for his brother's behaviour. Mr. Jones then went on to mention that Lucy had given him some information about Kelly. He was a bit hazy about it, but it was something along the lines of that Lucy had spotted Kelly while sweeping past her after the second wave hit. If I had been on my own with Mr Jones I wouldn't have passed that snippet of information on to Carlos. But when Carlos was up and about *two* mornings later (because he was still unwell on 2nd January), Nico told him what Tom's father had said and passed on the news that Jones had flown back to the UK the previous afternoon.

'Lucy didn't say anything like that to me,' Carlos said. 'I think I'll have to have another little word with her.'

I was at the makeshift morgue again later that day when I received a phone call from Carlos. *'Lucy discharged herself from the hospital this morning. I'm at the airport now but there's no sign of her. Can you get out here and take over from me, keeping an eye out for her.'*

I wasted the next two days at the airport without catching sight of anyone who might have resembled Lucy Jones. Carlos had shown me a photo of the woman which had been taken when they were all having a meal together, but I wasn't sure if she'd be identifiable anyway. Tom's father had told us she'd had to have facial reconstructive surgery, her face was covered in dressings; she had one arm in a sling and could only get around using a wheelchair. I didn't see anyone like that anyway.

Nico and I were booked to fly out the next day – on the 6th. He had to get back for business, I had to get back to my family. My eldest daughter was having an eye operation the following day and I was not prepared to stay for what was increasingly looking like a lost cause. Kelly was probably dead.

'I'm going to stay on and continue with the search,' Carlos told us. He wouldn't believe that Kelly was gone.

'If I don't have any luck, then I'll return to Melbourne and hunt down Lucy,' he added.

His words chilled me to the bone.

10
Kim

Melbourne, January 2005

I was across at my neighbour Janine's place with Freddie and Clara when I noticed a taxi pull up outside our block of flats. I watched as the driver removed a wheelchair from the boot and helped a woman, with short dark hair, out of the cab into it. He then took a small case and positioned it on the pavement near the front door for her. It was Lucy! It had to be. We weren't expecting her home this soon.

I asked Janine to watch the kids while I went across the road. 'Lucy?' I called out as she was struggling to open the main door. 'Why didn't you let us know you were coming home? Laurie would have taken the day off and picked you up from the airport. Tom's father told us you'd be in the hospital for at least another couple of weeks.'

She turned around and I was horrified. The state of her face. She looked dreadful. Her face was swollen and bruised and she had dressings over her nose and down her cheeks. My hand flew involuntarily to my mouth and I let out a stifled screech.

'Oh my God Lucy. You look terrible. You poor thing.'

'I know. I was badly smashed up in the tsunami.'

'Tom's father told us about your injuries, but we didn't realise how bad it was. You look so different. Clara won't recognise you.'

She sat there not saying anything for a minute before finally asking, 'How is Clara?'

'We're all over at Janine's place over the road. The kids are all playing together. I saw the cab arrive and realised it must be you when the wheelchair came out. I'll help you in. Do you have your keys on you? I've left my set to your place upstairs.'

'Yes, thanks,' she said handing me her keys. I picked up her hand luggage and led the way, holding the entrance door open for her. She was slow to follow me into the flat and I wondered if it was because she was struggling with the wheelchair.

'That's a snazzy chair you have there. Did they give that to you in Phuket?' I asked as I watched her steer into the flat.

'No, I've just hired it from a local company – I'm still learning how to use it. I had the cab driver take me straight to a company he knew. Otherwise, it would be impossible for me to function.'

'Yes, I can see that. So how are you going to manage to look after Clara with all your injuries?'

'I don't know. Perhaps we can talk about that.'

That was music to my ears. She was going to ask me

to continue looking after Clara while she recovered! Freddie would be thrilled. He'd become so attached to her. And if I'm honest, I had as well.

'Look I imagine you are dying to see her,' I said. 'I'll nip across the road and get her. I won't be long.'

When I returned with Clara and Freddie, Lucy reacted in the most unexpected way when she saw her daughter. *She laughed*. And then cried, before starting to interact with her. She seemed very caring and attentive, a side of Lucy I'd not seen before. I hoped this wasn't going to interfere with me continuing to look after Clara. But Lucy seemed happy enough for me to take Clara back to Janine's and later to my place for the kids' afternoon naps. We chatted for a while about how she'd been. She even *apologised* to me about how she'd been before she left for Phuket.

Lucy explained that she had to eat liquid foods while her surgery healed, so I offered to take her shopping after the kids' nap. Tom had done most of their shopping and I knew their cupboards and freezer were always stocked up with largely unhealthy, pre-prepared food. Tom heated a meal for them most nights when he returned from work. Later, at the supermarket I was therefore surprised to see Lucy stacking her disabled trolley with fresh healthy food – apart from some chocolate and ice-cream. I challenged her about that and she told me she'd always cooked healthy meals before … and then she paused, and rambled on a bit before declaring that she intended to eat healthier food now.

Back at the flat I helped Lucy unpack her shopping

and was about to take the kids back to mine when Lucy announced that she wanted Clara to stay with her. *I knew it!* I could sense her attitude changing every time she was with Clara. It was utterly absurd. How the hell did she think she could look after a child with her disabilities? She had one arm out of action and was unable to walk. It was crazy. She told me she'd look after the kids while I popped up to collect Clara's things.

I'm so angry with Lucy I could scream. In fact, the urge was so great I had to let it out. I threw myself down on our bed and screamed into the pillows while pounding my fists against them like a child throwing a tantrum. Tears followed my screams. I realised, while Clara was sleeping this afternoon that I didn't want to let her go. I know she's not mine, but she *feels* like she's mine. I'm the one who has been looking after her much of the time since Tom and Lucy moved into our block. I know I'm not really being fair, as Tom shouldered a lot of the responsibility as well. *She* did very little. She either stayed in bed or lolled on the couch each day, ignoring that beautiful little girl. Grieving the loss of her son, while she had a living child!

I couldn't see how it was going to work with her physical difficulties. I'd give her two days at the most and then she'd be screaming for help. I'd been convinced that she was going to ask me to keep looking after Clara when I first encountered her. I don't know what changed her mind.

Resigned to the situation, for now, I dragged myself up and went into the children's room. Children. I had already begun to think of it as *their* room, not Freddie's room. Freddie had been sleeping in his little bed since Clara had come to stay and Clara was in Freddie's old cot. How they would miss each other. It wasn't fair! I knew I was being unreasonable, but I had begun to wish that both Tom *and Lucy* had died in Phuket. Then perhaps we could have adopted Clara. But that probably wouldn't have worked anyway as Tom's parents would have demanded custody of her. Or Lucy's sister. Eva, I think she's called. The career sister from what Laurie told me.

I reluctantly began packing the bag that Tom had brought up with Clara's clothes and toys. I decided to leave a few back just in case.

Before returning to Lucy's, I gave my face a good wash and then sat on the side of the bath staring into space for a time. Finally, I dragged myself up, picked up Clara's high chair and bag and trudged wearily back downstairs.

The door was still open and I found Clara and Freddie sitting on the couch listening to a story Lucy was reading them. *Now she wants to play the attentive mother!* I put the high chair near the dining table and interrupted her reading asking, 'Shall I put these things in Clara's bedroom for you?'

'That'd be great thanks,' she replied and resumed reading as though I was a servant she'd dismissed!

I dumped Clara's things haphazardly on the little bed in the room. Let her sort them out, I wasn't tidying them away for her.

When I returned to the living room, Lucy had finished

the story and was sitting back in her wheelchair chatting to the children. She turned to me and said, 'Would you like to leave Freddie here for a while? Is there anything you'd like to do? Alone I mean. Pop out to do something? Have a few quiet moments to yourself upstairs? I don't imagine you've had much time for yourself recently.'

I bristled at her offer. I knew she was trying to be helpful, making a gesture towards returning all the favours I'd done for her. But instead, I felt offended. Trying not to show it, I gave her a false smile. 'Thanks for the offer, but there's nothing I particularly want to do.'

She steered herself over to me and whispered, 'When you take Freddie back upstairs, don't turn back if you hear Clara cry. No doubt she will do. Ignore the cries and leave her to me to sort out.'

I looked at her in silence for a moment. I wanted to slap her face but of course, there was no justification to do so. And with her injuries I couldn't of course, so I clenched a fist behind my back.

'Right, well we'll be off then. Good luck with it all,' I said. 'Come on Freddie, we're going home now.'

Clara automatically jumped down off the couch to follow Freddie and me, but Lucy caught her and held her back. She immediately started howling.

'Just go,' Lucy said, nodding her head towards the door. 'She'll be fine after a while.'

Freddie started to protest and turned holding his hand out for Clara. I had to drag him out of the door and quickly close it behind me before he freed himself from my grasp and ran over to her. I could hear loud wails on the other side of the closed door. Freddie was chorusing her on my side of the door. I picked him up and climbed the stairs.

'Lara,' he cried over and over – the name he used for Clara. It broke my heart to see him so upset.

'Clara has to stay with her mummy now,' I told him. 'You know that is Clara's real home. She was only staying with us while her mummy and daddy were away.' It did little to console Freddie and he continued to cry out for 'Lara.'

In the kitchen, I turned the radio on to drown out Clara's cries and distracted Freddie with a biscuit while I set about preparing his tea. His tears had stopped, but I could see he was still really upset by his downturned mouth. I heated a packet of savoury food and served it up to him in his high chair. Despite his upset at Clara's absence, Freddie loves his food and demolishes every scrap. He was never one to hurtle food about the room as I had seen with other kids. He never viewed it as something to play with. It was for his stomach and always a matter of serious concentration; transferring the food from the plate to his mouth. Even when he and Clara ate together, Freddie ignored her while his attention was on filling his stomach. Clara had learned to eat all her food while staying with us, realising that there would be no interaction with Freddie until he'd finished eating.

I gave him a banana to munch on and an apple juice to drink while I cleaned up and turned the radio down to listen for a moment. No sound of Clara's cries. Lucy had managed to quieten her. I wasn't sure if I was pleased about that.

Over dinner I grumbled and bitched to Laurie about Lucy, saying she was in no fit state to look after Clara. I also commented on how awful she looked with a swollen and bruised face. I expected Laurie to agree with me, so I was surprised at his response.

'Kim, think about everything Lucy has been through. Remember what you were like when you miscarried at four months into your first pregnancy. She also lost a child, a child she had a relationship with, and now she's lost Tom. She only has Clara. From what Tom told me at Christmas, Lucy had finally come out of her depression. Then the tsunami hit. We've only seen clips of the horror of it on TV. What she went through was horrendous. I think it was incredibly brave of her to discharge herself and come home to be with Clara. If she's determined to do it, then we should give her all the support we can.'

That put me in my place. But I couldn't help having a biased view of it all. Eventually, I said, 'You're right of course Laurie. It's just that we've all become so attached to Clara. I began to think of her as part of the family. I couldn't help it.'

'It was only ever meant to be a temporary arrangement. She was never ours. I watched you and Freddie become attached to her and was worried it was going to be difficult for you to let her go. We need to have another child of our own.'

'It took more than five years to conceive Freddie after I lost the first baby. If it takes that long again, Freddie will have little interest in a baby, and no playmate in his younger years.'

'He has friends in the neighbourhood now and Clara will still be there for him to play with.'

I snorted. 'I'm not so sure about that. Call it intuition, but I don't think Lucy will stay here when she recovers.'

11
Eva

Melbourne, February 2005

I was out for a drink with a group of friends tonight when a good looking dark-haired man came up and stood beside me. I'd just returned from the bar after ordering a round of drinks. I gave him a quick once over and considered he might be the type I might want to end up in bed with when the one word he uttered killed that stone dead.

'Lucy?'

So he was one of her old conquests was he? I raised my eyebrows at him. I'd let him think I was her for a moment to see where it went. He didn't speak, just glared at me.

'Have we met before?' I eventually asked him.

'Carlos,' he replied.

I hadn't heard Lucy ever mention his name. Had she been seeing his man on the sly since she'd gone off with Tom? I wouldn't have thought Miss Goody Two Shoes would do that. But she stole Tom from me and I hadn't expected *that*.

'What's going on Lucy? Why are you acting like you don't know me?'

'And where am I supposed to know you from?' I asked him.

'Phuket. Christmas. Remember?' he said clenching his teeth.

'Phuket at Christmas?'

Lucy was in Phuket over Christmas? The whole world knew what had happened in Phuket on Boxing Day. Was Tom there with her?

'What's going on Lucy? Why are you pretending not to know me?'

'Because I don't know you, asshole. I'm not Lucy. I'm her twin sister Eva.' I stood up then. I needed to know more. 'What's this about Lucy being in Phuket at Christmas? Was Tom with her? And the babies?'

He looked shocked. 'You don't know?'

'If I knew I wouldn't be asking you.'

'Tom and Lucy were there on their own. Tom's dead.'

'Tom's dead?' I asked, suddenly feeling faint. I had to reach out and grab the back of my chair for support. I might have hated Tom for what he did to me, but he still held a special place in my heart.

'Yeah. I just said, didn't I? How come you don't know what happened to your sister then?'

'We're estranged.'

He frowned at me, looking confused. I don't think he understood what I meant. *Bloody idiot.* Not my type after all.

'We don't talk,' I explained. 'She sent me a card with

a photograph when the twins were born, but I haven't heard from her since and I haven't been in touch with her.'

'You're twins, but you don't have anything to do with each other?'

'It's complicated.'

'Do you know where Lucy lives?' he asked me.

'I have her address at home. Why do you want to know?'

'She was with my long-term girlfriend Kelly when the tsunami struck. The last I saw of Kelly, she and Lucy were being swept inland by the water, holding on to each other. Kelly has never been found. I spoke to Lucy in the hospital – through a bathroom door, I might add. They wouldn't let me see her. She told me they were separated and she didn't know what had happened to Kelly. I was then thrown out of the hospital. When I went back they told me she'd left. Discharged herself to come home. Presumably to her kid.'

'Don't you mean kids?'

'No, I don't. Their son died last year. There's only the daughter left now.'

Shit. Why hadn't they told me? I wondered what had happened to the boy. Christopher I think they called him.

'What were Lucy's injuries?'

'Lots of fractures. She was pretty badly smashed up.'

Good. 'And Tom?'

'He died instantly with one of my employees. We found his body later the same day. His father came out to Phuket and took his body back to the UK for burial.'

Involuntary tears ran down my face on hearing about Tom.

'Look, I want to meet up with Lucy and talk to her about Kelly. Can you give me her address?'

'No,' I said, wiping my eyes. 'But I will come with you to visit her. Perhaps it's about time Lucy and I were reconciled.'

'When could we do that?' he asked.

'Not until the weekend. I'm very busy. Say Saturday?'

'Okay. Give me your number and I'll phone you to make arrangements. I can pick you up.'

'No, I'll pick *you* up,' I said. 'Give me your number. A landline number where I can reach you. Not a mobile.'

He paused and frowned. I suspected he was the kind of man who was used to being in charge and having people do what he said. Well that wouldn't work with me. I took out my mobile and stood waiting for him to make his choice. He eventually reeled off a number which I entered into my phone.

He leaned over and whispered in my ear, 'You're a bit of a bossy bitch aren't you?'

'Yep, you got me in one,' I said smiling sweetly at him.

'You will call me, won't you?'

'Yes, I'll call Friday afternoon, to finalise arrangements,' I replied before turning my back on him and re-joining my friends.

I picked Carlos up on Saturday morning at 10am, turning up in my Peugeot 206 Coupe Cabriolet. He sneered at it before climbing in.

'What, you don't like my car?' I asked him sarcastically.

'It's just the type of sports car I'd expect a sheila like you to drive. I drive a Porsche myself.'

If he thought that would impress me it backfired.

'Where are we headed?' he asked me.

'Richmond. They have a rental house there.'

'So what's the story with you and Lucy? From our conversation the other night, it seemed like you were more concerned about Tom and didn't even know one of the kids had died.'

I wasn't sure I wanted to give this nosy bastard details of my private life. But then I decided it didn't really matter anymore.

'Tom and I used to be together.' I told him. 'You could say that Lucy stole him from me.'

'Is that why you fell out?'

'Yes.'

He didn't say anything else for a while and we drove on in silence.

'How long were you with the woman, Kelly, you mentioned?' I asked him.

'Up until the tsunami, five and a half years. They have been the happiest years of my life.'

'And how old are you if you don't mind me asking?'

'I'm thirty-seven.'

'And how old was Kelly?'

'Kelly *is* twenty-five.'

He'd told me Kelly was missing. She was probably dead, but he didn't seem to want to accept it.

'So she was nineteen, and you were thirty-one when

you became involved?'

'Yeah, what of it?'

'Nothing, just asking.'

'Kelly lied about her age when we first met. She said she was two years older than her real age.'

'Mm.'

'After the tsunami I spent a few weeks in Phuket looking for her without success.'

'Well she's probably dead then. What's the point in talking to Lucy?'

'I want to know what happened to them. Lucy didn't tell me much when I spoke to her. I want *details*.'

'Right.'

We travelled the rest of the way in silence. I didn't really have anything else to say to him.

I turned left into a street of terrace houses and pulled over. 'This is it. I've never been here but it was the address listed on the card Lucy sent me. I looked it up in my street directory the other day.'

'Good thing you kept the card then. You weren't tempted to throw it away?'

'I did, but then I retrieved it from the bin and put it in a drawer where it's remained out of sight ever since.'

Carlos followed me up to the front door. The small front yard was a mess with weeds everywhere, bushes that needing trimming and overflowing bins. It didn't look like Lucy took care of it, but to be fair to her I guess if she was recovering from injuries it would be difficult for her to do any maintenance.

A young woman, either of Maori origins or from one of the Pacific islands, answered to my knock. With three young kids hanging around her legs. Urgh! All those kids. It looked to me as though we had the wrong place, or they'd moved.

'Hello, I'm looking for my sister Lucy. She was living here in two thousand and three, but it looks like she's no longer here.'

'No, we've been here since September last year. There was a young family here before us, but I don't know their names.'

'Do you know where they've moved to?' Carlos asked pushing past me.

'No, sorry, no idea,' the woman said, stepping back as though afraid of him.

'Well thanks for your time, and sorry to bother you,' I said and turned to walk back to the car.

'Hang on a moment,' Carlos called out to me. 'Maybe some of the neighbours would know.'

'Well, you can knock on their doors if you like. I'm not. They moved and didn't let me know their new address.'

'Can you hang on a bit while I knock on some doors?'

'You've got five minutes, then I'm leaving.'

'*Bitch*' I heard him mutter. I watched as Carlos knocked on doors either side of Lucy and Tom's old house, but I could see from their shaking heads that they didn't know anything.

When I pulled up outside his apartment block, Carlos turned to me and said, 'Look I was planning to hire a private investigator, but after I met you I thought I wouldn't need him. It now looks as though I will. Give

me your number and I'll let you know what he finds out.
I can pass Lucy's address on to you.'

'I'm not interested,' I told him. 'I don't actually give a
damn whether I ever see Lucy again. But good luck with
finding her.'

12
Eva

After meeting up with that man Carlos, I spent the rest of the weekend shedding tears on and off for my beautiful Tom. Sometimes I raged at him and Lucy. If he'd stayed with me then we would never have been holidaying in Phuket and he'd still be alive. It was no doubt Lucy's idea to go there and now she'd caused his death, taking him away from me forever. And what happened to the little boy they had? Carlos said he'd died as well, months before the holiday. I hoped his death wasn't the result of something negligent that Lucy did. She would have been charged if that was the case. She might have received a suspended sentence. If she had, and my employers found out it might reflect badly on me. Being a firm of lawyers, they wouldn't be too happy to discover I had a criminal twin sister.

Over the next few weeks I searched through back newspapers and on the net every spare moment I had. Trying to find out anything I could about what happened to Tom and Lucy's son Christopher.

I finally found a small article attributed to a local paper from the Richmond area. It said that Tom and Lucy Jones had been cleared of any blame for the sudden death of their son. He wasn't a tiny baby. He'd been eight months old when they'd found him dead in his cot one morning. I was pleased to discover they'd not done anything wrong. I recalled seeing I had a voice message from Tom that I'd deleted without listening to. It would have been around the time the boy died. Perhaps Tom had been ringing to tell me about his death and wanted a shoulder to cry on. I wish I'd listened to the message now. It might've changed things. I'd deleted his and Lucy's numbers after that last call Tom made to me so I no longer had numbers for them.

In a way, I'm relieved that I don't know where Lucy lives now. If she'd been at the Richmond house, I wasn't sure how things would've been between us. We haven't spoken since the night I returned home and found the two of them about to jump in the shower together. And they'd clearly been in bed before that. I'd always known that Lucy was in love with Tom and relished the idea *I* had something *she* wanted. With her high bloody morals, it never occurred to me that she would attempt to steal him from *me*.

Throughout our teen years, all the boys I was interested in went for *her*. *I* always attracted them with my extrovert personality, but then when they got to know us a bit, they always fell in love with *her*. God knows what they found so attractive about her. Perhaps it was her nauseating bubbly sweetness. I'd never been able to be like that so if that's what they wanted good riddance to them I thought. But I *hated* Lucy for it sometimes. Everyone preferred Lucy to me. Including, Mum and Nana. Only Dad and Pop had ever liked me, but then that was spoilt as Noel grew. Well I sorted that problem out.

It didn't matter that I came top in everything at school and Lucy only averaged out in 15th place across most subjects; my parents would gush over *her* achievements. We were always in the top set and every year I came first out of the whole year group – with little praise. I complained to Mum about it once and she said it was because they *expected* it from me and that they always knew they didn't have to worry about *my* results. It might have been nice if they showed their appreciation once in a while.

I considered calling my own private investigator to try and track Lucy down. But I soon dismissed that notion. If she was still recovering from injuries, she might expect me to help out with her daughter. That was something I wasn't prepared to do. And there are some things you just can't forgive. Twin sister or not.

13
Kim

'Kim, there's an envelope addressed to you that's been shoved under our door,' Laurie shouted. 'I'll leave it on the kitchen worktop.'

I heard the door slam, signalling he'd left for work. Curious I walked into the kitchen and examined the envelope. I didn't recognise the handwriting. Opening it I found a short letter from Lucy telling me she'd decided to take Clara away for a road trip holiday. She said that creepy Carlos had come around again last night knocking on her windows, trying to open them and ringing her buzzer. It had spooked her a little, so she wanted to get away for a while. I looked out the kitchen window and could see that her car was gone. He must have really spooked her as she'd recently admitted she was nervous about getting behind the wheel after such a long break.

I'd told Laurie about finding this Carlos outside the block when I returned from Janine's yesterday.

'Don't speak to him if he comes around again Kim. Tom mentioned him when he phoned on Christmas

Day – he didn't think much of the bloke.'

Hearing this confirmed everything Lucy had told me. But it was easy for Laurie to say this when he's out at work all day and I'm here alone.

'I won't be here tomorrow anyway. If you remember I'm going to Sophie's,' I told him.

Laurie nodded, adding 'Good.'

I returned home from my sister Sophie's at 3pm, exhausted after dealing with her boisterous kids and Freddie. Freddie was grizzly and in need of his afternoon nap after all that physical activity. I was about to open the gate leading from the car park when I heard running footsteps behind me. I turned to find that man, Carlos, behind me.

'I'll come in with you to knock on Lucy's door,' he said in a tone that indicated he wouldn't take no for an answer. He'd no doubt already been buzzing and knocking at the front without success. Did he think Lucy was in there hiding from him and that a knock on her flat door might entice her to open it?

'There's no point I'm afraid. She's gone away.' I stood in front of the gate, determined not to let him in.

'Gone away where?'

'I have no idea, she just left me a note saying she and her daughter were going away for a few weeks. She'd been planning to have a holiday as soon as she was well enough to drive again. And now she can.'

'That's a bit of a coincidence, isn't it? That she goes away straight after I come around wanting to talk to her? How long is she going to be away?'

'She'd been planning to go on a holiday as soon as she was free of her wheelchair. As I've already told you, she said a few weeks.'

'So where's she gone?'

'I've already told you that as well. *I. Don't. Know.*' I spoke each word out slowly for him. To make the point. He seemed to be hard of hearing as he kept asking me the same questions.

He stepped closer to me and in an intimidating manner said 'You trying to be funny? I will ask you one last time. Where's she gone?'

'And I have told you, she didn't tell me. I'm not sure that she knew herself. She mentioned a road trip. That could be to anywhere. Now I need to get my child inside. I'm sorry, you'll have to leave. This entrance is for residents only.'

'You'd better not be lying to me or I will ..., ' he trailed off not finishing the sentence, but I sensed the implied threat. 'One more thing,' he added. 'Was she living here alone?'

'She was here with her daughter of course. No one else. And I'm not lying to you. Quite frankly wherever she's gone is none of your business. You have no right to come around hassling Lucy. She told you all she knew in Phuket. What more do you want?'

'The truth.'

'What do you mean, the truth?'

'I have a suspicion that Lucy knows more than she's letting on about what happened to my girlfriend and if she's not being honest with me, I won't be happy. There will be consequences.'

I lost my temper then. Probably not the wisest thing to do given his character. 'It sounds to me as if you are threatening Lucy. Why don't you just bugger off and leave her alone? Don't you think she's had enough to deal with? First the death of her son, then Tom – all in a matter of months. She's had to recover from terrible injuries and is grieving. You have no right to be bothering her like this.'

'And what about me, what do you think I'm going through?'

'I'm sorry for your loss, but it's nothing to do with Lucy – or me. Leave us alone.'

Freddie was crying now. He must have picked up on the threat from this man. I unlocked the gate, lifted him up and stepped through – half expecting to be pulled back by Carlos or for him to push in after me. But he remained standing where he was. The gate has an automatic lock and I closed it with a hard kick. I unlocked and entered the back door, checking it was also locked behind me, before hurrying upstairs to the safety of our flat.

No wonder Lucy was scared of him. Yesterday, when I'd bumped into him outside the flats, he'd been all charm and playing the part of a man suffering. Today he showed his true colours. I shuddered at the potential threat this man posed to Lucy. And possibly Clara. I could understand why she took off. And if I was right he was also threatening *me*!

Whilst I'm not Lucy's greatest fan, this man's behaviour was seriously out of order. She's a vulnerable single mother. Although, if I'm honest, it's more Clara's welfare that concerns me. Really I should phone Lucy and warn her of Carlos's visit. I tried her mobile but it went to voicemail.

Once I'd settled Freddie for his nap, I nipped downstairs to Lucy's and let myself in with the spare key. I thought she might have left clues about where she'd gone. The place was clean and tidy and the bedding removed from both her bed and Clara's cot. That indicated she planned to stay somewhere where she'd need bedding. Not a motel or hotel then. A cabin probably. There were plenty of those on the highways, and you could pay a reduced rate if you had your own bedding. But there were no clues pointing to where she'd gone. As I turned to leave the flat I spotted her mobile phone lying on the kitchen worktop. Either she'd forgotten it or didn't want to be contacted. I wondered how long she'd be away. The threat from this man wasn't going to disappear. He seemed obsessive and dangerous. Yesterday when Lucy said she might have to move, I thought that was a bit extreme, and dismissed her concerns. Now I understood why she was so worried.

14
Eva

Melbourne, March 2018

I've just come from a meeting with my boss who's issued me with an ultimatum. He said if I don't get my act together the partners will have to let me go. Get my act together! I've been doing fine – despite everything. And they'd let me go after working for this firm for twelve years, the ungrateful bastards! I should have moved on to another company five years ago when they refused to make me a partner or started my own practice. It was sheer laziness that prevented me from doing so. I hadn't wanted the responsibility of running my own business. Now my boss claims I lost a valuable client through underperforming. I don't believe that. The client just got a better offer somewhere else.

'Take the long service leave you have owing and have a holiday somewhere,' my boss said.

'I don't want a holiday, Greg,' I told him. 'It's only two months since I had one.'

What a disaster that had been. My boyfriend of

seven years split up with me on that holiday – leaving me alone on the Sunshine Coast in Queensland while he headed back to Melbourne. I *have* struggled to come to terms with Drew no longer being in my life, but I know it hasn't affected my work.

Returning to my apartment from Queensland to see all his belongings gone hit me badly at first. I went into a rage and smashed a few things up. The affair I had with a stunning man up at the resort once Drew departed, consoled me for a short time. I posted pictures of us on Facebook hoping Drew would see them and realise that I didn't give a toss. But I did. I don't like being duped like that.

Of course, it was the issue of children that finished it for me. Drew always claimed he didn't want them either. But most men have an overwhelming desire to procreate which eventually surfaces. It's the same old story. Tom was the first one who I lost for that reason. Others followed. I thought Drew was an exception. Seven years of my life I gave him. He'd never proposed, but we lived as man and wife, so I wasn't that bothered. I imagined we'd spend the rest of our lives together.

While on that holiday, Drew announced that a woman he'd been seeing secretly over the past year was pregnant with his child. He claimed she only told him *after* we'd arrived at our holiday resort. So he left me, with indecent haste I might add, and has now set up a home with her playing *happy fucking families*.

It's said that 'wives' normally know when their husband is having an affair. I had no clue. He'd completely fooled me. He claimed I didn't know her and said he'd met her at the club – a club where he supposedly played a lot of squash. I envisioned one of those sporty types. I enjoy walking, cycling and swimming in the summer months but I'm not what you would call 'sporty' by any stretch of the imagination. I'm better looking than most *sporty* women. I make sure I only take enough exercise to keep my body trim – but not so that it becomes hard and muscly. I think women should remain *soft*.

Moaning about my situation to my girlfriends only served to push them away. They started making excuses about why they were unable to meet up with me. No doubt fed up with my endless rantings. They'd heard it all before.

Having been forced to take long service leave, I was at a loose end most days with all my friends working. Apart from a few work colleagues, there was no one in my life who had children. I'd never seen Lucy's kids. Well her one surviving child. Never wanted to. But now it wouldn't be too bad as her daughter Clara would be a teenager. Most parents complain that teenagers are a nightmare. At least you can hold a conversation with them; unlike tiny children. It used to make me sick seeing my parents, Lucy and my grandparents, gushing over my brother Noel when he was a baby and a toddler. I would've considered having children if someone had taken them away and returned them to me as young adults.

Somewhat begrudgingly I began looking for Lucy in Melbourne. At first, it was simply to pass the time. However, as my search went on I realised I really did want to find her and my niece, Clara. I didn't think Lucy would ever leave Melbourne, but where could she have moved to? She wasn't listed with a landline anywhere. Of course, she could have an unlisted number or only a mobile phone. I searched social media. There were plenty of women called Lucy Jones but none were her. There were no listings for a Clara Jones either. Lucy could have remarried by now.

Tom's parents would probably know where they were – if she'd kept in touch with them. I had Tom's parents' address somewhere; they own a hotel in some seaside town in Wales. I recalled Tom telling me the town wasn't a huge place, so even if the parents were now retired I was sure I could find them.

With little to do, I began contemplating a trip abroad. I could travel to the UK, take in the sights of London and then make a trip to Wales and look up Tom's parents. That would use up some of my long service leave. I had almost three months to fill – with full pay. I could also visit Paris and other European capitals. Maybe meet the man of my dreams.

I've booked my ticket and I'm due to leave for England on 4th April. I dug out the phone number of Tom's parents' hotel last week. It's in a place called Llandudno in Wales. When I phoned the number there was an answering machine that said the hotel wasn't open until the first of April. Hopefully I can make a booking before I leave Australia. I've drawn up a will in case anything happens to me on my travels. You never know these days. I've left everything to my niece Clara. I wouldn't leave Lucy anything on principle.

15
Eva

United Kingdom, April 2018

London is an exciting city! Much, much larger than Melbourne. I trudged around seeing all the usual tourist sights. I also joined a tour that took us quite a way out of London, to a large palace called Hampton Court. It's been a bit lonely some days but on that tour I teamed up with some Canadian women. We're all heading off to Bath tomorrow to see the Roman Baths and explore the Georgian city. From there I plan to make my way to Wales.

It was so complicated finding my way to this Welsh town from Bath, but I finally arrived – four trains later.

I jumped into a cab at the station which eventually pulled into a car park at the rear of the hotel I was booked into. A woman, who looked to be in her 40s, met me at the reception desk. I gave her my name and completed all the formalities of checking in. After a quick glance at their brochure I could see Tom's parents no longer owned the place.

'I wonder if you could help me – the parents of my brother-in-law used to own this hotel. Would you know if Mr. & Mrs. Jones still live in Llandudno?'

'Yes, they do,' the woman said. 'Well for part of the year anyway. They'd be in Spain right now. They usually return in early June, just after the school half-term holidays. You said they were your brother-in-law's parents. You don't mean Tom do you?'

'Yes, that's right.'

'So you must be Lucy's sister? I can see the resemblance.'

'So you've met Lucy then?' I asked her, thinking Lucy must have come over to the UK at some point on a holiday.

'I *know* Lucy. She was running the hotel with Tom's parents before we bought it. She owns the Deli Kitchen in town now. Didn't you know that?'

'No … er, we haven't spoken for many years.'

'Gosh, she'll be surprised to see you then! I could ring her if you like and let her know you're here.'

I bristled at her suggestion. 'No, I'd rather you didn't contact her,' I said emphatically. 'I would like to surprise her. Is my niece Clara living with her?'

'Yes, of course.'

'What did you say the name of her place was?'

'The Deli Kitchen. Lucy and Clara live up above the business. They're open until 5 pm. If you head down there now you should catch her.'

'I'd rather wait until after they're closed. I don't want to meet up with my sister after all these years in front of other people.'

'Yes, of course. You're right. Well, I hope you enjoy your stay at our hotel and that your reunion with Lucy goes well,' she said, handing me the keys to my room.

After showering and changing I walked down to the town, following the directions I've been given and found 'The Deli Kitchen' as she'd described. It was shut now, but I could see some staff inside still clearing up. One was stacking the tables and chairs I'd seen him take in from outside. It looked impressive. So, Lucy had finally put her business degree to good use. I hadn't expected to find Lucy here in Llandudno, but perhaps without Tom she felt the need to be near 'family'. She'd always been needy like that.

I couldn't see Lucy anywhere but I spotted a door next to the deli that, presumably, led to the upstairs. I walked over to it with the intention of pressing the buzzer but I felt all sweaty with nerves and left my hand hovering for some time. I wasn't sure what kind of reception I was going to receive from her. *Do it!* With a shaky hand I pressed the buzzer. After a short interval, I could hear someone coming down the stairs and a woman about my age opened the door. She looked at me with a quizzical expression for a moment before exclaiming, 'Oh my God. Eva!'

I peered closely at her before asking, 'You know who I am?'

'Of course I do silly. I'm Lucy!'

No that wasn't right. This woman had some resemblance to Lucy and me but I knew with absolute certainty she wasn't Lucy. Being her twin, I should know. I see myself in the mirror every day. 'Oh no you're not,' I replied, 'but I'd like to know just who the fuck you are!'

16
'Lucy'

Llandudno, April 2018

Clara returned from school in an aggressive mood today. After stomping into the kitchen, without any greeting, she immediately opened the fridge. 'What can I eat? I'm, like, starving!' she declared scanning the contents.

'*Clara*' I said sternly.

'What?'

I raised my eyebrows and she realised what I was intimating.

'Oh, alright. I'm not starving like thousands of poor kids around the world. I'm just a privileged western teenager who is, like, very, very hungry! Is that okay?' she asked.

'Better,' I said attempting to keep a straight face.

'So what can I eat then?'

'Not too much before your dinner. There are some scones in the pantry. There's a range of fruit and there's some home-baked ham in the fridge and plenty of bread.

You could have a sandwich.'

'I'll have a sandwich *and* a scone. I didn't eat much at lunchtime. I'll, like, still eat my dinner. Promise. What's for dinner tonight? Leftover specials I imagine,' she said with resignation while cutting some thick slices of bread. I was about to protest at the size of her slices, but closed my mouth, having second thoughts.

'No, I made a Bolognese sauce last night. I just have to cook the pasta to go with it.'

'Great. Give me a shout later when it's ready. I'm, like, off to do my homework as soon as I have all my goodies ready.'

Homework. I doubted that. At least not for the greater part of the time she'd be in her room. Although Clara was pretty sensible at completing her homework – eventually, she spent far too much time closeted in her bedroom looking at her tablet or surfing the net. I monitored the sites she visited and didn't always approve of some of them. We'd argued about various videos she'd watched on 'YouTube'. Clips of young women or men in their homes. One particular young woman, who girls like Clara thought was their 'friend', was simply promoting cosmetics. Other clips showed mindless hours of people doing very little, while endless advertisements flashed up on the screen. When I asked her what was so interesting about these people she just gave me her usual teenage shrug.

After she'd gone I cleaned up the kitchen, still in a bit of a daze about my news this morning. I'd recovered from my earlier sickness and was looking forward to eating something. I grated some fresh parmesan, took a pan out, and filled it with water for the pasta. I retrieved the sauce I'd made last night from the fridge and put it in another pan ready for heating. It was still too early to start cooking. I decided to have a small glass of wine and do today's codeword and quick crossword from the Guardian, to pass the time and take my mind off my 'little problem'. I sat looking at the glass of wine I'd poured. Was it okay to drink alcohol when I'd been feeling so sick? I took a few sips and waited to see if my stomach reacted. It didn't, but I left it beside me while I tackled the crossword.

I was halfway through it when I heard the buzzer sounding. I wondered who it could be. Staff usually texted me first if they wanted to pop in for a quick word. I went downstairs, opened the door and stared at the woman standing there in puzzlement. Instead of the expected familiar face of one of my staff, another familiar face stood before me. Eva. *Shit! After all this time!*

'Oh my God, Eva,' I said foolishly.

'So you know who I am then?' she asked.

'Of course I do silly, I'm Lucy,' I said laughing – although I could feel every bone in my body tensing. Of all the times to turn up – why now?

'Oh no you're not, but I'd like to know just who the fuck you are,' she said.

17
'Lucy'

Eva's hostile accusation left me in shock. I needed to remain calm, otherwise there might be great ructions. Eva had always caused trouble and it was the last thing I needed today.

'Come in, come in,' I said – although every part of me railed against it. She followed me upstairs to the kitchen and pulled out a chair, sitting at the kitchen table.

'Would you like a glass of red wine?'

'Yes, thank you,' she said.

I poured her a glass hoping she wouldn't notice the slight tremor in my hand.

'So, who are you then? You're certainly not Lucy. Did the woman from the hotel phone you and warn you that I was here.'

'No. Who are you talking about?' I asked puzzled. 'And I am Lucy, I've just changed.'

'*No you're not!*' she shouted at me. '*I am Lucy's identical twin and you look nothing like us!*'

'Of course I do, it's just that—'

'You know Mum, like, got her face completely

smashed up in the tsunami in Phuket. She had to have facial reconstructive surgery. That altered her appearance. But then, like, you wouldn't know about that, would you? As you didn't bother to keep in touch with us,' Clara said coming into the kitchen. She must have heard everything Eva had been saying.

'Oh, I didn't know that,' Eva said, her tanned complexion paling. She picked up her glass and gulped down some wine, bringing more colour back to her cheeks. 'So what happened to your face?' Eva asked me.

'It was smashed to bits. I had two broken cheekbones and a flattened, broken nose. I was lucky that my skull wasn't broken. My forehead received quite a hefty battering and was very swollen. You can see the scars on the side of my face if you look closely where the surgeon inserted metal plates and screws.'

'They weren't mum's only injuries,' Clara added.

Eva looked at me quizzically and I so I went on to tell her about all my injuries in detail.

'My God, so many broken bones. You must have spent months recovering.'

'I did.'

A couple of times she looked like she was about to say something, but then stopped. No word of sympathy from her. She hadn't changed then. Finally she turned to her niece.

'So, you must be Clara then,' she said. 'I can see bits of Tom in you – and me, or how your mother used to look.'

'Why didn't you, like, help mum after she returned from Phuket?'

'Well to start with I didn't know and I would have been no help at all I'm afraid,' Eva said waving her arms around. 'I'm no good with little kids. Never have been. Which is why I don't have any.'

'Did you ever marry?' I asked her.

'No,' Eva said. I could see from her reaction this was a sensitive issue for her. She drained her glass of wine and looked around expectedly for more. I re-filled it for her.

'I came close to marrying, but no, it didn't happen. Of course, Tom and I might have married, except you *stole* him from me,' she said looking at me accusingly. 'Did your mother tell you that she stole *my* boyfriend?' she continued turning to Clara. 'He was *mine* first.'

'Yes mum did tell me that, but like, you didn't want children did you? That's, like, why my father preferred mum. So, like, what are you doing over here?' Clara asked. 'Why now, after all these years?'

For God's sake Clara, stop saying 'like' all the time. It was a habit of hers that drove me mad.

'I've been very busy practicing corporate law,' Eva said with a touch of arrogance. 'I'm currently on long service leave and I thought I'd try to find you. I couldn't locate you in Victoria anywhere. I decided while I was touring Europe and, in the UK, I'd look up Tom's parents to see if they knew where you were.'

'They're, like, in Spain,' Clara said. 'I don't think they would have been happy to see you anyway. They mentioned you to me some years back saying, like, it was shameful that you didn't support your sister after the tsunami.'

'As I said, I didn't know your parents were in Phuket,' she told Clara. 'Not until I bumped into some creep called Carlos,' she continued, turning back to me. 'He told me about Tom's death and that you were badly injured but had discharged yourself to return home. He thought I was you at first and it took me a while to convince him I wasn't. I *did* go out to your old Richmond house with him after that to see how everything was and see if you needed help, but you'd moved and didn't let me know where you were.'

So she went with Carlos to the old address. If she'd really wanted to know where we were, she could have kept in touch with him. He discovered where we were living.

'We moved from Richmond after Christopher's death. Tom and I couldn't stay at that house. That's where he died.'

Eva looked at me, her face devoid of any emotion after I mentioned Christopher's death. Was she really that heartless?

'Tom and I didn't think to make contact with you again after we moved,' I continued. 'We were a little preoccupied with our grief. Tom left you a message about Christopher's death and you never replied. You never responded to the card we sent you after the twins were born either. We assumed you still didn't want anything to do with us.'

'I didn't want anything to do with you – until I heard about Phuket that is. And I didn't hear Tom's message about Christopher. I might have seen a missed call from him and deleted the message without listening to it. I was still very angry with you both. Then, as I said, I didn't know how to contact you after discovering you'd moved. I'd deleted both of your mobile numbers.'

'If you knew where Tom's parents lived all this time, like, why didn't you make contact with them then?' Clara challenged her.

'I didn't … I just didn't think of it until I came across their address while clearing out a cupboard. I'd forgotten I had it.'

'So when did you discover their address then? Like, was it ten years ago? Five. One? How long ago?' Clara kept on at her. *Calm down, Clara. God, she was in an aggressive mood today.*

'Recently. It was the hotel address I had. That's where I'm staying. I was still expecting to see them there. The new owner of the hotel told me where to find you. Seems she knows you.'

'Yes, we worked with the new owners for a few weeks before they took over. Look I was about to start preparing dinner before you arrived. Would you like to join us for a meal?' I asked her, hoping she'd refuse.

'Yes, that would be nice thank you.' *Damn!*

Clara plonked herself down at the table, folding her arms, all the time shooting hostile looks at Eva. I could tell, by Clara's behaviour that she didn't like her. In an effort to divert attention from me I asked Eva when she'd arrived in the UK and what she had seen so far. She prattled on, all the while replenishing her glass of wine without asking. I had still barely touched mine. I even opened a fresh bottle for her as I needed some for the meal. Her monologue was all me, me, me. Her usual narcissistic behaviour. Nothing had changed there then.

Clara retreated to her room after dinner, citing homework as an excuse. I could tell that she didn't want to sit in the same room as Eva a moment longer than was necessary. Once she'd gone, Eva dropped her next bombshell.

'I'm still not convinced you're Lucy. Facial reconstruction aside. So I'd like to play a little memory game and see how well you do on that. Tell me what happened during the summer holidays when we were ten and were out playing one day at Nana and Pop's place?

I frowned, trying to recall what she was talking about.

'Do you mean when we came face to face with an eastern brown snake and you nearly shat yourself?' I asked.

'So did you!'

'No, it was me who remained calm and told you not to move a muscle while we waited for it to move on. Pop always told us not to run or make sudden movements if we came across a snake like that.'

'You put your hand over my mouth to stop me making a noise,' Eva said accusingly.

'Yes, because I knew you were going to scream otherwise,' I replied.

'And so you left me in front of you so the snake would have bitten me.'

'No, it was just to keep you quiet. But it slithered away much closer to me.'

'Okay. Another one. What happened on our twelfth birthday?' she asked.

I had no trouble remembering this one, jumping straight in with my answer. 'We celebrated it the day before our *actual* birthday at Nana and Pop's. You blew out all the candles before I had a chance to do *any* and we had a stinking row, throwing cake at each other. You later pushed me under the water in the creek and held me down. I thought you were going to drown me.'

'Alright, Enough. You've convinced me. I just can't get over how *different* you look.'

'I don't look *that* different.'

'I can see a resemblance between us, but to me, you do look very different. Your skin is darker as well.'

'It's the same as yours,' I retorted looking at her healthy face.

'This is my left-over tan from the Australian summer. The warm weather continued into the autumn, so I was still catching the sun right up to leaving Melbourne.'

'Well mine is from a week we've just had in southern Spain,' I countered. 'We were over there at the beginning of the Easter holidays.'

'But you *hated* being in the sun too much, preferring —'

'I know,' I said cutting her off. 'I preferred my skin to be as silky white as possible. I was never the outdoorsy type like you Eva. But when you have children, things change. You can't keep children indoors all the time. Especially when we're in Spain. We spend a lot of time at the pool or beach.'

'Oh. No, I suppose not,' she conceded. 'The woman at the hotel said Tom's parents lived in Spain part of the year. Later I remembered Tom telling me they'd bought a place there. Do you go there often?'

I didn't want to get into this conversation with Eva. I rose from the table and said, 'Look it's been great seeing you again Eva, but I have to start work early in the morning. I need to get to bed.' I was also feeling quite queasy. 'How long are you going to be in Llandudno?'

'I'm booked in for two nights at the hotel. They're booked out after that, but I might find another hotel and stay another night or two.'

'I'll give you my number and you can text me. I have a business to run and so I can't promise what times I will have free.'

'But surely you can make time for your long-lost sister, *'Lucy'*,' she said making inverted commas in the air as she said Lucy.

'Of course,' I said as she rose from the table and began to make her way out.

'Don't bother seeing me out, I know the way.'

'I have to bolt the door anyway, so I will see you out,' I said following her down the stairs. 'Goodbye then,' I called out to her as she walked away. She waved with a half turn and continued on her way. Clara was in the kitchen when I returned.

'She's gone then. I hope, like, you're not going to see her again. She is such a *bitch!* Did she really do that on your twelfth birthday?'

'So Miss Big Ears was listening the whole time. And please don't use that word.'

'Well she's my aunt, like, and I wanted to hear what else she had to say. I couldn't stand being in the room with her. I felt like slapping her face at times. And what's wrong with calling her a bitch. We, like, use that word at school all the time. And she *is* a bitch.'

While I agreed with Clara, it was not language I wanted to encourage her to use. Hypocritical of me no doubt. 'It's a poor habit to get into Clara. How would you like someone to call you a bitch?'

'My friends call me 'bitch' all the time. In, like, a joking way of course. We only use it in a derogatory way when we don't like someone. And I don't like her.'

'I could see that. You made it plain. If she comes around again, please attempt to be more polite and civil to her. She's only going to be here for a few more days. It won't hurt you.'

'Okay, I'll, like, make an effort for *you*. Not her.'

'Now off to bed miss and put that tablet away. I'm off to bed now too. Don't stay awake for hours on that damn thing. Ten more minutes and then you can hand it over to me actually. And your phone. I'll return them in the morning. I can imagine you staying up for hours sending messages about Eva to all your friends. You can tell them tomorrow. Not tonight.'

'Okay, okay. Ten minutes.' She raced off then, no doubt to make contact with friends.

I tossed and turned in bed later that night concerned about Eva's presence in Llandudno. With the startling news I'd had earlier today it really seemed too much to be dealing with.

I had been violently sick this morning. And again after going into the business kitchen at lunchtime. I'd made it to the loo in the nick of time, losing the food I'd just eaten. *Great! I must be coming down with something,* were my first thoughts.

'Not in the family way are you? After your recent tryst?' Catrin, one of my staff had asked me as I'd emerged from the toilet.

'What?'

'Pregnant. You couldn't be pregnant, could you? You also said you were sick this morning. Looks familiarly like morning sickness to me. I should know. It hit me badly with my two, almost from the moment I conceived.'

Pregnant? Oh God, surely not! Not at my age! I was going to be thirty-nine later this year – with a fourteen and half-year-old daughter and no partner. Well, there was a potential partner but he lived on the other side of the world.

I'd left the Deli after my lunchtime vomiting bout and rushed out to buy a pregnancy test. It was only four weeks since that careless night. Would a test be able to tell me yet? Was it too soon? I hoped Catrin was wrong and that I wasn't pregnant.

The test proved positive. Oh God, what an impossible situation. What was I going to do? What would I say to Clara? To the father, who was now back in Australia? Should I tell him? It was all too complicated.

I spent the afternoon pacing, trying to remain calm and considering my options. The afternoon flew by and, before I knew it, I heard Clara climbing the stairs. Then my world went even crazier.

18
Eva

I found my niece extremely confrontational and aggressive. Challenging me about not helping her mother after the tsunami. As if I could have when I didn't know where she was? Lucy seemed a bit nervous and she's so different. Not just in her appearance. When we were growing up, I was the dominant one. I was the first born after all. Lucy would only assert herself at odd times, otherwise, she let me be in charge of most things. I suppose, because I haven't been in her life for so long, she has become more independent and assertive. She was certainly assertive tonight, but she was definitely nervous as well? Why?

The following morning, I explored the town – what there was of it. It was tiny compared to seaside resorts in Australia – streets of cramped terrace houses. How could they call this a resort? It was laughable. And it was so small. How could Lucy stand living here after Melbourne?

A cold wind blew up as I walked along the pier,

forcing me to turn around and retrace my steps. Melbourne can get cold, but this was something else. I couldn't live here.

I went along to 'Deli Kitchen' for a spot of lunch. I had to admit the food and coffee were good. I sat on one of the lounges in the warmth and read a paper at leisure. I spotted '*Lucy*' flitting in and out to presumably, the kitchens or something at the rear. She hadn't seen me. Should I call out to her and ask to see her kitchen operation? I wasn't sure I'd be welcome. I couldn't decide whether to stay on in Llandudno. Was it worth trying to re-connect with her or getting to know Clara a little better? Perhaps I should buy them a present, maybe then they'd appreciate me more.

Before going shopping, I went down to the seafront hotels and found one which had a vacancy. The place was huge and I couldn't believe all these hotels accommodated tourists coming to visit. Why on earth would they do that when they could go to Europe? I booked in for a two further nights. I'd give it that long. Then, I don't think I could stand to be here any longer. Paris was beckoning and I'd decided it would be next on my itinerary. The hotel was displaying brochures of trips to different parts of Wales. To break the boredom of this town I booked a trip to Snowdonia.

I traipsed around the shops trying to find suitable presents for the two of them. I didn't have a clue what to buy, so I settled on some flowers and a leather-bound notebook for Lucy. The notebook wasn't dated, but it would be suitable for use as a diary. I was sure she still kept a diary.

I couldn't decide what to get for Clara; choices in Llandudno were limited. So I decided I'd give her one of the smart phones I'd bought in Bangkok during my stopover. I'd spent one night and almost two full days there looking around. When I saw smart phones were so cheap, I bought a couple for spares, in case I lost mine on the trip.

I'm sure she'll be happy with the phone - all young people like 'smart' phones don't they? I decided I would invite them out for dinner as well. A treat on me.

I returned to the hotel, wrapped the presents and sent Lucy a text, inviting her and Clara out for a meal. That and the presents might sweeten them up a bit. An hour later she still hadn't answered so I had an afternoon nap.

When I woke I checked my phone. Lucy had accepted my invitation and suggested that I call for them at 7 pm. It was 6 pm already, so I texted confirmation back to her, showered and changed.

Clara answered the door saying I should come upstairs and wait for them, they weren't quite ready. Her tone was a little friendlier than it had been the other night. I presented both of them with my presents as soon as I entered the living room. They both looked embarrassed as I encouraged them to open their gifts. Lucy expressed delight with the flowers.

'You remembered that I loved gerberas,' she exclaimed. 'And my favourite colours.'

I hadn't remembered, not consciously anyway, but perhaps some part of my brain had. After all, I'd chosen those particular flowers for her at the florist shop.

'What a lovely notebook,' Lucy also declared when she unwrapped it.

'I thought it might be suitable as one of your dairies,' I told her.

'I stopped writing my diaries after Christopher died,' she said. 'But it'll still be very useful for the business,' she added.

Clara let out a squeal of delight at her smartphone. Perhaps she would be nicer to me now. They both thanked me and then Lucy asked what type of meal I would prefer to eat.

'There's a good Italian restaurant and good Indian restaurant in town,' she told me.

'Urgh! Not Indian. Too spicy for me. I would prefer Italian.'

'I forgot you don't like spicy food. You always complained when mum cooked any spicy meals.'

'Yeah, and I haven't changed.'

'We, like, love spicy food. Mum often cooks Indian meals, don't you mum?'

Lucy nodded. She always did prefer mum's spicy dishes.

'So where are you going next on your travels?' Lucy asked me over dinner. I noticed she'd barely touched her wine. She'd only had a few little sips from her glass and she'd toyed with her food a bit as well, whereas Clara and I ate everything on our plates. I'd consumed most of the wine I'd ordered.

'I thought Paris. Have you ever been there?'

'We went once when Clara was about seven, with Tom's parents. It was during the February half term when the hotel was still closed. We met up with them there – they flew over from Spain. It was very cold though.'

'What, colder than this place?'

'Yes. February is one of the coldest times of the year. It snowed while we were there. Clara loved the snow – being so close to the sea we don't see much of it here.'

'I forget that the weather in Europe is the opposite of Australia,' I said. 'Don't you miss the sun?'

'Yes, and no. We do have lovely sunny days here and we get out to Spain every year. There's plenty of sun there.'

'When will you go there again?'

'Probably in Clara's summer holidays. It's almost too hot there in the summer, but that's when Clara has her main school holidays. Late July and August. Now that Gwyneth and Howell aren't tied down to the hotel we can all go there anytime we like. Within reason that is. I can't waltz off from the business anytime I want – and I don't take Clara out of school during term time.'

I noticed that Lucy looked more relaxed and animated when talking about Clara. My colleagues in Melbourne often made proud statements about their offspring. I suppose that's what it's like to be a parent.

'Don't you miss Australia?' I asked her.

'Yes, of course, there are lots of things I miss. Including practical things. I miss fly-wire screens in the summer. The flies here are a bloody nuisance. We have to have fly swats in every room. I looked into having screens fitted, but I couldn't find anyone who could make them. They don't have them here. We like to have the windows open, so we have to put up with the flies.'

'Mum likes to save the dead flies and she puts them in the scones,' Clara said with a straight face.

'What?' Surely I couldn't have heard her correctly?

'Just a little joke. We call fruit scones, scones with dead flies. Only between ourselves of course. We don't let customers hear us saying that,' Lucy added.

'Oh. They put dried fruit in scones in Wales as well? I've only ever seen that back home in 'English' type tea rooms, and not always then.'

'Yes, some people like fruit scones. Not us I might add.'

'Anyone for dessert?' I asked when the waiter approached to clear our plates.

'No thanks,' Lucy said.

'Not for me either,' Clara added.

'I'm surprised to hear you say that Clara. Come on, I thought all young people liked sweet things.'

'I, like, had some cake this afternoon so I don't fancy anything. I'm quite full thanks. My pizza was very filling. I don't get the chance to have pizza very often. Mum seldom makes them and they're not served in the Deli Kitchen, so I like, jumped at the chance to have one tonight.'

'What about some ice cream?'

'No thanks.'

'Okay. How about coffee or another drink?'

'None for me thanks. I'll have a herbal tea back at home,' Lucy said. Clara shook her head as well. I actually wanted a coffee, but I could see they wanted to leave. Clara, to get back home and play on her new phone no doubt. That reminded me. I wanted to ask about social media.

'When I was looking for you, I couldn't find either of you on Facebook.'

'Why would I do Facebook?' Lucy asked. 'I don't have the time and Clara is too young. I don't agree with young people being on Facebook. It potentially leaves them exposed to things like grooming.'

Grooming. I suppose she meant paedophiles. But I wasn't convinced that was her real excuse.

'You could keep in touch with friends on Facebook,' I suggested.

'If I want to keep in touch with friends I use email or the phone. You know, talk to them in person?' she said with sarcasm. 'This nonsense of having hundreds of friends on Facebook is a joke. It's not real.'

'No I suppose not. I have some real friends on Facebook, but the rest are acquaintances. I've had people asking to be my friend who I've never heard of. I usually ignore them.'

'Glad to hear it. Look I need to get back. And Clara needs her beauty sleep.'

'Yes, of course. I'll have coffee back at the hotel.'

'Thank you very much for the meal. Will we see you tomorrow?'

'I'm booked on a trip to Snowdonia tomorrow. The coach is leaving early in the morning. I have to leave my hotel tomorrow, so I'll be busy checking into my new one when I return from my trip. I'll see you the following day I suppose.'

'That would be nice,' Lucy said giving a fake smile. Her tone was also unconvincing. I should know I've done it a million times myself. So what was going on with her?

Sipping my coffee back at the hotel, I wondered if Lucy and I could ever connect again. I couldn't conjure up any feelings for her – she seemed so alien to me. When she came to live with me in Melbourne – before Tom, our relationship wasn't easy, but we had a sisterly connection. Now it seemed even more strained. I guess that's because we spent so many years apart. I'd like to get her to tell me more about her life with Tom and details of what happened to him in Phuket.

19
Kelly

Phuket, December 2004

I woke in a hospital bed, in a semi-upright position attached by wires to a range of machinery. I was alive!

'Good morning Lucy,' a nurse said leaning over me. Her English was almost perfect with only a slight trace of an accent. Was I home in Australia?

'*Lucy?*' Oh yes, I'd had Lucy's passport in my pocket. So it must have survived. Even though I remembered my dress ripping at one point and thought the force of the water was going to tear it off me. I tried to speak to correct her, but my throat felt like someone had scraped it with sandpaper. And I had a strange nasal sound that echoed in my head. My 'no, I'm Kelly,' didn't sound right.

'Don't try to speak at the moment. You're in Phuket International Hospital with a lot of injuries I'm afraid, plus many cuts and abrasions. Some of your injuries have been dealt with but you're going to require some reconstructive surgery to fix your face. You need to

127

breathe through your mouth due to nasal injuries.'

My bandaged right hand instinctively went up to my face but there were compresses there. It hurt across my forehead, nose and cheeks. I *was* finding it difficult to breathe.

'Don't touch,' the nurse scolded me.

Reconstructive surgery might not be a bad thing, I thought. At least Carlos wouldn't recognise me if he came looking for me. And perhaps I'd come out of it so ugly that he'd be repulsed by me – if he managed to find me. If Lucy survived they'd soon realise that I wasn't her – if she was conscious enough to speak. I hoped it was Lucy I saw passing me and that she was being treated somewhere like me.

Talking hurt too much, so I decided to remain quiet. I'd correct them later. I nodded gently at the nurse. Even that hurt.

'The facial surgeon came down to look at you earlier; you'll be going to theatre later today. I have to keep checking that your airways are clear. We had to intubate you at first, so your throat might be sore from that as well as from all the muck you spewed up.'

Was it the same day, I wondered? She mentioned 'morning' when she greet me. Surely it couldn't still be the same morning of the tsunami?

'You were lucky,' she continued, 'some local people pulled you to safety and managed to get an ambulance to you once the second wave of water receded. Many, many people are still out there with injuries, missing or dead. And we have many others admitted here to the hospital, but not yet identified.'

I nodded, tears trickling down my face. What she'd said made sense. If I hadn't had the passport on me, they wouldn't have had any idea of who I was; not that I was the person in the passport. Lucy had put the passport and money in a sealed plastic bag, so they must have withstood the water deluge. I imagined there might have been a lot of people out that morning without any identification on them. Like Lucy. People who had popped down to the pool or the beach for a swim.

The nurse left me then and went to tend other patients. I was in a small room with five other beds squashed in.

It was then I noticed that my head felt odd, a lot lighter. I carefully moved my right hand up and felt short hair. They'd cut my hair off! The nurse glanced around and seeing the startled look on my face said, 'I forgot to mention, your hair had to be cut off. It was full of thick gluey sand and debris.'

Later that morning I was woken by the sound of a raised male voice saying, 'I'm sorry sir, you cannot come in here. We have told you that we have no patient by the name of Kelly O'Brien admitted to this hospital.'

I froze at the mention of my name. Carlos. It had to be. And I soon had all my fears confirmed when he opened his mouth. I couldn't see him, as there was a screen beside my bed, but I heard him.

'Yeah well, I want to check for myself. What about all the ones you haven't identified? She had no identification on her when the tsunami hit. She was down at the pool.'

'There is no-one in this room who hasn't been identified. I have told you. You need to check with admissions down at the entrance or with the Bangkok Hospital Phuket.'

'I've already been to that hospital. They say she's not there either, so I came back here. I want to check things out for myself.'

'Well I'm sorry to hear that you haven't found her, but we cannot help you. I must ask you to leave sir.'

I heard the door close and breathed a sigh of relief. So Carlos was on the hunt for me. Well, he would be of course, wouldn't he? He had no Benny to issue orders to now and no Kelly to control. A sliver of guilt passed through me. I'd wanted to escape from Carlos, and this disaster was providing me with exactly that opportunity. So far. It wasn't what we'd planned though. Neither Lucy, Tom nor Benny were supposed to die. I knew Tom and Benny were more than likely dead. But what of Lucy? Had she made it? Was it her I'd seen?

They took me for surgery later that day. When they removed the compress I could feel my face was badly distended. My forehead felt like someone from a special effects movie set had plastered extra layers on it. Whatever had hit me must have caused a lot of damage. I was woozy from all the drugs they'd given me but I had a vague recollection of a doctor leaning over and chatting away to me before I went into surgery. He spoke poor English with a strong accent and in my woozy state, I couldn't understand anything he was saying.

I could see it was dark outside when I woke following the surgery. I was in a different room now, with only one other bed. It must be a 'private' room. Again I was in a semi-upright position – I suspected it was to help with my breathing. This must be costing a fortune, was the next thing that popped into my head. How would I pay for it? How long would I need to be here?

I had the answer to my enforced hospitalisation later that night. A surgeon came to see me telling me he was the maxillofacial surgeon who had operated on me. In broken English he told me that I'd need to remain in the hospital for at least two weeks following my surgery to ensure the injuries were healing and that no infections arose. I also had to have the compress and dressings changed each day. No chewing was allowed – all my food would need to be pureed or in liquid form which I could suck through a straw. I had broken cheekbones he'd had to operate on and he didn't want me moving my jaw too much. He said he'd had to reconstruct my nose, using my passport photograph to help him – but found it difficult to reconcile the image in the photograph with my face after my injuries. I said nothing; just smiled at him. Had he realised I had a different face?

The orthopaedic surgeon, who spoke excellent English, came to see me early the following morning, explaining my injuries and the operations he'd had to perform on my collarbone and arm socket. He explained that he hadn't needed to operate on my pelvic fracture, but I was not to bear weight on my left leg for at least six weeks and would need a wheelchair or crutches to move around.

Move around! How was I supposed to do that with one arm immobilised and one leg out of action? I felt sick with everything he'd told me. God, I was full of metal! Would I set off alarms when I went through customs, I asked him with difficulty?

He laughed and said everyone thinks that, but no, I wouldn't set off alarms. He suggested that it would better if I had a wheelchair until I was more mobile and that I should rest as much as possible. Who was going to supply the wheelchair I wondered? And how was I going to shower or wash? So far I had only experienced one wash from a nurse – in bed. I made a mental note to ask the next time a nurse came to my bedside. And to ask about removing the new catheter they'd inserted after this latest surgery. It felt extremely uncomfortable.

I drifted off to sleep again and when I woke a strange man was sitting beside my bed.

'Ah, good morning Mrs. Jones. My name is Keith Stapleton. I'm from the Australian Embassy in Bangkok. I'm er …very sorry about what has happened to you and I'm afraid I have some bad news. Your husband's body has been found and identified by another resident who was staying in the same hotel. But the British Embassy is responsible for him and they have made contact with his family in Wales. I know he was an Australian resident and lived with you in Melbourne. However, because he has British Citizenship, matters concerning him fall under their jurisdiction. No doubt his family will be coming to Phuket to do a formal identification and help sort out his legal affairs with you.'

'I'm … not …,' I trailed off struggling to speak. My head was fuzzy from the strong painkillers they were giving me and my throat was still incredibly sore. I swallowed a few times and then began again.

'I …need …your …help. I …want …to … go … home,' I croaked. It took me forever to speak each word. He shifted awkwardly in the chair and pulled a face. I couldn't judge whether he felt embarrassed by my slow speech or whether it irritated him.

'We haven't even considered repatriation processes. I know that a number of able-bodied Australians and a few walking wounded are flying out in the next few days. As far as I know, they've made their own arrangements. We are flying in several other consular people tomorrow, so we will no doubt be looking into these matters. I can see you are in no condition to be travelling anywhere. From what I understand you've had numerous operations. I suspect you'll need to remain here for several more weeks.'

'But … can't ….I … be … transferred … to … a … hospital … back in … Australia? I really … need to …'

He cut me off before I could finish. 'It is not something that the Australian Government is in a position to deal with I'm afraid. That will be up to your insurance company.'

Insurance company? What did that mean? Was I supposed to have insurance? I didn't have a clue about any arrangements Carlos had made. I wouldn't be contacting him to find out either. Tears streaked down my face. I *had* to leave Phuket and get away from Carlos. 'Please … you … don't … understand … my … name … is ….

'Mrs. Jones,' he said standing. 'I'm sorry, but I have to be going. Someone else will pop in to see you another day. I hope you get better soon.'

It was hopeless. He didn't want to listen and left my room as though propelled by a rocket. What was I going to do? I'd never felt so alone in my life. Not even after all my family died. Then, at least, I was with Kylie and her family when they brought me the news. Here, I was lying incapacitated in a hospital bed in a strange country with no one to talk to. I prayed that Lucy had been found and we could escape together somehow. Maybe she could get Tom's family to help us if they were coming to Phuket. I just hoped that the next consular person would be more approachable and sympathetic. I had to get out of the hospital and Phuket before Carlos came looking for me again.

20
Kelly

Another man from the Australian consulate group dropped into my room this morning. 'Morning Mrs. Jones,' he said. 'I'm from the Australian Embassy. I've just popped in to tell you that your father-in-law arrived this morning. He will no doubt call in to see you at some point.'

I stared dumbfounded at him without answering. He called me Mrs. Jones, so they obviously still thought I was Lucy. Did that mean that Lucy hadn't been found? Could she be in the hospital somewhere, but still unconscious? Or had her body been found but not identified?

Now was the time to be honest, but I was terrified. How could I explain the real reason I had Lucy's passport on me? And all that money? I could be charged. And so could Lucy. What we had been planning was a crime. No, better to let him think I was Lucy for the moment unless Lucy suddenly materialised. But if Lucy didn't re-appear, pretending to be her might the only way I could return to Australia, avoiding any contact with

Carlos.

I just nodded at him and he excused himself saying he had other people to see.

Now I had another dilemma to deal with though. Tom's father. Had he ever met Lucy? I tried to remember what Lucy had told me about their wedding. I'm sure she said that none of Tom's family were there, as they had arranged it at the last minute. Impulsively – with only a couple of their friends present. But surely they would have been sent photographs? Could I use the excuse of my facial injuries and surgery to explain my different appearance?

That afternoon an older version of Tom approached my bed. He had less hair than Tom and a thicker body – otherwise they looked so similar this man could have been Tom's older brother. He didn't look old enough to be Tom's father. 'Lucy, Howell Jones, so good to meet you at last,' he said leaning over to give me a kiss on my forehead before realising that wouldn't be wise with the swelling he could see there. 'Sorry,' he mumbled, pulling back and clearing his throat. 'I'm just sorry it is under these circumstances. I got here as soon as I could. How are you? A silly question I know,' he rattled on, 'I can see you are in the wars.'

I liked his lilting accent. This must be how Welsh people spoke. 'I'm full of metal and strong painkillers,' I croaked, doing my best to imitate Lucy's posher accent. I told him about my different fractures, what they'd done to correct them, and that I had to remain in the hospital for at least another fortnight.

'God it's a wonder you survived. I've been hearing and reading about remarkable survival stories. It's apparently the world's worst natural disaster. Places all over the Indian Ocean have been hit. Some with absolute devastation. Much of Phuket was not affected as badly as other places, due to having a greater number of high rise hotels. But places with low-level buildings, bungalows or beach huts were wiped out. The death toll and the number of people missing are horrendous.'

He looked at me and said, 'Sorry Lucy, perhaps I shouldn't be telling you all this. I'm still in shock. I imagine you are as well.'

I nodded.

'I've carried out a formal identification of Tom. Let's just say I'm glad neither you nor his mother had to do it. They told me his death was instantaneous, due to the nature of his injuries. At least that was one small blessing.'

I nodded again, tears streaming down my face. It must have been so hard for him to identify the body of his son. You don't expect to have to do that in your lifetime.

'I'm sorry, Cariad,' he said taking my right hand. I'd never heard that expression, but assumed it must be some form of endearment. We sat in silence for a few minutes. I could see silent tears running down his face.

'Which hotel were you in?' he finally asked, releasing my hand and wiping his eyes.

'The Regent. Third floor. You could stay in our room, it's all paid for – if it survived the tsunami,' I added. I still found it difficult to talk; my throat was sore and my voice gravelly.

'I had wondered about that. I haven't booked anywhere as yet. Perhaps that might be the best solution – if your room is habitable. I'll need to sort out yours and Tom's belongings anyway. Have you let people know in Australia?'

'No. It's not been feasible to do anything from here. I don't have anyone's number and our mobiles are back at the hotel.'

'Okay, I'll deal with that. There's also the matter of insurance. You'll need to make a claim to cover your health costs. Do you know who you were insured with?'

'No. Tom took care of all that.'

'Well, leave that to me. I'll see to everything. What about Clara? Who's looking after her? Tom did mention it, but I didn't really take it in.'

'A couple called Laurie and Kim. They live in the same block of flats as us back in Melbourne.'

'Ah yes. Presumably either you or Tom will have their number in your phones. I'll make contact with them and let them know what has happened. Tom works with this man Laurie doesn't he?'

I nodded. What was it with these people? Mr. Jones seemed concerned about the dog as well!

We chatted for a few more minutes and I filled him in on all my injuries and operations. He nodded sympathetically at me and sat in silence for a few moments before saying, 'If you don't mind, I'm going to head off to the hotel now. There's lots to sort out. We can talk some more when I come back later.'

It was a relief to have someone to deal with things

like the insurance, but I wasn't looking forward to discovering what he meant by "lots to sort out".

Mr. Jones returned later that afternoon and told me 'our' room was fine. He'd made contact with Laurie, who had been trying to find out what had happened to Tom and Lucy.

'He was pretty upset about Tom but pleased to hear that you survived. I told him about your injuries and various operations. He told me to tell you not to rush back before you're up to it. Everything is fine at home. Clara is doing well. She and Freddie, Laurie and Kim's son, apparently get on really well.'

Perhaps they would like to keep the dog then, I thought. But didn't say anything as Tom's father seemed to think this was important news for me. I'd suggest that possibility if I made it back to Melbourne. I know I promised Lucy I'd take her, but if the dog was happy with this couple and their son had become attached to it, then it might be better for them to keep it. I just nodded and smiled. We had dogs when I lived with my family at the stud farm. Of course, all of us kids adored them and I was upset about never seeing any of them again. But when it came down to it, it was my family that I missed the most.

'I found your insurance documents by the way,' Mr. Jones said. 'They were in a zipped compartment of Tom's case. I made contact with the company and started the claim process. I've also been to see the hospital administration and passed on all the details. Everything will be covered by the policy so you don't have to worry about that.'

'I'm relieved to hear that,' I replied. 'Was there any trouble with the hotel? Gaining access to our room I mean?'

'No, they were very understanding. Some floors are still in a bit of a mess where the water entered. The lifts aren't working. It was the lower ground floor area that copped the worse of it though with a number of casualties. Apparently, the hotel lost power for more than a day. Which made it awkward for guests getting in and out of their rooms with their electronic keys. We don't have any of that nonsense at our hotel back in Llandudno. Anyway, they have things back up and running again, but the restaurant still isn't open. I found these at the hotel. Yours I assume?' He handed me two rings, a diamond engagement ring and a wedding ring. Lucy's. She must have taken them off to come down to the pool. I couldn't remember if she'd worn them at the pool other days.

'You weren't wearing them that day?'

'I usually took them off when I went to the pool,' I lied quickly. 'I was just about to have a swim when the tsunami struck.'

He nodded, satisfied with my answer.

'Now we need to decide what we're going to do about Tom,' Mr. Jones said after a few minutes of silence.

'What do you want to do?' I asked him. I'd been thinking back to his comment of "our hotel back in Llandudno". Did he mean there is just one hotel there and it didn't have electronic keys or was he referring to a hotel his family was involved in? I couldn't ask Mr.

Jones any questions about it because presumably I was supposed to know.

'His mother would like him to return home and be buried in the family plot there.'

'Then that's what we should do.'

'Are you sure you don't mind? You wouldn't want to bury him with Christopher?'

'I did think about that, but it is probably best that he goes home. I think that is what Tom would have wanted.' *Besides I had no idea where Christopher was buried.*

'His mother will be pleased to hear that.'

He sat and held my hand for a while and then jumped up. 'I must get back to the hotel and phone Gwyneth. And I'll have to make arrangements for transporting Tom back.'

'Okay. And thanks for organising everything,' I said.

'It's the least I could do. Is there anything in particular you want me to bring in from the hotel? Personal items? I thought it might be best, given your physical condition, to send your larger case back to Australia. Keeping the bare minimum here with you in the hospital. I noticed you both had quite good-sized hand luggage bags with wheels. I could bring your one here. Then when you are up to flying back it won't be so difficult for you. What do you think? Oh, that's the other thing, I've let the airline know you won't be travelling on the flights on the 2nd January. They wanted me to book another ticket there and then, but I said I didn't know when you would be able to travel. So ....what do you think about that idea? About your case I mean? I could bring everything in here for you to go through and let you choose what you want to keep. I doubt you'll be going back to the hotel, will you?'

'No, I have to stay in here. When they discharge me I'd like to go home.'

'Sounds like the best thing to do then. I'll bring your cases in in the next few days.'

'Thanks,' I grimaced. I wasn't comfortable with all this, but as I was supposed to be Lucy I had to go along with it. 'But could you take my rings back to the hotel and put them in my handbag. We aren't allowed to wear jewellery.'

'Right. Well, it's probably best I do take them back then. I saw your handbag. I'll put them in there for you. Look, I'll leave you for now. I can see that you are in a lot of pain. And I have much to do.'

He kissed my right hand and gave me a sad smile before walking out.

I watched him leave and lay there contemplating this crazy situation I'd now got myself into. Having been directed to my bedside, Mr. Jones had just assumed I was Lucy and I'd managed to play the part well enough to convince him. Could I continue to take on Lucy's identity, or was it total madness?

21
Kelly

Mr. Jones turned up at the hospital the next day with two cases. One large case and one that would be allowed as cabin baggage. I asked him to place the large case on the bed. I perched beside it sifting through everything with my one usable hand. My throat was better today, but my voice was still quite croaky and I let him chat on while I sorted the clothes; nodding every now and then. The less I said, the better.

'I didn't see your passport amongst everything at the hotel,' he suddenly said. 'Tom's was there, but not yours.'

'No I had it with me. We'd been to the bank to withdraw some cash. I hadn't worn the dress for a few days and forgot the money and passport were still in the zipped pocket. Luckily they were inside a plastic wallet so miraculously survived intact. The hospital have put them away safely for me. That's how they knew who I was when I was brought to the hospital – because I was unconscious.'

'Oh, well that was lucky then.' He sat there frowning

and I was worried whether he'd accepted what I'd just told him. It was true that the hospital had put the passport and money away. I'd raised the matter with hospital staff and they confirmed they also had the rings Carlos had given me. I knew they were worth a bit and I could sell them. I would need money while I was recovering and to make a new start somewhere else. I had the cash Lucy gave me, for the time being. I had my savings account that Karen had the passbook for, and I had Carlos's rings. It ought to be enough to make a new start. But what would I do with Lucy's rings? I couldn't sell them. It wouldn't be right. Perhaps I could post them to Tom's parents sometime in the future.

'I noticed your medication in the hand luggage. Do you need it?' he asked pulling a packet of Lucy's anti-depressants out of the zip compartment.

'No. I'd stopped taking the tablets after we arrived here. The hospital has me on strong painkillers now.'

'Okay well I'll put them back in case. I'm worried about leaving your smaller case here though,' he remarked as he packed my choices into it. 'It could easily be stolen. Why don't I take it back to the hotel and you can collect it before you leave Phuket?'

'No!' I croaked loudly.

He looked at me with surprise.

'I'm sorry, I don't think I can face going back there.'

'Of course. Sorry Lucy, I didn't think. Well, what about left luggage at the airport? I could send the large case back to Australia, then leave the smaller one at the airport. But you'd need something here with you at the hospital. For some toiletries and the clothes you will wear when you leave. And your handbag with all the paperwork – your airline ticket, insurance etc.'

'I did have a soft woven basket that would have been ideal for that, but I lost it when the wave hit us.' And that was true. Both Lucy and I had had a basket that morning. Both long gone – either buried under a mound of debris or lying on a sea bed.

'I could pop out to some shops and find you another one? What about that?'

'Yes, that would be perfect. Thank you. Ideally, one that that either has a zip top or some form of closing mechanism.'

'Okay, that's what I'll do. If you pick out the essential things you need here, then I will take the smaller case back with me as well today and deal with them both tomorrow.'

I chose a few things which he placed in my locker.

'Now what about Tom's things?'

'What should we do with them?' I asked him.

'I see no point in hanging on to them. Unless there's something special amongst them – a special shirt or something you want to keep?'

'No. There's still plenty of his things back home.'

'Well from what I've seen around Phuket, many people lost all their belongings in the disaster. What do you think about me donating Tom's clothes to some local organisation? It's the locals I'm thinking of. Holidaymakers would have other possessions at home. It's the poor locals, who've lost everything, who'll be in real need.'

'That sounds like a good idea,' I said nodding and smiling. 'Tom would approve of that.'

'I think so too.'

'Are there still a lot of people missing?'

'Yes, about 500 in Phuket from the boards I looked at. A lot more in some other places.'

'That's a lot. Why are they still missing? What do they think has happened to them?'

'They say some will have been dragged miles out to sea. Their bodies drifting off to other places or attacked by sharks. Some they think are still buried in the mess that's still around. No doubt many of the bodies will turn up, but they say that some never will. Now I'd better get off and find you the right kind of basket. And deal with Tom's clothes.'

'How long are you planning on staying in Phuket?'

'I am provisionally booked on a return flight on 2nd January – if I can arrange a casket for Tom and transport for it on my flight.'

I could hear his voice choking up when he mentioned Tom's casket. He cleared his throat and continued.

'I'm worried about you though. Would you like me to stay on? I could alter my flight. Tom's brother could take care of things at the other end. I don't necessarily have to accompany Tom.'

'But you'd like to, wouldn't you?'

'Well yes, but it's not essential. How will you manage? I could, of course, travel back to Melbourne with you. It would make everything so much easier for you.'

No, it wouldn't as I don't really know where I am going!

'It's very kind of you to offer, but they want me to

remain here in the hospital for another few weeks. That would run up huge costs for you. I'll be fine. I'll get them to order a taxi when I'm ready to go. They can also get someone to meet me with a wheelchair at the airport.'

'If you're sure ... I—'

'Yes, absolutely sure. Thank you anyway.'

'Right you are then. I'll be off. I'll either see you this afternoon or tomorrow morning, depending on my success with basket shopping!'

I smiled and waved to him as he headed out of the room. Talking so much had been a strain, so I gulped down some water. The whole thing was proving so bloody difficult. God, what was I doing? It was crazy! But the other option was to admit who I really was and inevitably be reunited with Carlos. I shuddered at the prospect. Although in physical pain, the past few days away from Carlos had been liberating. I simply couldn't return to that life. So I had to persevere at being Lucy. At least until I managed to return to Melbourne. Then I would have to think about taking off to some other place. As quickly and as decently as I could. With the bloody dog if need be.

Tom's father returned with a hideous basket the following morning. But I smiled and said it was perfect. It had a zip top so would do the trick. And it was soft and pliable, meaning I could fold it over to fit in the locker beside my bed. It had some very ugly flowers all over one side of it and was a dirty brown colour. I was grateful though as I'd been told they're moving me to a larger room tomorrow, and I'd need something to put my things into.

'It's the only one I could find with a zip,' he said apologetically as I inspected the interior of it. 'I wasn't sure you'd like it because of the colour and those awful flowers, but it looks very practical.'

'Yes it is, it's exactly what I need. What it looks like doesn't matter,' I told him.

He heaved a sigh of relief. I doubted he'd ever had to buy a basket for a woman before.

'By the way, I met a man at the hotel this morning who seemed to know who I was and he was asking about you. Carlos or something his name was. He was a rather unpleasant man.'

I froze. It was typical of Carlos to stick his nose into other people's business. With an agenda though. He knew Lucy and I were together when the tsunami hit and I was sure he'd want to question me about her. I can't have him coming here again! I didn't say anything, so Mr. Jones continued.

'I took an instant dislike to the man,' he said. 'I told him that only family could come and visit you after he said he wanted to come and *question* you about his girlfriend. Very pushy he was. He didn't want to take no for an answer. You and Tom spent time with him and his girlfriend from what he told me.'

'You're right. He *is* an unpleasant man. Very controlling. Tom and I didn't like him. We liked his girlfriend though and spent time with her at the pool of a morning while he watched from a balcony above. He always had a bodyguard watching the woman in case she ran off.'

'That's a bit extreme, isn't it? I can't imagine any young woman would be happy being with someone like that.'

'No, she wasn't.'

'Well, apparently she's missing. Claims he's not going home until he's found her – or her body. I told him he might have a long wait then, imparting some of the things I'd been told. He said you were with Kelly when the tsunami hit'

'Yes, we were together until the first wave of water receded and then were separated. I thought I saw her struggling in the water when I swept past a woman after the second wave, but I couldn't say for sure it was her.'

'I could tell him that.'

'Yes, that would probably be helpful. I don't want him coming here.'

'No. I agree.'

'I'm being moved sometime tomorrow. I don't know where to as yet. A bigger ward or something.'

'Well, I'll still be here tomorrow. I'll find out where you are and tell the staff there, and on this ward, not to let him in.'

'Thanks.'

'I found a group that I'm donating Tom's things to. I need to go now and deal with that. I thought I'd drop the basket in first.'

'Okay thank you very much for buying this for me. I'm sure it's not something you'd normally do.'

'No. It was a new experience for me.' He winked at me then. It was the first time I'd seen a less serious side to him. I smiled back at him.

'In case I don't make it back today with all I have to do, Happy New Year, Cariad,' he said, bending over to kiss my head. I hadn't realised it was New Year's Eve!

He left shortly after and I sat worrying about Carlos. I was sure he'd attempt to force his way in to see me. Perhaps I ought to discharge myself and take off. I didn't think I could do that while Tom's father was around though. It would seem strange. But as soon as he flew out that's what I planned to do.

I was resting that afternoon with a face compress on when I heard him. Carlos. He was out in the corridor arguing with a woman. In a panic I lowered myself off the bed and hopped over to the wheelchair that had been left in the corner of the room. I could hide in the bathroom, an en suite attached to the room but what if he came in and waited? He'd be forcing himself in here any moment now. I was clumsy and awkward as I frantically dragged the chair into the bathroom. Once inside I locked the door. There was no other choice but to sit it out. I'd grabbed the face compress which I could stick over my face if a nurse came in and asked me to open the door. Carlos could be standing behind her. He was unlikely to recognise me with the short hair and my face covered. He probably wouldn't recognise my croaky voice either if I was forced to speak. But never underestimate the enemy.

I waited for what seemed like hours (but was only minutes) when sure enough I heard him barge into the room.

'I *have* to talk to her,' he insisted. 'Where is she? I was told by admissions that this is where she was.'

I could hear the woman shouting at him in her own language. 'Fuck you. I want answers,' Carlos said.

The handle of the bathroom door moved down. He was trying to get into the bathroom. The cheek!

'Lucy?' he called, banging aggressively on the door. 'Lucy? Are you in there? It's Carlos. I need to know what happened to Kelly!'

He was never going to go away. Not until I told him something. Surely he wouldn't recognise my voice? I decided to take a risk. I'd practised mimicking Lucy's intonations when I had been with Tom's father, convinced he would have spoken to her on the phone at some point. He hadn't noticed.

'I'm sorry Carlos,' I croaked through the door. 'We were separated when the first wave receded. I don't know what happened to her.'

'No!' he screamed. He banged on the door some more. And I could hear him sobbing. Then another male voice said, 'Sir, you must leave now or I will have to have you arrested.'

'And stuff you too. I'm leaving!'

I could hear his aggressive voice fading into the distance, but I didn't dare leave the bathroom in case he came back. I sat there quivering until finally there was a knock at the door and a voice called out that she was leaving my meal in the room. It was dinner time. I'd been in the bathroom for at least three hours. Luckily the woman who had been sharing my room had been moved the previous day so there had been no-one else to make demands on the bathroom.

Had I done enough to convince him for now? One thing was for sure. I had to get out of here as soon as possible. I knew Carlos well enough to know that his obsession with 'Kelly' meant he'd be back. As he had said, he wanted answers – no doubt in detail. That meant a face to face encounter; something I could not do.

22
Kelly

Phuket Airport, January 3, 2005

I managed to discharge myself from the hospital very early this morning – after a great deal of arguing with hospital staff. My nerves couldn't take another day of being there. It was three days since Carlos had been in. I hoped he was gone but, realistically, I knew Carlos would still be hanging around searching for evidence of me and that he could return at any time. I wasn't waiting around for that to happen. I'd been put into a larger ward on New Year's Day where he had easier access to me – with no nearby bathroom to hide in. There were only shared bathrooms and toilets in the middle of the ward. You had to pass the ward entrance to reach them.

The nurses had called a doctor up to the ward when I said I wanted to discharge myself. The doctor argued that it was too soon for me to leave the hospital. Especially to travel unaided on the long journey to Australia. He was right of course. A manual wheelchair was extremely difficult for me to manage as I could only control it one-handed. My free right hand was also bandaged with minor wounds on my palm and it hurt putting pressure on it to turn the wheels. I ended up wobbling all over the place. But I was sure I could sort something out. It was better than remaining in hospital exposed to a visit from Carlos.

I was dressed and ready to go, adamant that I was leaving. I told them I had urgent family business to deal with back in Melbourne. They made me sign a form and I wondered if discharging myself early would invalidate the insurance claim. They returned my belongings and I stuffed them into my handbag. I'd retrieved Lucy's rings from the handbag earlier when preparing to leave and had stuck them on my left finger. My hand was exposed from the sling over my arm and so it made sense to put them on.

Mr. Jones had flown out with Tom's coffin yesterday. I said I'd phone them when I returned to Melbourne. Before he left the hospital he'd asked why I didn't call him 'dad' anymore. I wasn't sure what Lucy had called him so I hadn't called him anything. I'd managed by speaking to him without any form of address. I'd muttered, embarrassed, that I wasn't certain that he'd still want me to call him 'dad'. He'd assured me that both he and his wife were fine about it.

'Okay dad,' I had muttered. A word foreign on my tongue. My father had always been 'da'.

According to Tom and Lucy's airline tickets, they were due to leave yesterday. Of course, I'd forgotten that Tom's father had cancelled the seats and not booked a new flight. So when a kind man wheeled me up to the airline information desk, they told me that no seats were available. They said that so many people were trying to get home and wanting to change their tickets. I argued my case for a while, insisting I had to return to Melbourne urgently. After highlighting my medical needs they finally booked me on a business class seat to Kuala Lumpur. From there I would pick up a connecting flight to Melbourne.

I retrieved my cabin baggage from the left luggage kiosk and was wheeled over to the check-in. They agreed to check my case into the hold so that I only had to worry about the basket and my handbag for the flight.

I'd decided that I would return to Melbourne and go to Lucy's place for now. In my condition it was my only real option. I wasn't in a position to be looking after a dog for the moment but perhaps in another few weeks that would change. There was also the possibility that Laurie and Kim would be happy to keep it or continue looking after it until I was better.

As far as I knew, Carlos had no idea where Tom and Lucy lived, so I'd be safe there.

They took me onto the plane by a special lift and removed my wheelchair once I was seated near the front.

I looked out from the window as the plane banked and turned towards Kuala Lumpur. You could see the devastation the tsunami had caused along some parts of the coast. I was very lucky to be alive. I thought I could see a figure floating way out to sea. Was that a body? Surely they had boats or helicopters scanning the area looking for some of the missing.

The missing – Lucy among them. I wondered if she'd turned up alive, but unconscious somewhere. If so, she would remain unidentified. Or alternatively, I wondered whether her body had been found. Again remaining unidentified. Would Kim and Laurie take one look at me and know that I wasn't Lucy? From what Lucy had told me, Laurie was Tom's colleague from work. They'd never socialised with them as a couple. Lucy had told me that Kim started coming around to their flat on a regular basis – after they'd moved in there following Christopher's death. Kim wanted to be friends, but Lucy hadn't been interested because she was so depressed. I remembered her saying that she just sat or lay on the couch much of the day. Greasy hair spilling over her face. With any luck, neither Kim nor Laurie would have had a good close look at Lucy. With my bruising and swelling from injuries and my facial surgery, I could claim that I looked different because of that. At least Lucy and I had a similar shaped face, brown eyes and almost black hair. I wondered what Christopher had looked like. Presumably, there would be photographs of him in their flat.

My physical appearance was one thing that concerned me. The other was my physical ability. While I was in the hospital or using an airline, I had access to wheelchairs. I wasn't sure what I would do back in Melbourne. What I needed was an electric wheelchair on a temporary basis. Were they available to hire? That was the first thing I would have to sort out when I arrived.

As we landed in Kuala Lumpur I wondered if this was where surviving members of my mother's family lived. I couldn't remember my mother ever saying what part of Malaysia she had come from. I also had no idea of my grandmother or aunts married names, even if I'd wanted to search for anyone.

There was a six-hour delay before my flight to Melbourne. I was provided with a wheelchair and 'parked' by a helpful staff member, at a restaurant/bar that served soup. I ordered a bowl; it was unlikely that I was going to be able to eat any of the food served on the plane. How I longed for a decent meal, but I still wasn't able to chew. That was going to be another problem I had to face when I arrived at Lucy and Tom's place. I would probably have to put up with buying cartons or tins of soup for the next few weeks.

After my soup I managed to take myself off to the disabled toilets and then make my way back to the restaurant to be collected. Using the manual wheelchair was so frustrating I wanted to scream. I would have to improve my situation once I arrived in Melbourne.

23
Kelly

Melbourne, January 2005

My plane landed in Melbourne at 7.20am. As I required wheelchair assistance, I was the last one off the plane. I didn't clear customs until shortly after 9 am. I also had to exchange my American dollars before I could leave the airport. I was wheeled to a taxi and asked the driver whether he knew of a wheelchair hire company. When I told him my final destination was Yarraville, he said there was a rehab hire place in Port Melbourne he could take me to.

The hire company had the ideal lightweight foldaway electric wheelchair. But there was an issue with the hire as, under their terms and conditions, they required a card, not cash. I had a card that I'd found in Lucy's handbag but hadn't spent any time practising her signature. I was concerned about using it as well, as I had no idea if there was money in her account. This was only a debit card. Not a credit card. Tom had had credit cards, but his father had cancelled them back in Phuket.

It also felt like a step too far to use her card. The passport was one thing, but her card? Would that be theft? In the end, I had no choice, but to use the card. They didn't even look at the signature when I signed their documents so it wasn't an issue and they telephoned the bank to gain authorisation.

The cab driver was marvellous and waited for me while I completed the transaction. I tested the hire chair, steering myself out to his vehicle and he then folded it away, stowing it in the boot.

I gave him the address listed on the insurance policy Tom had brought with him. Lucy had said their place was on the corner of two intersecting roads. That meant four corners. I hoped there was only one block of flats at that junction. I'd look pretty stupid if there were flats on each corner and I had no idea which was mine when I supposedly lived there. When we arrived at the junction of Ryde and Rudge, there was only one block of flats at the intersection – thank goodness. Each of the other three corners had large single storey houses sitting on wide blocks of land. Assuming it to be correct, the driver pulled over to the block's entrance. He helped me out and I paid him a generous tip on top of the fare. He offered to help me in with my bag, but I insisted that I could manage. I wasn't sure where flat 2 was. I prayed it was on the ground floor. I was going to be in serious trouble if it wasn't; it looked like one of those cheap builds that wouldn't have a lift. It was only a low-level building that went up a further two floors, but still, I wouldn't be able to manage stairs.

When I steered myself towards the entrance I

discovered there was a step up to the main door that the wheelchair couldn't glide over. I had to climb out of the chair, stand on one leg and pull it up with my one good arm. Luckily it was lightweight. I was attempting to insert the key in the front door (after discovering which key it was) when I heard a woman cry out behind me.

'Lucy? Why didn't you let us know you were coming home? Laurie would have taken the day off and picked you up from the airport. Tom's father told us you'd be in the hospital for another few weeks.'

This was Kim I assumed. Tom's father had told me that Laurie had offered to collect me when I travelled home. As I didn't know what Laurie looked like, that would have proved awkward.

I turned around to face this stranger. She shrieked and told me how terrible I looked.

Thanks. I already knew that from the glimpses I'd caught of myself in bathroom mirrors at the hospital. My face was swollen and discoloured with bruising and I still had a dressing over my nose. The ones from the stitches on my cheeks had been removed.

I smiled weakly at her and mentioned my injuries, thinking I ought to bring them up straight away to explain any difference in my appearance.

She commented on how different I looked and said Clara wouldn't recognise me – which I thought was a bit strange. Dogs would be more concerned with smell, wouldn't they? She wouldn't recognise my smell anyway.

I asked her where Clara was and she said they were all over at someone called Janine's place with Freddie.

Was I supposed to know this person and where she lived?

Kim helped me in through the front door after I passed her my key. But then I stopped, fumbling about with my basket waiting for her to lead the way. I didn't know where I was going. I followed her, looking around surreptitiously. After passing the staircase to the upper floors, we came to two different flat entrances. The door on the left had a number '1' on it and the one on the right had a '2'. This was it. I was feeling quite nervous as she opened the door. I had no idea what to expect.

She stood back as I steered into the flat while commenting on my snazzy chair. I filled her in on where I'd acquired it from while again innocently looking around. Kim asked how I was going to manage Clara with my injuries. She looked happy and excited when I suggested we could talk about this.

Before I could ask whether she'd be willing to hang on to Clara for the time being, she said she'd pop over and fetch her. She disappeared out the door, leaving it open. I looked around the flat. We'd come straight into a large open plan living-room with a kitchen/dining area at the rear. I steered my chair over to a door across the other side of the room that I found led into a hallway. Off it to the right, fronting the building, there was a large bedroom with a queen-sized bed. I could see Lucy's larger suitcase in there. So it had arrived. Immediately to the left was a very small laundry room. There was a separate toilet beside the bathroom and straight ahead was another room. The door to that room was shut and I assumed that would have been Christopher's room if he'd survived. I would look at that later. I imagined Lucy and Tom might have kept some of his things that were still in there.

I steered myself into the bathroom. It was a good size and had a separate shower cubicle as well as a bath. In desperate need of the loo, I reversed out of the bathroom. Parking my chair outside the toilet door, I stood up and hopped in.

I was about to re-enter the living room when Kim walked in the door holding a little girl in her arms and a toddler trailing behind.

'Here she is,' Kim announced.

Here who is? I couldn't see any dog.

'Look Clara, there's mummy.'

The little girl in her arms looked at me then turned her head away, burying her face in Kim's shoulder.

What? A little girl? Not a dog! I burst into nervous laughter. What a bloody idiot I was. All this time I'd thought Lucy, and then Tom's father had been talking about a dog. At no time had it occurred to me that it was a child. I'm not sure why I'd made that assumption. It was something to do with Lucy saying she didn't take Clara for walks or a run around the park. Lucy never actually mentioned she had a *daughter.* Only a son. And Tom's father never mentioned the word grand-daughter. Clara and Christopher must have been twins! That was what Lucy must have meant when she said Clara was born soon after Christopher. Shit! What on earth had I let myself in for? What was I going to do now?

To cover my laughing, I coughed and apologised

to Kim. I told her I was laughing with relief. And that, although I hadn't wanted to leave Clara behind, with hindsight, it was very lucky that we had. Involuntary tears began to trickle down my face.

'Yes, Laurie and I thought that. Otherwise, you would have probably lost her as well.'

I nodded, swallowing back tears. 'Can I hold her for a minute?' I asked.

'You can hold her for as long as you want, she's your daughter,' Kim said with a deep sigh.

I'd have to remember that. Not ask permission for anything to do with her. This little girl who was a stranger to me, was supposed to be my daughter!

'Let me move to the couch first.' I steered myself across and standing, I lurched onto the couch, settling my weight back into the cushion – wincing with pain as I did so.

Kim placed Clara onto my right hip; her legs stretched at an angle across mine. The little girl looked up at me in wonder for a moment, then her face crumpled in distress, her mouth opened and she let out a howl. My heart wrenched hearing her cries, bringing tears to my eyes again. This poor little girl had lost her parents and here I was masquerading as her mother. She clearly knew I wasn't. Lucy's last words to me had been about caring for her daughter. I had to pull myself together.

'I suspect she's frightened by the state of my face. And she's probably forgotten me already,' I murmured.

Remembering what Lucy had told me I added, 'It's not surprising really, the way I felt before we went away. I didn't really give Clara enough attention. It was mainly Tom and you that she spent quality time with. I'm sorry Clara,' I whispered into the little girl's hair, 'and I'm sorry Kim that all this was dumped on you.'

'We understood. God if anything ever happened to Freddie, I'm sure I would have been much the same as you were. How are you now?'

'Nothing like a tsunami to shake you out of your problems, and put everything into perspective.'

'Yes, I imagine it did. When Tom phoned on Christmas Day, he said you were much better. Said you'd met a woman – Kelly I'm sure he said her name was, who'd been very helpful.'

I was about to protest that I hadn't done anything to help when I remembered that I couldn't say that. *I was not Kelly.*

'Yes, she's one of the missing,' I said in a sad voice thinking of Lucy.

Clara had settled and was now looking up at me with curiosity. I chatted to her and she reached up with one hand and touched my face. I ceased talking and let her explore me until she pressed too firmly on my nose and I yelped. Kim raced across and pulled Clara off me, who immediately started to howl. She placed Clara on the floor next to her son who was absorbed in a small wooden puzzle he'd found. He'd tipped out the pieces and had made a start on re-assembling them. He immediately moved the puzzle closer to Clara to share it with her. Clara quietened and looked at the little boy (who I assumed must be Freddie), a huge smile spreading across her face. She was beautiful. A cross between Tom's fair complexion and Lucy's dark beauty.

Clara had huge hazel eyes and light brown wavy hair. There was a hint of a Eurasian appearance about her eyes. Her hair would no doubt darken in time. I was already smitten. *Careful!*

'You'll have to be so careful around her while you are recovering,' Kim said, satisfied that the kids were fine. 'How long before you'll have full mobility again?'

'About a month. Even then I will have to take it easy.'

'Why don't I take her for now and leave you time to settle in? The kids were going to have a paddle in the toddler's pool that Janine has set up in the garden. You could have a rest and then come and join us if you wanted to.'

'It's very kind of you. But I'd prefer to freshen up and relax for a bit. Will you bring Clara back later?'

'Yes, of course. But she can stay with us tonight. Look why don't we sort that out later?'

'Yes, okay. I'm feeling quite exhausted.'

'Righto, we'll leave you to it then. I'll come by with the kids later.'

'Thanks. That'd be great.'

With that, she gathered the two kids up, taking Clara in her arms and Freddie following behind. I steered over to the window and watched as she crossed the road; Freddie holding her hand, Clara clutched firmly in her other arm.

The image she created was one of a happy little family. A mother and her two children. But Clara was not hers. My thoughts were already beginning to be possessive towards her. Clara was mine. Hadn't Lucy made me promise to take care of her – or deliver her to her grandparents? I don't know why I hadn't twigged what Lucy was talking about when she mentioned taking Clara to Wales. I thought she was just being hysterical. And what was it she had said about her sister Eva? *She'd get rid of her or put her in a home.* So Eva wouldn't want Clara. That would mean that lovely little girl going into care. I couldn't bear to see that happen. Not after what I went through.

It was crazy. Crazy to think I could get away with it. But why not? I was Lucy now. I could live my life as Lucy. If Lucy miraculously re-appeared surely she'd be happy that I'd kept my promise. I could simply slink off. Or we could take off together.

Lucy's driving licence might prove an issue when I was more mobile. I'd never learned to drive. Before I became involved with Carlos, it was not something I'd even thought about. I lived near the city and public transport was excellent, so why would I need a car? After I met Carlos and mentioned that I would like to learn to drive, he wouldn't agree to it. Naturally. As I arrived in the cab, I noticed there was a car park around the back of the block. Did Lucy or Tom have a car there?

My father had allowed me to drive tractors on the stud farm as a child. With the seat pushed as far forward as it would go, I found that easy. I had watched Carlos driving his flashy manual-geared sports cars often enough to understand gear changes. But there was no way I could drive a car on Melbourne roads without lessons. How would I explain that when I supposedly had a licence? Perhaps I could claim that I had lost my confidence and needed some revision lessons. From what I recalled listening to Lucy, she hadn't gone out much since Christopher's death and so she probably hadn't driven for a while. As Tom and Lucy had only lived in the flat for a short time, it was feasible that she hadn't driven since moving here.

I decided it was time to explore the flat further. I turned away from the window, steering the chair down to what must be Clara's room. I opened the door and was surprised at the crisp clean décor. Tom must have decorated it after they moved in. There was a subtle red and cream wallpaper on a feature wall and the rest of the room was painted in a light cream. A single bed and a white cot sat along one wall and, as you would expect in a modern block, there was a built-in wardrobe. There was also a small white chest of drawers on the right as you walked in and what I assumed was some kind of 'nappy changing table' with shelving underneath. Under the window, there was a small child's table with two chairs. The floor was carpeted and there were white wooden blinds on the window. Looking out onto the rear of the property, I could see a fenced off shared garden area, with several fold-down clotheslines. Beyond that was the car park. I'd noticed a door at the rear of the main entrance hallway that led to out to the back, but there was no direct access to the yard from the flat.

I turned and steered back into Lucy and Tom's room – now to be my room. The bed was stripped – presumably they'd done that before they left. It was going to be fun attempting to make that up later. I needed to discover where the clean linen was stored. I'd noticed a cupboard in the hallway outside the laundry and hoped this was where it was. I'd also spotted a 'dirty linen' basket in the laundry so I imagined there was washing in there waiting to be done.

I was about to turn back to the hallway to inspect the cupboard when I noticed framed photographs of two babies adorning the wall. In the first one, looking like new-borns the twins lay side by side. Another one showed them smiling – clearly some weeks later. In the final one, they were sitting up, about six months old. Christopher had much darker hair than Clara and there was a similarity about their faces. But they were not identical twins. This must have been one of the last pictures taken of them together. Lucy said Christopher had died close to six months before we met. Such a tragedy for the family to lose one of the little babies. If Christopher hadn't died, then both Tom and Lucy would still be alive. It's unlikely that they would have taken the holiday to Phuket. Lucy told me Tom had booked it in the desperate hope that she might pull out of her depression.

I returned to the hall, opening the cupboard there. It *was* a linen cupboard. I pulled out what I needed, steered back to the room and threw the items on the bed. I would ask Kim to help me make it later. The duvet on the bed was a lightweight summer one, but I wasn't sure I would need it at present with the current heat. A top sheet would be enough. The flat smelt musty so I opened windows to air the rooms.

Retrieving my small suitcase from the living room, I took it into the bedroom. With some awkwardness, I selected clean clothes to change into after showering.

At the hospital, I was taught how to remove the sling for showering but had to be very careful. They had provided a special stool to perch on for showers. I'd have to buy one for showering here but today I'd have to manage without.

Refreshed from my shower, I went to explore the kitchen. I found some cans of soup in the larder which would do me for now. I wasn't eating a lot at present but I was beginning to detest soup.

Lucy's kitchen was well equipped with modern appliances. I would be able to make myself some wholesome pureed food when I had the opportunity to go shopping. I'd spotted a small local IGA supermarket on my journey here. First thing tomorrow I'd be heading down there in a taxi.

The one good thing about my time with Carlos was that I'd become a very decent cook. With little to do most evenings while Carlos was at the Club, I'd taught myself to follow complex recipes. Once I gained confidence I'd experimented with ideas of my own. When I first arrived in Melbourne as a teenager I only knew how to cook basic meat and two/three veg meals. Not that I'd had much experience, but being the eldest girl, I used to help my mother out in the kitchen. Mum would sometimes cook Malaysian food but as a child, I hadn't understood the ingredients she used when making the exotic flavours she created. She cooked lots of vegetarian meals, but always some meat for my father. He preferred eating meals with meat, potatoes and two other vegetables.

I was looking forward to buying some interesting

food. Thinking about it made my mouth salivate.

I'd noticed a desk, with a large filing drawer, in the main bedroom. I went back there to see if the desk provided any information that would expand my knowledge of Tom and Lucy's life. Lucy had mentioned that they owned a block of land which they planned to build on one day. I had no idea where this was. I was hoping to locate paperwork that would give me a clue. I wasn't sure if rates had to be paid or what the situation was. It was Clara's inheritance if Lucy didn't return, and I needed to ensure it was safeguarded.

The large drawer held a number of files, all ordered and tidy. I found a file on the land. The deeds seemed to be held by the couple's bank – not because they owed money, but for safekeeping. It wasn't only a block of land. It was a large bush property with a house on it, in Mount Martha. Was it derelict? There seemed to be no indication in this file. Only an outline of the plot – which amounted to approximately three acres, showing the house situated towards the back of the land.

Mt. Martha? That was out past Mornington I believed. I remembered seeing a road sign for Mt. Martha when Carlos and I were in Mornington once; a pleasant seaside suburb on the Mornington Peninsula where we'd stopped for lunch before returning to the city.

Further exploration of the files revealed that Lucy and Tom had several bank accounts. Lucy had a savings account with a little over $310,000 dollars in it. The account dated back many years. The large balance must have been her remaining share of the proceeds from selling her parents' and grandparents' properties. Her parents' place, Lucy had said, had been only a short distance from Melbourne city centre. The grandparents' property had been a large livestock spread with a house in the country. There was a large withdrawal back in 2003. That must have been when Tom and Lucy purchased the Mt. Martha property.

Lucy had another account in her name, the one linked to the card I'd used this morning. It had a little over $4000 left in it – not for much longer though. Tom and Lucy had a joint savings account. It had $97,000 dollars in it according to this last statement. Tom also had his own account that had a balance of $7300. So much money! What should I do about these accounts? I'm sure the balances would be less now – especially after they'd withdrawn money for me. There were credit card statements in the file, but it looked as though they cleared the balances each month. I wouldn't know if any charges were outstanding until new statements arrived.

Howell Jones had given me Tom's death certificate to produce to anyone relevant, including the bank. Should I go to the bank and have Tom's money transferred to Lucy's account? I could see regular direct debits going out of his account. For payments to various insurance companies, gas, electricity and probably the rent. I needed to find the details of their rental agreement. A few files later I found what I was looking for and it confirmed that one of the direct debits was for the rent. The last payment went out on 2nd January. That left me with almost a month to sort out how the next payment was going to be made. I found a car file which had details of only one vehicle. It was registered in Lucy's name but insured for both of them to drive. There was a bill of purchase from 2002 for a silver Hyundai Accent. It was registered until September 2005, so there was no urgency to deal with that and the insurance was current. No flashy vehicles for this family – although Lucy would have purchased it long before her pregnancy.

There was a box file with plastic sleeves for recent gas and electricity charges. There were also plastic sleeves for the landline telephone and Tom and Lucy's mobile phone details. I'd have to remember to cancel Tom's mobile. I tucked that file away.

The next two cardboard files were marked as 'Tom Personal' and 'Lucy Personal'. Tom's held his degree and his employment records. Laurie would have informed the Company of Tom's death, but I needed to contact them to see if there were any outstanding monies owed to him. I discovered a life insurance policy for Tom where he was insured for $250,000. I guess I would have to make an official claim in respect of this.

In Lucy's personal file I found a life insurance policy matching Tom's. It also held her Business Studies degree and letters from her previous employers. She'd still been on maternity leave when Christopher died. According to correspondence in this file, she had now officially resigned from her job. A good thing for me. I didn't have to worry about contacting any employers. It would have been impossible for me to 'return' to a job that I knew nothing about. The problem I was facing though was how I was going to earn an income. Before the tsunami, my plan had been simple: retrieve my belongings from Karen and then take off. Far away from Carlos. I'd intended to find a job in a restaurant in one of the other states until I decided what I wanted to do. That was no longer feasible. At least not for the immediate future. Not now I had a child to consider as well as my lack of mobility.

The final file I came across was a document file which held birth certificates, for Lucy, Tom and the twins. Also, Tom's old passport, Christopher's death certificate, the funeral invoice and his burial details. Now I knew where Christopher was buried. I hadn't even looked at Lucy's date of birth on her passport. The birth certificate showed she was born on 18th October 1978, so she was almost a year older than me. I was born in late September 1979. I needed to memorise Lucy's date of birth as it was bound to come up in medical matters. I was surprised I hadn't been asked already. They must have registered my date of birth from the passport at the hospital. According to Lucy's birth certificate, she was born Lucy Ann Harrington.

Clara and Christopher were born on 7th October 2003, making Clara almost 15 months old. She was old enough to be able to follow basic instructions I thought, recalling my sisters at that age. That would make life easier.

I closed the drawer and sat back, thinking about all that I would have to deal with from now on. Was I going to be able to manage it? I wasn't stupid, but I'd never managed my own household before. Nor had I ever impersonated someone and had to absorb the complexities of their lives. And the lies that would entail, not to mention crimes. When I'd left the Hills as a teenager on the run, I'd increased my age by several years. But I'd stuck to my own name and birthday, only altering the birth year when anyone asked. This was going to be an entirely new situation for me. Could I pull it off? And with a young child?

I heard the key in the door a few minutes later and so I steered the chair back out to the living room. Kim was there with the two children again. I was keen to see Clara and was surprised, given our last encounter, to see her toddle towards me with a smile on her face. I stopped the wheelchair and bent down attempting to pick her up, but I couldn't manage it with only one arm. Kim stood watching for a moment before she moved across the room and helped Clara up onto my lap.

'So did you have a lovely time at Janine's? I asked Clara. I knew she probably couldn't answer in sentences but I thought she might understand. She did and nodded her head in the affirmative.

Kim answered vocally for her. 'Yes, they had a great time in the pool, and then pigged out on cake and ice cream after.'

'Oh dear, we'll have to find you something healthy to eat this evening then,' I said frowning at the unhealthy contents of her 'lunch'. I wondered if it was common for her to eat this type of food.

'Talking about food,' I said turning to Kim. 'I don't have any fresh food in the house, of course, that I can use to make a meal for Clara – or me for that matter. I'm not allowed eat solids yet with my cheekbones healing.

There are cans of soup I can eat today, but I really need to get some fresh food in. I'll probably call a cab and go to the local supermarket.'

'I could take you to the large Woolworths over at the shopping mall later. I need to buy some stuff anyway. The kids need their nap first though. I thought I'd take them upstairs and I could also feed them both later. I have plenty of kiddie food upstairs.'

No doubt out of packets as there was no mention of fresh food. 'Okay, that'd be great. What time do you think you'll be back?'

'Around three thirty. Is that okay?'

'Yes fine. Thank you.'

'By the way. I hope you don't mind, but when I learned about events in Phuket, I came down here the other day and washed your linen and all the clothes that were in the wash basket. I did a few loads here in your flat, using your soap powder. It was all dry and folded away the same day, the weather has been so hot.'

'That was very kind of you Kim. Thank you. I'd been dreading looking in the wash basket, not wanting to see all the work I had facing me.'

Kim lifted Clara off my lap. She'd been quietly preoccupied with the buttons on the front of my dress. Attempting to pull them off – without success.

It dawned on me after they had left, that looking after Clara with only one arm was going to be seriously tricky. But I wanted her here with me. Not upstairs with Kim. I steered the wheelchair into Clara's room to practise on her cot and the changing table. I spent some time working on different methods in her bedroom, then moved to the bathroom and lounge. I would manage I was sure. I'd seen a potty in the toilet and wondered if Tom or Lucy had attempted to train her before they left for Phuket. That was something I would have to get cracking on.

I was enjoying the freedom of shopping without bodyguards that afternoon when Kim almost caught me out.

'Since when have you been into such healthy foods?' she asked, peering at the goods stacked in my disabled trolley. 'I didn't know you cooked elaborate meals. Tom always said he did most of the cooking.'

'I've been cooking …' I started, then stopped myself in time. I was about to say I had been cooking fancy meals for years but realised that didn't fit. I amended my statement to say, 'After the twins were born I didn't have as much time for preparing meals. When Christopher died I couldn't face it. We always used to eat well before that. I plan to eat better from now on.'

She nodded, seeming to accept what I'd said. Lucy must have been a decent cook at some point in the past. The way her kitchen was equipped was evidence of that. They didn't look unused, so either she or Tom must have cooked healthy meals.

After dropping the shopping to the car, we returned to the Mall and popped into one of the large pharmacies, to see if I could find a shower stool to buy. Kim had mentioned that some pharmacies stocked these items. They had exactly what I needed. She carried it back to her car for me, pushing Freddie and Clara in a double stroller. Tom, Kim said, had given the double stroller to her shortly after he and Lucy had moved into the flats. She'd used it to take the two children out when she looked after Clara.

When we returned to the flat Kim helped me to pack away my shopping while Clara and Freddie played together. I wasn't sure how to broach the subject of Clara staying with me from now on, so I just came out with it.

'I want Clara to stay with me from tonight on,' I said not looking at Kim. I suspected she wouldn't be too happy about that. She behaved in a proprietary manner around Clara, as though *she* was the mother. I could understand that she had become attached to Clara in the weeks of having her so close. Plus prior to the Phuket trip, Kim had looked after Clara on many other occasions. But I was here now and I had to wean her away from Clara. Kim was silent for a moment before answering.

'I'm not sure that you are in any fit state to be looking after Clara yet,' she replied, her voice a little strained.

'Oh I know it will be difficult, but I want Clara here. In my grief, I didn't spend any quality time with her before the holiday. I want to make it up to her. I realised while I was away, that time with her is precious. We've only got each other now both Tom and Christopher have gone.'

'Yes, of course,' she said after a further pause. 'But if you need any help, I would always be only too happy to help out.'

I nodded. 'You and Laurie have been very generous

with your help and support. Thank you so much for that. Although physically incapacitated, I'm mentally well now. And Clara is of an age where she can understand me better.'

'Yes, she's a very bright little girl.' Kim sighed. 'Freddie will miss her.'

'I can see they're very close and they can see each other regularly.'

'Yes, okay. Do you want me to bring Clara's clothes and toys down now? Or should we wait and see how you go tonight?' Kim said.

'Now would be good thanks. I'll watch the kids here while you pop upstairs.'

24
Kelly

Clara screamed the house down for a good five minutes after Kim and Freddie finally left. She called out to Freddie a few times (calling him 'Eddie'). I spoke to her quietly and attempted to hold her, but nothing seemed to quieten her. Her little face was bright red. More with anger than distress, I thought, thinking back to my own younger siblings. Kim had brought Clara's high chair down but I didn't think I could manage that. There was another low chair next to the table with a tray attached. I pushed that over and, with some difficulty, lifted Clara into it. She stopped crying and sat staring at me. But her little chest was heaving in jerky spasms.

'It's just you and me now kiddo,' I told her, 'so you'd better get used to it. Let me see if I can find you something to keep you occupied while I prepare you a proper meal.'

I pulled a squeeze juice container out from the larder and put it in front of her.

While I had only one arm to use, it was going to be tricky preparing fresh food. I'd bought a batch of pre-

prepared fresh vegetables at the supermarket to make things easier. I set about frying the chopped onions with herbs before adding pureed garlic, other chopped vegetables, seasoning and a tin of tomatoes. Then I let it simmer. I'd had to prop the tin of tomatoes between my knees to pull open the ring tab with one hand and managed to spray juice everywhere. I was sure there were going to be many more disasters like this. Separately I fried some pre-cut slices of chicken breast. Later I tossed all the ingredients into a blender to puree them. Clara could have the same as me. I wasn't sure how many teeth she had and what she could and couldn't manage to eat. I would discover in time no doubt. I achieved everything at an agonisingly slow pace. The worktop and cooker were too high for my wheelchair and at times I had to prop myself up to manage. They hadn't built these flats with disabled people in mind!

Once the food cooled, I served Clara's meal with a soft roll and butter. I had to hold the roll down with my left elbow carefully while I spread the butter as best I could on a plate resting on my lap. I looked longingly at the roll. How I would love to savour the taste of bread again. It was one of the things I missed the most with my facial injuries. Clara looked at the food, then at me, in silence, after I placed it in front of her.

'Eat up Clara. Good girl,' I smiled at her encouragingly, pointing to the spoon. Finally, she picked up her spoon and took a mouthful. She paused and you could see her little mind thinking about the flavours she was experiencing. Would she accept or reject it? Had she tasted anything like this before? She must've found it acceptable as she then set about eating without further ado. She was very adept at using the spoon and, every now and then put it down to take a bite of the roll. Her neat eating habits were impressive and she made very little mess. I'd forgotten about things like bibs, so it was just as well. For dessert, I opened a packet of chopped fresh fruit and placed it in a bowl in front of her. She attempted to spoon it up, but it was proving difficult for her, so I told her she could eat it with her hands. I demonstrated by taking a small piece of pineapple and putting it in my mouth. It was so delicious I left it sitting there and squashed it gradually with my tongue on the roof of my mouth. I'd have to puree some for myself later. Clara copied me, picking up each piece. She seemed to squash it in her mouth, with light chewing before swallowing.

I cleaned her up after she'd finished and suggested she climb out of the chair herself. She seemed to understand me and did exactly that. I'd found some toys for her and laid them out on the floor for her to play with while I sat and watched her. She appeared to be having an imaginary conversation with her soft toys, changing expression in her voice from time to time – which I guessed were meant to be questions in her baby babble when she'd then answer 'yes' or 'no'. I'd gained the impression from my conversations with Lucy that Clara had often been ignored. She had, presumably, learned to just get on with it.

When Lucy had spoken about Clara, there had been little clarity, which is why I had been confused. Obviously with her depression and isolation Lucy wasn't used to talking and just let forth everything that had been in her head – in quite a jumbled way at times. For my part, I wasn't used to anyone confiding in me, so I probably didn't pick up on things I should have.

Later, with Clara's help, I stripped her and she followed me into the bathroom. The bath had a hand mixer shower attachment on it. Rather than running Clara a bath I turned this on until the temperature was appropriate for her and encouraged her to climb in. There was a small stool beside the bath which she could use to achieve this with my one-armed support. She was hesitant at first – unsure what I was asking her to do. Eventually, she seemed to understand and climbed into the bath, where I alternately rubbed liquid baby soap on to her and then showered her down while asking her to hold onto the side of the bath as I did so. We had a few water sprays that hit me and the walls as I placed the shower hose down each time. She found this all very amusing and giggled the whole time. It was the first time I'd had a smile out of her since Freddie and Kim had left. Lifting her out again was tricky. But we managed it without mishap. I towelled her dry, put a nappy on her and, again with her support, managed to get her pyjamas on. Thank goodness she was co-operative and well behaved! I doubted it would always be this easy.

I read her a bedtime story and when she finally drifted off to sleep I sat beside her cot resting quietly. It had been a long and exhausting day. Eventually, I left her to sleep and went to heat up food for myself.

Although I wasn't supposed to drink alcohol with

the medication I was on, I decided I deserved a glass of white wine. I'd bought several bottles of both red and white at the shopping mall. After few frustrating minutes, I finally succeeded in opening the bottle. I'd had to wedge it between my knees while I unscrewed the cap with my one hand. I sipped from the glass I'd poured while heating my food.

I didn't bother with dessert and straight after eating I went off to the bedroom, more than ready to crash, but realised that I hadn't asked Kim to help me make the bed! Fifteen minutes later I'd managed to slip a fitted sheet over the mattress, fit one pillowcase badly on a pillow and place another flat sheet loosely over the bed. After undressing with difficulty, I switched on the lamp, turned off the overhead light and crawled cautiously into bed. I was so tired I was asleep within minutes. I woke to lamplight sometime later. The digital clock beside the bed told me it was 12.37 am.

A full bladder forced me out of bed, and it was then I discovered I hadn't closed the window or the bedroom blinds and curtains. The blinds were the vertical kind and were slightly open. With the lamp on anyone standing outside the window could look in. Not that they could do that easily in the bedroom though, as it was shielded from the road by a fence. Still, someone could get around from the back and look in. I had to remember to shut everything up in future.

My stomach growled with hunger. I hadn't eaten a lot today. I steered into the kitchen deciding whether to suck on a slice of the dark mint chocolate thins I had bought or a piece of fruit. The chocolate won the argument. I didn't fancy fruit at this time of night and pureeing it would be too noisy. The chocolate did little to assuage my hunger though and I thought maybe I could manage some ice cream. I pulled out a large tub I'd bought earlier and sat spooning some into my mouth while, again, gripping it between my legs. When the icy coldness of the carton became too much to bear, I replaced it in the freezer. It wasn't as if I had to worry about my weight. Since the tsunami, I'd lost quite a bit.

The drugs they'd given me in the hospital enabled me to have painless sleep, but I didn't want to become dependent on them. Without taking a tablet I returned to bed and sank blissfully into sleep once again.

25
Kelly

Life was hectic over the ensuing weeks. I spent much of the time catching taxis to hospital and doctor's appointments, the bank, the shops plus dealing with a range of other matters. And of course, looking after Clara. We had fallen into a routine each morning. After washing and breakfasting, I'd spend some time sorting other issues while she entertained herself. Afternoons were devoted to amusing her in some way. Kim and I had developed a kind of truce; one that seemed acceptable to her. I often took Clara with me in the mornings, travelling by taxi, but when I had a hospital or doctor's appointment she stayed behind with Kim and Freddie. The physiotherapy I was receiving helped and I could feel everything gradually healing in my body.

Laurie visited me a few days after arriving 'home', telling me how everyone at work missed Tom. He gave me a sympathy card, signed by all Tom's co-workers. The firm had sorted out Tom's final monies owing and had paid it into his bank. I closed the account and transferred the money into Lucy's. Laurie was a lovely man, and I felt relaxed and at ease in his company. It was obvious that he'd spent little time around Lucy prior to the Phuket trip. He hadn't noticed I looked different. Either that or he assumed my injuries were responsible for the difference.

It was surprising how many people hadn't taken much notice of Lucy's appearance. Lucy's doctor didn't have a clue that I wasn't her – although to be fair, she had only seen Lucy a couple of times since moving to the area. And only about her depression. The doctor was pleased I no longer needed the anti-depressants. She was now prescribing me painkilling drugs – which I only took when I was in too much pain. It was lucky that I hadn't required blood tests for anything, as that might have exposed me. I had no idea of my blood group. Or Lucy's.

From the files, I'd discovered Tom and Lucy had lived in a different part of Melbourne before moving to Yarraville. That was actually a very good thing because there were no locals who knew Lucy well. I wondered about female friends Lucy might have had. She'd told me she had cut herself off from everyone after Christopher's death. Not great friends then, if they hadn't tried to maintain contact of some sort.

I was pleased with the way my new life was progressing but was mindful that it would have to change as soon as I was fit and able enough. I wanted to move right away from Melbourne – there was always the possibility that Lucy's sister Eva might appear one day. I didn't think Eva had the flat address, based on what Lucy had told me, but I didn't want to take any chances. There was also a real concern that Carlos might want to track Lucy down for a nice chat. That would be a nightmare.

When I was searching through a sideboard drawer one day I found printed e-tickets for a flight to the UK – for Tom, Lucy and Clara. They were due to fly out in June this year. Lucy hadn't mentioned it. Neither had Tom's father. Perhaps Tom hadn't told them and it was going to be a surprise. I'd have to think about that. I hadn't found a passport for Clara anywhere, so that was something they hadn't organised yet.

Further exploration of Lucy and Tom's belongings in the sideboard cupboard led me to Lucy's photo albums. There I made a frightening discovery. Lucy was a twin! An identical twin, unlike Christopher and Clara. There were albums full of photographs of two little girls at various stages of their life. Some with their parents, the younger brother she'd mentioned and presumably their grandparents. An older woman in the pictures must have been her Vietnamese grandmother. The woman I assumed was Lucy's mother still looked very Asian. And I could see Asian features on the face of the girls' father as well. The last picture of Lucy's sister Eva was of them as young adults, both still identical. I looked at my reflection in the mirror and compared it to Lucy and Eva. Although there were similarities between us, I could see a startling difference.

It would be tricky if I ever came face to face with Eva. She would know instantly that I wasn't Lucy. Perhaps I could blame the surgery, but I knew that wouldn't work. I needed to move on as soon as possible in case Eva turned up here.

I was vacuuming the bedroom awkwardly one day when I kept knocking a box under the bed. I'd noticed it before, but from my wheelchair, it was too difficult for me to reach it. Frustrated by my inability to clean under the bed properly, I tried to manoeuvre the box out using the long hose and metal ends of the cleaner. When I finally managed to dislodge it, I opened it and discovered it was packed with dairies. Lucy's diaries. The first dating from when she was nine years old. She'd kept up the practice from that point on as there were seventeen diaries. The last one ended a few weeks after Christopher's death. She'd stopped writing then leaving the remainder of the pages blank.

The diaries became my bedtime or spare moment reading, replacing books. They proved very insightful into Lucy's character and that of her sister, Eva. The Lucy I met was a warm caring person and she came across like that in her diaries – even when revealing her innermost thoughts. There was an entry about Lucy and Eva's brother's death that was a little disturbing, but as my reading progressed I was chilled by an entry I came across nine years later which Lucy had written while staying at her grandparents' property in the country following their deaths. I searched back through the diaries for the earlier entry and read them both through again.

26
Lucy

Tuesday 9th January 1990
Dear Diary,
I'm sorry I couldn't write anything yesterday. I was too upset.
It was the worst day ever for our family. Our little brother Noel
died. He drowned in the swimming dam on Nana and Pop's
property. My gorgeous funny little brother who had turned
six a few weeks before. Everyone is devastated. Mum and Dad
came back from the city when Pop called them with the news
and they went to see Noel in the hospital morgue before he
was taken away to a funeral home. Last night everyone was
too upset to even think about funeral arrangements. This
morning my parents decided he would be buried in a cemetery
back in Melbourne so we could visit his grave.

Eva had been teaching Noel to swim. She'd said it was
too dangerous for Noel to be running around the property
without knowing how to swim, with dams, a creek, plus a
river not far away. For three days they had been trekking over
to the dam for his lessons. Noel had been so excited about Eva
taking an interest in him. Normally she would swat him away
like an unwelcome, irritating fly. It was me who was close to

him.

At first I was suspicious of Eva's motives but she was the stronger swimmer out of the two of us. So it made sense for Eva to teach Noel to swim.

Yesterday I was so distraught about Noel drowning that I hadn't given anything much thought. Today, recalling everything I saw, I wasn't happy. Tonight I am going to talk to Eva again. When we are in bed and no one can hear us.

Wednesday 10th January 1990.

Eva refused to talk to me last night. She hissed at me, telling me to shut up. I forced her to take a walk with me this morning; away from the house, out of everyone's earshot. We ended up arguing and she walked off. Now we're not talking. Mum and Dad are returning to Melbourne tomorrow, following the hearse that will take Noel's body back to Melbourne. Nana, Pop, Eva and I will be travelling back down to Melbourne on Monday for the funeral. I don't think we'll be having much more of a holiday this summer. I plan to spend as much time as possible with Nana. Keeping right away from Eva.

27
Lucy

Friday January 8th 1999.
Dear Diary,
It is nine years today since Noel died. I can't stop thinking about it. I walked out across to the dam where it happened earlier this morning. I'm quite certain about what I saw that day. Eva and I argued about it many times back then. I didn't dare write too much in case Mum or Eva snooped in my diaries. I knew someone had been reading them. Mum denied it saying she wouldn't dream of doing it. Eva, I suspect, would.

If I'd written down everything I saw that day and mum had read my entries, it would have been too much for her to cope with. Planting seeds of suspicion in her mind that I doubt she would have ever recovered from. If I'd done the same and Eva had read it, my life might have been at risk.

I'm sure Eva was responsible for Noel's death. She hadn't actually drowned him herself, but I know she is to blame. She argued otherwise. And all her excuses seem very plausible — but I know what I saw.

The day Noel died, I'd decided I would walk over to the

dam to join them – despite Eva telling me I should keep away so Noel wouldn't feel inhibited by my presence. I thought that was a load of rubbish. I wanted to give Noel encouragement, knowing how critical Eva could be.

As I reached the crest of the hill looking down onto the dam I could see Eva lying on her side with her head supported by one hand waving her other hand and arm towards Noel – as though shooing him away. He was in the water and she seemed to be encouraging him to move out further into the dam. She was lying on a towel near the water's edge.

I'd tripped over at that point so I hadn't seen what happened next. When I was back on my feet I could see Noel's arms flailing around and he disappeared under the water. Eva was still lying as she was when I first saw her. She watched Noel disappear under the water and then laid down flat as though she planned to go to sleep.

Still some distance away I raced down the hill screaming her and Noel's name. At first Eva didn't respond. Then she sat up rubbing her eyes, pretending she'd just woken up. She stood and looked around, one hand shielding her eyes from the glaring sun. As I got closer I could hear her calling Noel's name. I was screaming at her that he was in the water. She took a moment to respond but when I kept pointing to the middle of the dam, she eventually rushed into the water and swam towards the centre. Eva dived from view and it seemed like hours, but was no doubt only seconds, before she resurfaced holding onto Noel.

I could tell he wasn't breathing when we both carried him out of the water. Eva started attempting to resuscitate him. She told me to run back to the house to ring an ambulance and tell Nana and Pop.

By the time help arrived it was too late. Noel was pronounced dead. Eva, through her tears, explained they'd spent quite a bit of time practising Noel's strokes and kicks, while she supported him. They'd then had a drink and some snacks sitting on their towels. Eva wanted to rest before any further swimming. Noel was keen to go back into the water, but she told him he couldn't without her.

Eva claimed she had then fallen asleep in the heat of the sun. She hadn't woken again until she heard me screaming her name. She'd done all she could to revive him, she cried. Adding that Noel must have become impatient and gone into the water alone.

At the time we all fell for it. I was so upset I hadn't taken in what I'd seen. It wasn't until the next day that I remembered. When I challenged Eva she denied everything.

'I saw you Eva. You were shooing Noel into the middle of the dam. You watched him go under before lying down,' I told her.

'No, Lucy. I didn't. I fell asleep and didn't wake until I heard you screaming my name. You only imagined it. It's possible that I roused for a second and then drifted back off to sleep, but I don't remember doing so. I only remember how tired I felt when I laid down.'

Eva was lying. I was sure of it. Unlike me, she lied with ease.

'How could you believe I would do that to our brother? You mustn't go around repeating any of this nonsense. You'll just upset everyone. Especially Mum. I feel guilty enough as it is. Don't dump your guilt on to me as well,' she'd said.

'You couldn't stand Noel. You were jealous of all the attention Mum and Dad gave him. You were jealous of the

relationship I had with him. And you were jealous of the time Noel was spending with Pop, when Pop took Noel with him some days while he worked around the property. You said that had always been your special treat. You were angry that Noel had usurped your position.'

'Yes, I was annoyed about that. Yes I found him irritating at times. But Lucy, he was our little brother. I would never have wished him harm.'

'You didn't want me to come with the two of you for the lessons. If I had been there it wouldn't have happened. Why didn't you want me to come?' I asked her.

'I told you why. Don't do this Lucy. You feel guilty because you weren't there to save him. I feel guilty because I fell asleep. I don't need this crap. Things are bad enough. You need to stop thinking and saying these things. It's just your mind playing tricks on you.'

Eva had tried to hug me then and I'd pushed her away. She'd shouted a few choice swear words at me before storming off. I sat and thought about it for ages and wondered if I had imagined it all and it was as she said. Eva could be very domineering and aggressive at times. But would she engineer my brother's death? I couldn't believe she would. So I let it go.

Today going over it all again in my mind, I wasn't so sure. I had strong doubts and began to wonder if Eva had persevered with resuscitating Noel after I'd run back for help. The incident when we'd been celebrating our birthday (actually the day before our birthdays) later the same year when we turned twelve showed me just how far Eva was willing to go at times. On that occasion she pulled up short of killing me. But had she been responsible for Noel's death? Had she offered him the swimming lessons with the intention of finding an *opportunity for him to die? That would mean a cold-blooded premediated murder.*

28
Kelly

Reading those diary entries sent shivers up my spine. Could Lucy's sister Eva have set up her own brother's death? I worked out that they would have been only eleven years old at the time. Was an eleven year old capable of such things? The more I read about Eva the more I disliked her. I know I was reading Lucy's biased view of her but Eva didn't come across as a very nice person. I took an instant dislike to her. I just hoped I never met her. She sounded dangerous.

A few weeks later I had my first driving lesson. It was much easier than I thought it was going to be. I told the instructor that I hadn't driven for over a year and had lost my confidence, but I tackled it as though I was an experienced driver. It didn't take long for me to master the synchronisation of gears and clutch. An automatic would have been easier, but Lucy's car had manual gears and so I needed to learn on one. I experienced mild pain in my pelvis at times when I depressed the clutch – no doubt it was not fully healed. But I was determined it wasn't going to prevent me from learning to drive. I'd spent years experiencing Carlos driving like a maniac, fearing a crash every time we went out. It was a relief to be in control of the wheel myself and although an inexperienced driver, I felt safer. A few more of these lessons and I might feel confident enough to venture out in Lucy's car.

Kim was looking after Clara while I was supposed to be at the hospital. I booked another double driving lesson for early next week.

I'd also finally had my hair cut into a decent shape while I was out today. The hospital in Phuket tidied it up a little once the mess in my hair was finally washed clean. I know they did the best they could but it looked like someone had hacked haphazardly at it, leaving a spiky, uneven mess. Now it was more of a short 'bob' style and would grow into a better shape. I preferred my long locks. I'd always had long hair, even as a child, so I couldn't wait to grow it again.

It's almost nine weeks since the tsunami and my fractures are healing well. It has seemed more like a year! I still have to be careful though. Whilst recovering, I had to do everything with agonising slowness – or explore different ways of achieving simple tasks. Now I was mobile, my inclination was to rush; not wise. I had to keep reminding myself that there was no need for speed! My body was still healing.

Clara is adjusting to life with me and we have an easy relationship because she's so well behaved. Her vocabulary is improving, she constantly repeats words I say to her. Although she appears reluctant to say 'mummy'. Kim keeps saying phrases like 'say goodbye to mummy', 'give mummy a kiss' or 'here's mummy'. Clara responds with a wave, kiss or smile, but doesn't use the actual word. I've not attempted to foist it on her, fraud that I am. When Clara wants my attention, she has often addressed me as 'lu-lu'. Freddie's term of address for me. He points to me saying 'lu-lu' and Clara imitates him. If Kim is around she will correct Clara and say, 'not lu-lu, it's mummy' which is confusing for Clara when Freddie isn't corrected. Kim eventually confessed that Clara had been calling her 'mummy' copying Freddie when she'd stayed with them. A few times when Clara had said 'where's mummy?' to me I didn't understand that she meant Kim. No wonder the kid was confused!

My second double driving lesson started badly. I was so nervous I kept braking without need and crunching the gears. The driving instructor was very patient. He spoke to me in a calm tone and after much encouragement I mastered it. Everything ran smoothly in the second half.

When I returned to Kim's to collect Clara, I received a frightening shock. Kim told me she had bumped into a man called Carlos ringing my bell and knocking on the lounge window. They'd had a nice little exchange.

How could he have found out where Lucy lived? I turned on her in fear and anger.

'Don't *ever* let that man into the flats. He is an absolute creep,' I shouted at her. 'You didn't invite him into your place did you?'

Surprised at my outburst she said, 'No, I didn't, although he was so sad I was tempted to. What's wrong Lucy? He said he wanted to talk to you about his girlfriend. Apparently, you were together when the tsunami struck.'

'Yes, we were. I told you that. Kelly and I had become quite good friends. She told me a lot about her relationship with that man. He kept her as a virtual prisoner and controlled every aspect of her life. Fortunately, he didn't swim and allowed her to come to the pool each day, with a bodyguard watching over her. The whole time she was at the pool, that man watched her from their terrace.'

'A bodyguard?'

'Yes, he had someone watching over her all the time. In case she tried to get away from him. From what I understood she tried it a few times and he was violent towards her. When we ate meals together you could sense his violence simmering below the surface.'

I found myself starting to shake. I'd thought I might be safe for a while but it seems I'd underestimated Carlos's obsession.

'That man came to see me in the hospital, behaving very aggressively. I had to go into the bathroom to get away from him. I can't have him here. To be quite honest with you, he frightens me.'

'God, Lucy, you make him sound like a monster.'

'He is a monster, and I don't want him around Clara.'

'What did Tom make of him?'

'Tom didn't like the man either, although he liked Kelly and appreciated that my contact with her had helped pull me out of my depression. I spent hours pouring out my troubles to her. Then when she told me her situation, I became very concerned for her safety.'

'What do you think happened to her?'

'I don't know, but when I watched her being swept away by the water, I didn't think she had any chance of surviving it. The water was so powerful Kim. You can't imagine it. The waves on our beaches here are nothing compared to what it was like that day.'

'Oh Lucy, I'm so sorry. It must have been a horrific experience. You're shaking.' She approached me and took me in her arms. It was the first sign of affection she'd shown me. A few minutes later she released me. Clara and Freddie had been watching the exchange between us. I turned and noticed that Clara had silent tears running down her face.

'It's okay Clara,' I reassured her. 'I'm fine. Just a bit upset about something,' I said, bending down and putting my arms around her. I told Kim I needed to take Clara home, but she insisted I stay for a cup of coffee first, to calm myself.

'Tom and I didn't tell Carlos where we lived Kim,' I told her a few minutes later. 'So you can see how obsessive and determined he is, to have found our address. I'm concerned he's going to try to insinuate himself into our lives. The last thing I want is for him to have any contact with Clara. I gained the impression he was one of these mafia types. He runs a club and is a property tycoon. He's not someone I want anything to do with.'

'No. I can see why you wouldn't, knowing how he treated his girlfriend. He seemed so sad though. I felt sorry for him.'

'I suspect it was an act he put on for you. He would be very angry about Kelly dying on him. He's lost control of her now.'

'Sounds like what happened was probably a blessing then. She is finally free of him.'

'It's a bit drastic that you have to die to be free of someone though. Life shouldn't be like that,' I snorted. Just thinking about my situation made me feel very angry. Yes I was happy to be looking after Clara for Lucy until I decided what we were going to do. But it was wrong that our lives had to be disrupted because of that bastard.

'No, I agree. Well, I promise I won't ever let him in the front door.'

'I won't ever be answering the door to him either.' I sighed. 'Looks like I might have to move Kim.'

'No, surely not! You could always call the police if he became a problem.'

I snorted again. 'In his line of business, he would have police working for him.'

'I can't believe that would be true. Maybe in the past, but not now.'

How naïve you are Kim. Yes, it does still happen today. Time to embellish so she will begin to understand how dangerous Carlos is.

'When I suggested that Kelly should go to the police, she told me that many policemen *did* work for Carlos. She didn't know what they did for him; she said she never wanted to know.'

'Jeez Lucy, you're worrying *me* now.'

'You ought to be worried. He's a very dangerous

man.'

When I returned to the flat I immediately ran around ensuring all the windows were locked. I pulled the curtains closed in the front rooms and shut the blinds as tightly as I could everywhere. I then furiously started packing bags.

Clara watched my panicky actions with a curious expression. I put the TV on for her to watch cartoons. The last thing I wanted was for her to become upset and cry. The sound was very low, so I hoped it couldn't be heard from outside. I needed to think things through in a calmer manner. He could return at any minute.

Where could we go? Heading to Shepparton, to Karen, was an option, but that might be dangerous. What if he was watching her? Or I could take off to another place that had no connections to me or Carlos where I could take some time out to think about the future. I'd have to do that soon, as my life, and possibly Clara's, was at risk. Carlos told me after my last attempt to escape that he would kill me next time and I believed him. It occurred to me then that I could go to the house at Mt. Martha. I hadn't had an opportunity to visit it yet. It could be derelict and not suitable for habitation. I had no idea. Or, I could alter the tickets for the UK I'd found in the drawer and take off there. After all, I'd promised Lucy that one of the things I might do is deliver Clara to her grandparents. But there was definitely no passport in the flat for Clara so I had to organise that first. I had a big decision to make.

* * *

I fed Clara early, putting her to bed a good two hours before her normal time without bathing. It was too great a risk to be in the bathroom in case he turned up. I knew she hadn't had an afternoon nap as talking to Kim, I'd kept her awake. I hoped she'd fall asleep quickly and thankfully she did. As soon as she dropped off, I ate my meal and when darkness descended, lay on the bed. Waiting. Sure enough at around 9 pm, the door buzzer went. Whoever it was kept constantly pressing it (and I knew it was Carlos). Next, there were loud knocks on the living-room window. He couldn't get to the bedroom window, there was a fence blocking his way. Unless he climbed it – which is exactly what he did. He started banging on the bedroom window. I could hear him calling out 'Lucy.' The sound of his voice chilled me to the bone. I slipped off the bed and crept into Clara's room. If he had access to the front bedroom window it meant he could now access the back of the block as well. He might start banging on Clara's window. I was worried she might wake and cry out.

The knocking at the front bedroom stopped and a few minutes later I saw a shadow passing Clara's window. The blinds were closed but the light from the car park projected his shadow. I held my breath praying that someone hadn't left the yard access door unlocked. I heard him try to open it; without success. It then sounded like he was attempting to gain access by the kitchen window. All the windows in the flat had slide openings. There were external fly screens fitted across the openings, which he could easily remove – if he had the right tools, but I'd checked all the windows were locked.

The shadow approached Clara's window where he stopped, attempting to loosen the screen. Every muscle in my body tensed ready for flight, and I held a shaky hand poised over Clara's mouth in case she woke. I could hear the sound of my heartbeat pounding away – far too rapidly. I conjured up an image of mountains – like the mountains that surrounded my hometown as a child in order to slow my breath and heartrate.

Carlos gave up and a minute later I heard him rattle the front bedroom screens as well. He couldn't gain entry unless he removed the fly screen, broke one of the windows and climbed in. But fortunately, he didn't do that. Tonight at least. I wouldn't rule out him doing it another time though. I breathed a sigh of relief when I heard him scramble over the fence again. He knocked a few more times on the living room window and then all was quiet. Would he sit outside all night and wait for me to leave in the morning? I didn't dare look out of the curtains in the living-room.

When I stopped shaking, I scribbled a note for Kim by torchlight in the kitchen – crouched down behind the peninsula, telling her that Carlos had been around again and that I was taking off with Clara on a road trip. I would drop it outside her door in the morning. I gathered some documentation I might need and after packing clothes for us, I returned to bed. After what seemed like hours I drifted off into a troubled sleep.

29
Kelly

The morning following Carlos's nocturnal visit I rose at dawn, had a quick shower and completed the packing I'd started the previous evening. Knowing Carlos's lifestyle I was pretty confident he wouldn't be up and about at this time of day.

I pushed the short letter I'd written for Kim under her flat door. I lugged the suitcases I'd packed out to the car. I then shoved our duvets and sets of linen into bin liners, throwing them into the car. We might be sleeping in it tonight. In the kitchen I left my mobile on the worktop, not wanting Kim to be able to reach me. Grabbing some food to keep us going, I packed as much as I could into the cooler box and shopping bags, and loaded them into the car, along with Clara's low eating seat and new stroller. Then I gently woke her and stripped her cot. I'd reclaimed Clara's car seat from Kim after our last shopping trip together earlier in the week. It was now fixed into Lucy's Hyundai ready for use. Clara was still sleepy when I strapped her in and she nodded off again within minutes.

The car turned over the first time. I'd been starting it some days over the past few weeks to ensure it still worked, but I hadn't driven it anywhere yet. Thankfully, the petrol tank was almost full. I sat letting it warm up for a minute before encouraging myself to get moving. Armed with the street directory and the property file on the front seat, I reversed back. Then in first gear, I kangarooed the car in fits and starts to the driveway out of the block and stopped. It wasn't a good start. I'd have to do better than that. A few deep breaths later, I checked the street. I couldn't see any cars parked in the immediate vicinity. Most houses surrounding our block of flats had driveways, so parked cars would stand out. Heaving a sigh of relief, I turned and accelerated down the street, reassuring myself that I could do this. I'd decided that I would head for the property at Mt. Martha in the first instance.

The roads were clear on the way out of Melbourne; most cars were heading into the city at this time of the morning. Once I reached the Mt. Martha area I had to stop and work out the way to the house.

I passed the entrance to it a few times before I realised; trees and bushes obscured the driveway which was a long dirt and gravel drive down to the house. There I found a single storey, rendered and painted house set back on the block. The land, neglected for some time, was knee high in weeds and grass gone to seed. It would be dangerous to walk there. It was still snake season. Thankfully there was gravel immediately around the house.

I could see why Tom and Lucy planned to build here,

rather than renovate. The house, like the land, had a neglected air about it. I'd found the keys to the house in a sideboard drawer in the flat, conveniently labelled in what I believed was Tom's handwriting from other organised files in the flat. Clara was still out for the count so I decided to leave her there for a minute and explore. I had to make sure the house was safe.

The door was stiff with disuse and I had to use my right shoulder to force it open. I couldn't tell what era the architecture was. If I had to guess I would say maybe 30s or 40s. From the door, I stepped into a hallway with rooms leading off to the left and right. A quick look confirmed they were both bedrooms. One had a foldaway camping style cot in it, with candle remains dotted around the room. Lucy and Tom must have come up here with the twins to work and camp out before Christopher died. A bathroom stood behind the bedroom on the left and then finally, it opened out into a large wide space at the rear, where I could see a very shabby kitchen and, what I assumed was the lounge and dining-room. Off the open plan space, a door led to a sunroom that looked like a 'modern addition' with a separate toilet and laundry to one side behind the kitchen. The toilet and laundry would have had an exterior entrance when the property was first built. They were now approached through the enclosed sunroom. It was just like the old weatherboard house I lived in as a child. With a partition wall in the sunroom it could have been my brothers' bedroom.

In the laundry there two large washing sink tubs and an old washing machine.

Large sliding coloured metal doors, with sliding fly-screen doors behind them, led off the sunroom onto a raised open veranda as the land sloped down at this point. I could see why Lucy and Tom liked this place. There was a beautiful vista at the rear looking down over sloping bushland and then to the sea. There wasn't another house in sight. I could have been in the middle of nowhere, not just over an hour away from a bustling city.

In the lounge, there were a couple of old armchairs set around an open fireplace, with folded sleeping bags, pillows and blankets on one of them. In the kitchen I found bits and pieces that matched things from Tom and Lucy's flat. A dirty old gas cooker had an old-fashioned whistling kettle sitting on top of it. I couldn't imagine that there was mains gas this far out, so it was probably bottle gas. I turned a jet on and heard a fizz, indicating there was still some gas. A very old fridge-freezer sat in one corner of the kitchen, but it was not plugged in. I switched on a light, but the power was either disconnected or turned off at the fuse box as no lights came on. I hadn't seen any bills in Tom's files for electricity here. Evidence of jars and bottles with candle remains suggested that there was no supply. Dirty brown water ran from the kitchen tap and I wasn't sure if it was on a mains supply or tank. In the kitchen pantry, I found a newish looking broom, dustpan and brush, plus mop and bucket.

The bathroom had seen better days, but with a clean and a paint, it looked usable.

With a good clean and some decorating the house

would do us for the time being. We could camp out here. There was a cot Clara could sleep in and I could bed down on the sleeping bags, using them as a mattress. I went out to the car and unloaded everything. I put the bin liners containing our bedding into the cot. It was the cleanest looking thing in the house. I left our suitcases in the same room and took everything else to the kitchen. Finally, I woke Clara and carried her into the house, settling her in her low chair. She looked around the room and smiled. I gave her some pieces of fruit I'd peeled and she looked at me with surprise. She normally ate cereal, fruit and toast for breakfast.

'It's all we've got kiddo, although there is a yoghurt for afters. I'm saving the bread for lunch. I didn't bring any cereal,' I told her.

'Toast?' she asked.

'No toast today.'

'Toast?' she repeated.

'No toast, sorry Clara.' Her mouth curved down and I thought she was about to cry. She eventually shrugged and demolished the fruit and the yoghurt. Later, holding her hand, we cautiously explored out the back. I spotted a large water tank, over to the left of the house. I was similar to the one we had when I was a child. There was a big shed in the grounds which one of the keys on the house set opened. In it, there were garden tools, building tools and a petrol lawnmower which all looked fairly new. I wasn't about to attempt to cut the overgrown grass with the lawn mower. It would need chopping down first. I decided that we'd go and find some shops shortly and see if I could hire someone to come and clear the overgrowth. If that was cleared and the house cleaned up it would do us for a while. I wondered if Laurie or Kim knew of its existence. Certainly, Carlos wouldn't be aware of it. It was not registered as Tom or Lucy's official address, so if he'd used his police friends to trace Lucy, he'd have no luck finding this place. Clara and I would be safe here – at least until I could make long term plans.

30
Kelly

Mt. Martha, Victoria March 2005

The old house and grounds have been transformed in the few weeks Clara and I have been here. I paid for the grounds to be cleared, old carpets and the kitchen lino removed and the floors stripped and polished after I'd painted everywhere. I'd bought many tins of white paint and set about painting every room. Even Clara helped to dab white paint on the walls with a small brush. I'd placed sheets of plastic awning under us (as I was a novice decorator) to avoid paint spills onto the unpolished floors. The kitchen cupboards were in good condition, so I sanded and painted them – just having the worktop, sink and taps replaced. I booked professionals to decorate the exterior of the house and replace all the window fly screens.

One of the first things I'd done was have the electricity connected. That enabled me to carry on painting into the night and gave us hot water. The whole process was exhausting but extremely satisfying to see the place gradually transform.

I carried out all this decorating to make the house more habitable and comfortable for us until I made a decision about our future. I gave notice on the flat and arranged for the remainder of the flat's contents to go into store in the first instance. I didn't want to take the chance of either Carlos or Kim following a removal van to Mt. Martha.

Clara ran around the land with delight most days, with me trailing after her. It was a shame that I couldn't invite Kim and Freddie to come and visit. But it would be too much of a risk for Kim to know where we lived – in case Carlos turned up and strong-armed her into revealing the location. Or worse still – followed her.

After spotting an advertisement in a local shop, I'd started attending self-defence classes. I was learning some moves in case I ran into Carlos. Clara came along with me and sat watching in fascination, barely moving. She really is such a good kid and much as I attempted to shut off part of my heart to her in case I had to hand her over to her grandparents and leave her behind, I couldn't stop myself from falling in love with her beautiful nature.

I didn't feel guilty spending Lucy and Tom's money on the house. It was an investment of sorts that could only improve its value for Clara in the future. If we travelled to the UK, the house would also be in a fit state to let.

After providing them with Tom's death certificate, the insurance company had paid out on his life insurance without any issues. So, we had plenty of money for now.

I was being careful not to waste it though.

I'd taken over the use of Tom's old mobile with a new sim card, but I'd only used it to call builders so far. I was tempted to call Karen and arrange to visit her. I still knew her old number that I'd memorised many years ago, having repeated it like a mantra over the years. I wondered if it was still valid. There was always the concern that Carlos might consider questioning Karen, but, if he was planning to do that, I figured he would have done it many weeks back. I wanted to collect my family's photograph. It was the only one I had. Also, there was my savings account. I could have gone to the Credit Union and claimed I'd lost my book. But I had no identification in my real name and believed it was unlikely they would allow me access to my money. With my savings book, I stood a chance. It would mean that I could use some of my own money to buy myself personal items and not have to constantly dip into Tom and Lucy's. Not that it was a huge issue for me. I was looking after their daughter after all. It was the future that concerned me. When I eventually took Clara to visit Tom's parents I would need my own money if I returned to Australia alone.

31
'Lucy'

United Kingdom, May 2005

The flights from Melbourne to London (with a change at Singapore) were a bit of a nightmare, seeming to go on forever. Clara was really good though. It was me who was the problem. I didn't like the meals they served and I struggled with the cramped space. They sat us at a bulkhead which at least gave me enough space to stand and stomp the numbness out of my legs. I'd barely slept though, I was very hungry and more than a little grumpy. We had to get from the airport to a station called Euston. Tom's father assured me the underground would take us to Euston without changing trains.

Mr. Jones had told me that the train journey from Euston would take over three hours. I couldn't wait that long for a meal. I'd need to sort something out for Clara later as well, although she'd eaten everything they'd served us on the plane.

I decided our luggage was too much to attempt on the underground train and elected to catch a black taxicab to Euston instead. The taxi driver assured me there would be places I could buy food there.

At the Euston ticket office a helpful attendant explained the different changes we'd have to make on the journey. He wrote it all down for me with the platform numbers we'd need at the various stops. Before boarding the train I stocked up on loads of food and drink for the journey.

I'd brought an unlocked mobile phone with me and so I also bought a British pre-paid sim card and installed it in the phone. When it was finally working (halfway to Crewe) I texted Tom's father as arranged, telling him what time our train would arrive in Llandudno so he could meet us.

Clara dozed off with the gentle motion of the train. She lay across my lap and I gazed, with interest, out of the window at the passing countryside. The train sped through many stations without stopping, but I couldn't catch their names.

Almost three and a half hours after leaving Euston and two changes later, we arrived at Llandudno. As soon as we walked out of the station I recognised Mr. Jones – although he was much shorter than I expected. In Phuket I'd only seen him while I was lying in bed, so I hadn't noticed he wasn't as tall as Tom. He came hurrying up to us and gave me a huge hug, declaring I was looking well, before scooping Clara up in his arms. I watched as he gabbled away to her, in both Welsh and English. She looked bemused and kept looking from him to me.

'What would you like her to call you?' I asked him.

'Tide. And Nani for her grandmother.'

'Tide as in the sea?'

'Well it sounds the same as tide, like the sea, but it's spelt, T-A-I-D.'

'This is Taid,' I said to Clara pointing at Tom's father. 'Taid,' I repeated. 'Your grandfather.' She looked at him and mimicked 'Taid'.

'Yes, that's right,' Mr. Jones said with seeming delight. 'Now let's get you in the car. I bought a child's seat for Clara as you requested.'

He strapped Clara in and we both loaded the luggage. 'I will give you a tour of Llandudno before we head to the hotel,' he announced. 'It won't take long.'

He was right. It didn't take long. There was one long main street of shops and a few side streets with further shops. Along the seafront, which he called the Esplanade, large hotels lined one side of the street. I wondered if this was where his hotel was, but he continued past them all without mentioning that one was his. He pointed to the rising cliffs we were approaching and said that was the 'Great Orme.' It was meaningless to me. I'd have to read up about it. He chatted on giving a potted history of the town, including that Llandudno was the largest seaside resort in Wales. It was so different to Australian 'resorts', but I liked it. It had an old-world charm. We passed what Mr. Jones called 'the Llandudno pier' which protruded quite a distance out over the sea (the longest pier in Wales he told me). I knew Clara would love to explore that. After doing a circuit of the main part of town, he drove up a hill and turned into a narrow lane that ran between buildings before finally pulling into a carpark. I could see there was a garden area behind it. I felt butterflies in my stomach. Tom's father had proven easy, but I was nervous about meeting Gwyneth, Tom's mother. Would she accept me? Could I pull this off?

'This is the back entrance to our hotel,' he said. 'We're not a huge affair, not like some of the big hotels down on the seafront. But we have 14 letting rooms and we're always fully booked during the peak season. That's more than enough for us. Our personal family accommodation is on the ground floor, away from the letting side of things. We don't have the glorious views, we leave those for the guests, although our living room has a sea view.'

It was a large, old, treble fronted Victorian building and as we entered the rear I saw what looked like closed corridors leading off all over the place. 'Fire doors,' Mr. Jones said as though reading my mind. 'We have to have all those doors for fire regulations.'

I nodded. We'd passed a small reception desk just inside the back entrance, before turning left off a hallway that I could see led to the front door. He led us down to a small double room near the end of the corridor, 'This is your room. It overlooks the rear. We've put Clara in the little room just past the bathroom which is next door – with a single bed as you requested. Clara's room used to be Tom's room when he was a child.'

Clara's room was small, dark and claustrophobic. It had a side window that looked out onto a fence and then the wall of the next property. My room looked out over a yard area, then the car park, but it was a double at least.

'Leave your bags and come and meet Gwyneth. She'll be in the main kitchen sorting things out for the evening meals.'

We re-traced our steps and he led us over to the other side of the property and into an enormous kitchen with a large wooden table in the middle. A woman with short brown wavy hair (who I recognised from Tom's photograph collection) was sitting at the table. I could see she was on the podgy side. She had a tired weary expression on her face.

'Gwyneth, this is Lucy at long last, and little Clara.'

When she stood I noticed she was only a few inches taller than me. She smiled, a kind of half smile, but her face lit up when she turned to look at Clara. 'She's the image of Tom!' Gwyneth exclaimed.

I thought that was rather exaggerated. I could see some aspects of Clara resembled Tom, but I thought Clara looked a little like Lucy as well. And perhaps a little like me, with our Eurasian backgrounds. Gwyneth immediately started speaking Welsh to Clara.

'Gwyneth,' Tom's father interrupted, 'It's better if we speak English around Lucy. We can gradually introduce some Welsh words to Clara over time. I've told Lucy that Clara should call you Nani.'

'That's fine,' Gwyneth answered.

'Clara,' Mr. Jones said taking her hand, 'This is your Nani. Nani,' he repeated pointing at Gwyneth. He pointed to Clara first saying 'Clara,' then me 'mummy', himself, 'Taid', and finally Gwyneth, 'Nani.'.

Clara repeated what he'd said, pointing to each of us as she spoke, leaving herself out.

'So what's your name?' Gwyneth asked her.

'My name is Clara,' she answered in a clear assertive voice. Clara had been able to say this phrase for some weeks and her ability to form short sentences was increasing daily. I'd heard her say her name like this several times, but for some reason, hearing it today brought a rush of tears to my eyes.

It had the same effect on Gwyneth. I could see tears forming in her eyes and she jumped up, picked up Clara and hugged her. Thank goodness. There were no hugs for me. Which I was actually relieved about. But until now she'd made no affectionate gestures towards Clara and I thought, *Come on this is your granddaughter. Welcome her properly!* Finally, she had.

'I'll put the kettle on,' Tom's father murmured. He asked what Clara and I would like to drink before suggesting that Gwyneth took us into their living room. I politely declined his offer of food, telling him that we'd eaten loads on the train.

I followed Gwyneth, still holding Clara, into their living room, back on the opposite side of the building again. It was a large space with a view out of the side bay window down to the sea. Photographs of Tom, both as an adult and a child, took up pride of place on the mantelpiece and shelves above built-in cupboards. In some photographs Tom was snapped with an older boy I assumed was his brother, whose name I didn't know.

'Daddy!' Clara exclaimed pointing to one of the photographs of Tom as an adult. I had spent hours showing Clara photographs of Tom in preparation for this trip. Explaining this was her 'Daddy'. I'm sure she already knew because the first time I opened an album containing photographs of him, her face had immediately lit up. She'd pointed to him, the word hovering on her lips, as though she once knew it, but it now escaped her. The first time I said 'daddy' she said 'yes, daddy,' and laughed. I'd helped her to remember. I should have done that from day one, but I'm ashamed to say that I was pre-occupied with other matters.

Recognising her father further endeared Clara to Gwyneth. As soon as Tom's father came in carrying a tray of refreshments, Gwyneth told him enthusiastically how Clara had recognised her daddy. Tom's father beamed at Clara. They were both smitten. As I'd hoped they would be. She was all they had left of their son.

I wasn't sure how I was going to address Tom's parents. His father had insisted on me calling him 'dad' back in Phuket and said Gwyneth would expect me to call her 'mum'. I couldn't imagine that in a million years, positive Gwyneth would bristle if the word 'mum' ever escaped my lips. I wouldn't be too happy about it either.

I bathed and changed Clara straight after our refreshments, providing an opportunity to escape from what was proving to be an awkward situation for me with Gwyneth. Tom's father then spent time with Clara in the garden and walking around the neighbourhood with her. They seemed to have formed a strong bond. Clara was so exhausted by the exercise that she ate very little for dinner and dropped off to sleep within minutes of me putting her to bed.

By arrangement, evening meals were served to guests

at 7 pm. After showering and changing, I spent the afternoon helping out in the kitchen. Later, after putting Clara to bed I offered to help serve the guests. Gwyneth asked me if I had ever had any experience of waitressing and I almost made the mistake of telling her I had many years of experience but caught myself in time. Instead I said that I'd done waitressing jobs during my university years.

Once we'd cleared up from our own meal, I excused myself and retreated to my room where after a short read I fell into a deep sleep.

A few days later I finally had 'the conversation' with Gwyneth, asking her how she wished me to address her. We were alone in the kitchen, relaxing over a cup of coffee.

'I've been dreading this,' she said, 'so I'm glad you've asked, rather than assumed. I know Howell wants you to call him 'dad', but I don't feel comfortable with you calling me 'mum'.'

'Well that's a relief,' I replied. 'I didn't feel comfortable with it either.' To me, it seemed like a betrayal to the memory of my mother to call anyone else 'mum'. It wasn't the same with 'dad' as we never called our father 'dad'. We always called him 'da'. 'So what about me calling you Gwyneth?' I suggested. 'Mrs. Jones sounds rather formal don't you think?'

'Yes, Gwyneth would be fine. I'm happy with that.'

I was pleased to hear that – it would make things simpler between us. I could see Gwyneth heave a visible sigh of relief. I'd sensed something about me was bothering her, but it seemed that wasn't the only thing.

'You look very different from the wedding photographs and the pictures Tom snapped of you after the twins' births,' she remarked casually.

'Well, you know that my face was badly smashed and I had to have reconstructive surgery, don't you? Also, they had to cut off my long hair because of the debris caught up in it and it hasn't grown back that much since.'

'Yes, I know all that,' she replied impatiently waving her arms about. 'But even so, you look different. You're much dar...' She trailed off not finishing the sentence. I suspected she was going to say I was much 'darker' skinned than she had expected. I could see that Gwyneth was embarrassed by her near blunder. Her face looked like a ripe tomato. I decided I would confront her on this matter.

'You think my skin looks darker than it does in the photographs? Is that what it is?'

'Um, ... no. That wasn't really what I meant.' *Liar*

'I caught the sun doing a lot of outdoor work back in Melbourne before we left,' I lied. The weeks before leaving were largely cold and wet. 'I have olive skin so it tans easily and I hold the tan for many months after. Our wedding was towards the end of winter in Australia. For many months before the wedding, I had been enclosed in an office with little exposure to the sun. I was also very happy back then as you can see. I'm not now. Which I am sure you can understand.' It was interesting that Gwyneth had noticed a substantial difference in my appearance when no-one else had.

'Hmm,' she said and paused. She appeared to be struggling to find the right words. 'You're also very different to how I imagined. After Christopher's death – you don't mind me talking about this do you?' She clearly didn't care whether I did or not as she ploughed on regardless. 'After Christopher's death, the one time I spoke to you, you sounded so ...'

'Depressed?' I suggested when she paused.

'Yes. And Tom seemed to be at his wits end about how to cope with you. He told us that this holiday in Phuket was a last desperate attempt to pull you back. And look how that turned out. My son arriving home in a coffin.'

She sounded bitter and accusing – but I knew I shouldn't react, reminding myself she was a mother who was still grieving for her son.

'I know, and I'm so sorry Gwyneth. We couldn't possibly have known that a tsunami would hit the resort. If it's any consolation, the holiday did change things for me. We were very happy in the short time we were there.'

'Yes, Tom said as much when we spoke to him on Christmas Day. He was so optimistic. Said you were like your old bubbly self again.'

'I was. That holiday changed everything for me – in more ways than one. I'm just so sad that Tom and so many others lost their lives.' When I spoke like this I had to imagine myself as Lucy. Speak like her. Speak *for* her. There were elements of truth in everything I said to Gwyneth. However, I was an accomplished liar – it was a survival strategy I'd used for years and I had to continue the lies if I was to convince Gwyneth.

'It's more than that Lucy. I can't quite put my finger on what I mean, except to say that you seem to have a *quiet* confidence about you now. The first few times I ever spoke to you, before Christopher's death, you seemed overly enthusiastic about everything, bubbly and very chatty. I know we only spoke a few times, but ...,' she trailed off shaking her head.

'After Phuket, I had to battle to remain strong for Clara. Especially with the injuries I still had when I returned to Australia. I couldn't cave into my feelings and fears again. And I couldn't be bubbly and chatty anymore. Not after losing Christopher and Tom. Their deaths have changed me.'

'I understand that. And it must have been very hard for you. It's just that I imagined—'

'Don't we all do that with people we've never met in the flesh?' I said cutting her off. 'I know, when I read a book, I create images of the characters in my head. If a film is made from the book, sometimes those characters match the actor playing the part. Other times they don't and it's a huge disappointment.'

'Yes, I suppose so,' she said with a sigh. 'On a different note, how long do you think you will stay with us? You know we're becoming very attached to Clara?'

'I know you are.'

'You're welcome to stay indefinitely. It's up to you.'

I nodded. But I wasn't so sure her comment was genuine. For Clara yes, but I doubt it applied to me.

The next few weeks followed a familiar routine. Tom's

parents had a small kitchen in their own apartment area. I prepared breakfast for Clara and me in there most days, staying out of their way. Then Tom's father, having completed many of his jobs, would collect Clara and take her out somewhere while I assisted Gwyneth in the kitchen and laundry. They had people working for them, but the workload was still unrelenting at times. When I asked if they did this all year round, Gwyneth looked at me in surprise.

'Didn't Tom tell you about our house in Spain?' *Oh shit!*

'Oh yes, I'd completely forgotten about the Spanish house,' I answered without faltering and turned back to the sink to give the pan I was washing an extra hard scour. I'd have to learn to keep my mouth shut and wait to hear things I didn't know about to unfold in general conversation. But I couldn't leave it there, after raising the issue in the first place.

'When do you go there?' I asked. *Was I supposed to know this as well?*

'Usually January to March. We often go in early November up to mid-December as well when we seldom have bookings and so will close up. Our house is right down on the south coast, near Malaga, so the climate is still warm in those months. I don't think I could stand the heat of the summer months there but it's great to escape the bleak winters here.'

That was why they hadn't answered on my second call. They were in Spain. The first time I phoned it was still early January and they'd had to organise Tom's funeral. They'd probably left shortly after that.

'What happens to the house the rest of the year?' I asked. 'Do you leave it empty?'

'No, we let it out much of the time. It covers all the overheads and leaves us spending money while we're there. Davey goes out there a few times a year with his friends.'

Davey, I'd discovered, was Tom's *older* brother. His name was David but he was always called 'Davey'.

I spent time with Clara after lunch most days, before I returned to work in the kitchen. We'd usually go out somewhere. I needed the fresh air and to escape from the confines of the hotel. I also needed time to think. I knew I couldn't stay at the hotel indefinitely. We didn't have enough space. Clara wasn't able to play like a normal little girl would, or with friends. I'd brought a few of her things with me and shipped other things over. Howell and Gwyneth had also bought more things for her. Every evening her toys had to be crammed back into her small bedroom. The private living room was a bit of a showroom and I knew Gwyneth would hate to see it become messy with Clara's things left out.

I didn't know anyone in the area and Tom's parents hadn't suggested anyone they knew who had young children. Clara needed to connect with children her own age.

I also felt quite isolated and lonely. Nothing new for me, but I didn't think it was fair on Clara. I had to do something about it.

Howell had bought Clara a new pushchair (which we

call a stroller at home) and one afternoon, on one of our walks I scoured around for other young mothers with children of a similar age to Clara. I spotted two women sitting outside a café – one with a toddler in a pushchair and approached them.

'Excuse me, sorry to interrupt you, but could I ask if you are from Llandudno?'

'Yes, love,' the one who I thought was the mother answered.

'Would you know if there is an under 5's kindergarten in the town? I've walked around all the streets here but found nothing.'

The women looked at each other with blank expressions clearly not understanding me. Then I could see one of them had worked it out.

'Do you mean a nursery?' she asked.

Now it was my turn to look puzzled. I had read about nurseries for young children in homes of the wealthy. Was that what they called kindies here? I'd come across communication difficulties like this with Gwyneth and Howell. We all spoke English but had different understandings of words we commonly used. Howell told me he was taking Clara to a nearby nursery one day. I thought he'd meant somewhere with babies, but when they returned carrying plants I was confused. He'd had to explain that garden centres are often referred to as nurseries because they grew plants from seedlings. 'Baby plants,' Clara had declared pointing to the box of plants Howell had dropped outside. That made sense.

'I suppose so. Is that what you call it?' I said to them. But just to clarify things I added, 'A pre-school for young children like my daughter.'

She nodded. 'There's nothing around the main town area. You need to go up Tow Hill. That's where you'll find one of the nurseries. There's also a drop-in play centre around the corner from that. We've been there this morning. They have morning and afternoon sessions. It's near the Great Orme Tramway.'

'Okay, great thanks.'

'Are you new to the area then? Where's your accent from?'

'I'm Australian. We've been staying with my husband's family who run a hotel here.'

'Not Tom Jones's family? You're Tom's wife are you?'

'Yes, that's right.'

'We went to school with Tom. Such a lovely young man. So sorry to hear about his death. It was in the local papers here. So you were in that dreadful tsunami thing?'

'Yes.' I wasn't going to be drawn into this conversation. 'Thanks again for your help, I'd better get on and see if I can find this place.'

I dashed off before they could ask any further questions. Small town syndrome. Everyone knew everyone else's business. It was very much like that where I grew up in a semi-rural area outside of Sydney. Llandudno almost seemed like a city in comparison to my home 'village'. We'd only had a small supermarket, post office, feed and hardware store, plus a garage. But still, here, everyone seemed to know about Tom. I'd had a few comments from staff at the Hotel and one or two of Gwyneth's friends who'd dropped in to see her. I made my excuses each time and left, to avoid their probing tsunami questions. The tsunami was just something they'd read about in the paper or seen on TV as a news item. For me it was real.

32
'Lucy'

The weeks at the hotel flew by. I enrolled Clara into a kindergarten - a nursery school a short distance from the hotel. The first day I left her there I lingered about the entrance to her 'classroom' to make sure she was okay. I needn't have bothered. As soon as she saw the other children and all the toys she was off, not looking back. Not even when I called a farewell to her. Ignored, I turned and left, feeling a little deflated.

Howell wasn't happy about the idea of Clara attending nursery at first. Howell was how I now *thought* of him. It was rather tedious to keep saying 'Tom's father' in my head all the time. When I addressed Howell, I called him 'dad' as he preferred. It didn't hurt me to do that and it made him happy. But I just couldn't *think* of him as *dad*.

Howell said he would miss his morning and afternoon sessions with Clara. When I pointed out that she needed interaction with other children, he agreed – admitting that he was just being selfish.

After Clara started attending kindergarten, I began to think about whether I should drop the Lucy charade and just take off – leaving Clara with her grandparents. I would have kept my promise to Lucy in doing so. I was satisfied that Howell was a good role model for Clara. Gwyneth, I wasn't so sure about. I could tell she adored Clara but I suspected she had a bit of a racist attitude towards people from other cultures. I believed that stemmed from growing up in a small, largely white town, not through malice. I'd seen similar attitudes towards my mother as a child in Australia – where the residents of our community had no idea that their comments and language use were, at times, offensive. I didn't want Clara to grow up developing any racist attitudes.

Indecision crippled me. Could I bear to leave Clara? I had become extremely attached to her. Some days I would forget that I wasn't Lucy and really thought of Clara as my daughter. The truth was though, she wasn't mine, and I was committing countless crimes pretending to be Lucy. I lay in bed at night planning my departure so that I wouldn't get caught. I could pack my rucksack and sneak out when Clara was at kindy, Gwyneth busy in the kitchen and Howell out on one of his shopping runs. I would leave them a note saying I had to leave and I would write further to explain all. Once I was safely back in Australia I would write with the full explanation, telling them about my promise to Lucy in the final moments we had together. How the actions I had taken were the only way I could keep the promise because of the danger Carlos represented.

Howell would remember Carlos mentioning me and might recall my name. If I explained it all, they might not do anything about it. It was a risk though. Gwyneth was the one who I thought might alert the authorities and have me traced back to Australia. I could go to prison. As it turned out, fate intervened – or more likely a human hand, and the decision was taken out of my control.

33
'Lucy'

Llandudno, July 2005

I'd begun half-heartedly looking for work in Llandudno. I needed to earn my own money while I made a decision about what to do. I had an interview lined up for daytime work in a café when Gwyneth had a serious accident. She'd been coming down the stairs carrying a bundle of dirty linen when she tripped over one of Clara's toys. The linen was usually cleared by the chambermaid who was off sick that day. The whole thing was very strange as Clara never played in the guest's quarters. I'd never taken her there and as far as I knew Howell and Gwyneth hadn't either. How the toy managed to find its way to the stairs was a mystery. A hotel full of guests had been up and down there that morning already and if the toy had been there, someone would have surely picked it up. I had suspicions of it being deliberately planted there by a particular member of staff. Intended for me, but again fate had intervened.

With the chambermaid off sick, Gwyneth had asked

whether I would go and strip the bedding in room 10, a family room where the guests had checked out that morning. She said either she or Bronwyn would clean the room later. Unusually, Clara and I had been in the large kitchen that morning. I agreed to do it as soon as I finished my toast. Howell had just left to take Clara to nursery. Bronwyn, a member of staff, had been in the kitchen when I'd agreed to do this for Gwyneth. She had then gone off to clear up the dining room. Gwyneth remembered I had my interview so said she would do it instead. As far as Bronwyn was concerned it was going to be me stripping the room. I wondered if Bronwyn had grabbed the toy when she left the kitchen (where Clara had been earlier with Howell) and placed it on the stairs after hearing someone trudging up the stairs a few minutes before. Perhaps with my blighted past, I thought the worst of people, but I had a reason for suspecting Bronwyn.

Gwyneth and I had been in the kitchen a week earlier when Bronwyn came in red-faced, asking me to go and serve some new guests who had come in for their breakfast. I told her I was scrubbing pots and asked why she couldn't do it.

'I'm not serving them darkies,' she'd said contemptuously.

'Darkies? What on earth are you talking about?' I asked her. I'd never heard the expression.

Gwyneth just sighed after Bronwyn's announcement and eventually said, 'She means coloured people. That's what some people around here call them.'

'And do *you* call them 'darkies' Gwyneth? Those

coloured people?' I'd challenged her, raising my voice. 'Neither the word 'darkie', nor 'coloured', is an acceptable way to describe people. They're just *people*.'

Gwyneth turned beetroot red at this point. 'Please lower your voice, Lucy. Or our guests will hear you.'

'Perhaps they ought to hear how *you* and your staff refer to them. You ought to be ashamed of yourself Bronwyn,' I said, glaring at Bronwyn with hostility.

I then turned to Gwyneth. 'How can you let her talk about *your* guests like that? She's not fit to be working here. Do you call *me* a darkie?'

'No, no ...of...of...course not,' Gwyneth stuttered.

'I'm one of your so-called 'coloured' people. You also referred to your guests as *coloured*, what colour are they?' I challenged Gwyneth.

'They're black,' Bronwyn piped up. 'You're brown, no ... no, Indians are brown, you're ... more yellow,' she said flippantly. She beamed at me with a self-satisfied smirk. The urge to wipe it off her face was overwhelming. I clenched my fists in readiness.

'Bronwyn! Enough!' Gwyneth shouted at her.

I stormed out of the kitchen then and into the dining-room. Otherwise, I was going to do Bronwyn some serious damage. I don't think the couple in question had heard us. They were standing by the window at the front of the lounge admiring the view. I readjusted my features from furious to friendly, showed them to a prepared table in the dining room and took their order. They had distinctive accents that were unknown to me. After I'd brought them their breakfast, they asked me where *my* accent came from. I told them I was Australian and that was where I was born and grew up. I always added this in case people thought I'd immigrated to Australia. I'd come across other guests making that assumption about me and asking me where I'd originally come from. The couple mentioned they were from Birmingham. Where they were born and grew up, they added. I guessed people also made assumptions about them. They were only in Llandudno overnight.

'The people Bronwyn wouldn't serve are English,' I told Gwyneth, when I returned to the kitchen. 'They were born in Birmingham. But it wouldn't matter if they had just flown in from the West Indies or Africa. It's offensive to refer to people as "darkies".'

Bronwyn was not there at the time – Gwyneth told me she'd disappeared off to the toilet behind the kitchen after she'd told her off.

'I don't think Bronwyn should be working here. Not serving people anyway. I don't think a 'telling off' is good enough.'

'I can't sack her if that's what you're implying,' Gwyneth had moaned. 'She's the daughter of a friend.'

'That's no excuse.'

'I've told Bronwyn that if she wants to keep her job she will serve any, and all, of our guests with equal courtesy. Please don't get into a squabble with her Lucy. I've dealt with it.'

'Humph,' I snorted.

Gwyneth apologised to me, saying she hadn't realised that the term 'coloured' was offensive to anyone. Explaining it was language she'd grown up with and always used.

'You hear it used on television all the time,' she said.

'It doesn't make it right though, does it? I know some people don't mind being called *coloured*, but personally I find it offensive. There's no need for it to creep into the language you use.'

She asked me how she should describe people then.

'Do you mean generally or in the business?'

'Both.'

'If you need to refer to them because of a specific order they've made you could refer to them as "the couple from Birmingham". Or "the couple from whatever room they're in" or "the couple from table number X"– as Howell does. If they're from another country, you *could* mention the particular country. How do you refer to people who are visiting from, say, Scotland or Ireland?'

'I might say "the Scottish family" or "Irish family" – whatever is applicable.'

'Well, it's exactly the same with *anyone*.'

'But what if they are col…'

'Gwyneth, please. Don't,' I said cutting her off. I was sure she was going to ask, "But what if they are coloured?" I couldn't bear it. I'd turned and walked out of the kitchen to avoid any further conflict.

Now, a week later, Gwyneth had this mysterious accident. I heard her scream and went running through to find her moaning in pain at the bottom of the stairs. Bronwyn was standing at the door to the dining-room, a horrified look on her face.

I told Gwyneth not to move and asked Bronwyn to call an ambulance. She just stood there, not moving, staring dumbfounded at Gwyneth.

'Bronwyn!' I shouted at her. 'Call a bloody ambulance. *Now!*' I emphasised.

She finally stirred herself and ran through to the kitchen where there was a phone. Gwyneth ended up in hospital with a broken pelvis and a broken leg. Needless to say, I cancelled my interview and ended up taking over Gwyneth's duties from that day on. It would be many months before she would be able to work again.

While we'd been waiting for the ambulance, Gwyneth had murmured through her pain that she'd tripped on something. She swore that whatever it was, it hadn't been there when she went upstairs. I looked up and noticed the toy, halfway down the stair run, lying to one side. One of Clara's, which I was sure she'd taken into the kitchen earlier.

I elected to wait for Howell to return from the nursery rather than travel in the ambulance with Gwyneth. I told Bronwyn to go with her and white-faced, she'd complied. I didn't want her around when I spoke to Howell.

When I expressed my suspicions about Gwyneth's accident, Howell insisted that Bronwyn wouldn't do anything like that. Gwyneth hadn't told him about the incident with the Birmingham couple. So I enlightened him, citing that as my reason for suspecting Bronwyn of placing the toy on the stairs. I also added that Bronwyn thought it was *me* who would be stripping the bedding.

Howell departed for the hospital with a worried look on his face. I offered to stay on to finish the jobs that needed to be done as new guests were expected. As I worked I thought about what had happened. Had

Bronwyn just made an attempt on my life? Or was she so ignorant she thought I might just end up with a broken ankle or something? People died from falls down staircases all the time. Hadn't she realised how dangerous it was? I really didn't want her to return to work here. How could I trust her? How could I trust myself? I knew if she came back I would confront her and there'd be an unpleasant scene.

Howell returned from the hospital with news of Gwyneth's injuries and that she was having surgery. He'd dropped Bronwyn home as she was feeling very unwell. She'd told Howell she'd heard Gwyneth scream and ran out of the dining room to see Gwyneth tumble down to the bottom of the stairs. Howell said Bronwyn was suffering from shock. The hospital had given her something for it, but he said she was still shaking when he'd dropped her home. He doubted that she would be in tomorrow.

'Good,' I said. 'I would prefer it if she never stepped foot in here again. I'm sure it was her that placed Clara's toy at the top of the stairs. I *know* I saw it in the kitchen earlier. And I'm sure it was intended for me.'

'Where's the toy now?' he asked. I went into the kitchen to fetch it, Howell following.

'This is it,' I said picking up the toy – a large, hard-plastic giraffe, 'but as you can see it's broken. This is the only thing that was on the stairs. Gwyneth maintained that she'd tripped on something, something that wasn't on the stairs as she went up. She would have seen it and picked it up if it had been there.' The giraffe's head was now twisted at a strange angle. It gave me the creeps looking at it.

'I took this off Clara just before we went to the nursery this morning,' Howell said.

'Where did you leave it?'

'Here in the kitchen.'

'So someone definitely put it on the stairs.'

'I don't understand. Okay, maybe Bronwyn was angry at you suggesting she shouldn't work here. *If* she heard your conversation with Gwyneth about it. But to do this! Gwyneth could have died. Broken her neck or something. Or one of our guests could have had a serious accident. I just can't imagine Bronwyn doing it but I think you're right, she must have.'

'Are you going to call the police?'

'The police?' Howell looked surprised and I could tell the idea had never occurred to him.

'Yes. The police. If she put the toy there to deliberately trip me, then it's a criminal offence.'

'I was thinking more along the lines that it might be a sacking matter. Although we have no absolute proof that she did it and it's highly unlikely that she'll admit to placing it at the top of the stair run.'

'No I don't suppose she will, but she's the only one who went into that part of the house this morning. I was only in the big kitchen and the private apartment. Gwyneth didn't go in there until she went up to strip the bed.'

'I'll wait and talk to Gwyneth before we do anything. We have a full house tonight, with some dinners to cook so we'd better get to work. I'll need to draft someone in to help. There's too much for both of us to do and I have to return to the hospital later.'

I spent the day doing an assortment of jobs: cleaning the vacated rooms, completing the work Bronwyn had abandoned in the dining room, then preparing the evening meals. Not all the guests ate in of an evening. Sometimes there might only be two people. It seemed such a waste for Gwyneth and Howell to be stuck in all evening for two people. There were often other guests who, after returning from evening out wanted an after-dinner drink or coffee and tea in the lounge. Guests had tea and coffee making facilities in their rooms but some liked to be served downstairs. Especially the smokers, so they could pop outside for a puff and then return to their drinks.

Howell only served drinks between 6 pm and 11 pm. He left me the keys to the 'bar' to serve people that evening, thinking he might not be back in time. Howell's mate, Hugh, turned up at 5 pm and we worked together catering to our eight guests. Hugh held the fort at one point while I put Clara to bed earlier than usual. I thought she might protest, but with her room darkened she soon drifted off.

Bronwyn didn't return to work at the hotel. She pleaded illness in the first few days and then gave notice. Gwyneth and Howell had made a decision they had to let her go, so were relieved when she handed in her notice. They decided against involving the police, believing she'd been so shocked and frightened by the incident that she'd never repeat anything like it again. That was all very well I thought, Bronwyn was obviously very upset when she realised it was Gwyneth she'd tripped up. If it had been me, or another person of 'colour', I doubt she would have felt so upset. But who was I to view Bronwyn so critically? Hypocrite that I was. The crimes I had committed might be considered just as serious. I kidded myself that I was only keeping a promise. Some promise. Staying in Wales meant I was continuing to live my life as someone else. Pretending to be the mother of a child who was not biologically mine. The police would have a field day with all the different charges they could make against me if my crimes ever came to light.

Howell left it up to me to find Bronwyn's replacement. I hired a lovely young Polish woman called Anna who had recently settled in the town. She lived with her boyfriend, her brother and his wife. What a pleasure it was to work with her. Her English was not brilliant, but passable. With little lessons from me, she improved daily (and I could hear the odd Australian intonation emerging when she pronounced some words).

Gwyneth remained in the hospital for more than a month. As her pelvic injury was so serious the hospital sent her to a rehabilitation unit for the final stages of her recovery. This meant further distances for Howell to travel and more time away from the hotel, leaving me to take over his duties. It was difficult juggling everything and I often worked late into the night in their little office off the main kitchen entering the computerised accounts as Howell (another of his duties) had taught me. I was supposed to have a business degree. But I was sure that being thrown in at the deep end running a business was better training than any degree. I was learning new things daily – sometimes through trial and error.

In consultation with Gwyneth and Howell, I expanded the evening meals on offer and opened the hotel to the public. After placing a large advertisement in the local paper we soon began having a full dining room. We only opened Wednesday to Saturday evenings and opened for Sunday lunch. We didn't offer in-house guest meals on Mondays, Tuesdays or Sunday nights. Nor after dinner drinks. That meant we could all have some evenings off. Anna worked extra hours in the evening now and drafted her sister-in-law Katya in to work in the kitchen with me. We also had a local girl, Alwyn, who came in to wait on tables.

Gwyneth and Howell were extremely pleased with the success of the 'restaurant'. They insisted I should draw a wage so I was no longer having to dip into reserves I'd brought from Australia. When Gwyneth finally returned home, she was happy for me to continue with my enterprise. The only problem for me was that Clara and I were living in someone else's home and I craved our own place. When the British Home Office granted me leave to remain indefinitely in the country, I thought about renting a place away from the hotel. When I tentatively mentioned it to Howell and Gwyneth, they became very upset. It looked like we were going to be at the hotel for the foreseeable future, so I decided to grin and bear it. It would provide an opportunity to save at least and I wasn't sure if it was safe for me to return to

Australia. Not after everything that had happened.

34
Kelly

Shepparton, Victoria, March 2005

With most of the jobs in the house completed, I decided we would head off to Shepparton to see Karen; driving at night so there might be less traffic on the road. I didn't want Karen to know about me replacing Lucy. No-one could know that. I decided I would tell her that I was minding Clara for a friend I'd met in Phuket. Basically the truth, without letting on that Lucy was dead. With no word from Lucy, I had to assume that she *was* dead. One of the missing or unidentified.

We arrived in Shepparton at 12.30 am making good time. I found a 24hr motel and booked us in. I hadn't expected to do the journey so quickly. The real challenge had been navigating my way out of Melbourne with stops and starts at traffic lights, and loads of gear changes (with only one stall and one gear crunch). Once out of Melbourne, we'd cruised along at a steady pace encountering little traffic. Clara slept most of the way and I was looking forward to sleeping in a proper bed again after spending weeks camping out on just a few sleeping bags as my 'mattress'. I slept like a log at the motel and woke refreshed.

In the morning I bought a street directory for the area and located Karen's parents' place. I knocked on the door but was told by the woman who answered it that Karen's parents didn't live there anymore. They'd moved three years ago. She didn't know where they'd gone but said the neighbour to her left might know where I could find Karen when I explained that I was actually looking for their daughter.

The elderly neighbour, who claimed to have known Karen all her life, told me with obvious pride, that Karen owned 'Marshall's Real Estate'. She went on to say it was an independent real estate business, dealing in sales and lettings. Not one of those chain groups, she added. She couldn't remember the name of the street but was able to give me vague directions, reassuring me that I'd have no trouble finding it as it was next door to the 'Spotlight' store.

Good for you Karen, I thought. She'd endured the unpleasant side of the club scene for quite a few years but had left with her dignity intact, creating a new life for herself and her son. I'd forgotten that her surname was Marshall.

I was concerned about rolling up to Karen's office and have her screech out my real name for all and sundry to hear. Following the directions that were given to me, I was able to find her agency without too much difficulty. I pulled into a parking spot nearby and decided to see if the old mobile phone number I knew was still valid. She answered in a very business-like manner after three rings. Saying *'Karen Marshall speaking, how may I help you?'* I paused for a second and she said *'Hello?'*

'Karen,' I said. 'It's Kelly. Kelly O'Brien. I'm almost outside your office and plan to come in, in a few minutes. Only you can't call me Kelly. You have to call me Lucy. Lucy Jones. I will have a little girl with me. Could you spare me some of your time to speak in private? I'll explain when I see you.'

'I understand,' she said. *'That would be fine.'*

Clara was excited about finally leaving the car and holding her hand we strolled into Marshall's Real Estate. Karen, who was talking to a member of staff near the front of the office, looked up as I walked in and exclaimed, 'Lucy Jones! How wonderful to see you.' She gave me a hug, then invited me through to her office, shutting the door for privacy. She looked very different to the Karen I knew, but I recognised her because she still had the same face framed by glasses as she used to at home away from the club (where she wore contacts).

'What's going on *Lucy?'* she hissed emphasising the 'Lucy'. 'I thought you were supposedly either dead or missing. According to Carlos anyway.'

Shit. So Carlos *had* been in touch with her.

'Did he come up here to see you?'

'Yeah, a couple of weeks ago. Suspicious and threatening. Which is the last thing I need. I told him, in all honesty, I hadn't seen or heard from you since the last time I saw you, which was the day you moved in with him. And I wouldn't recognise you now if I passed you in the street. You look quite different.'

'That's because of the injuries I received in Phuket. And not many people have seen me over the past five plus years, especially those from my club days. I've been virtually a prisoner.'

'I did try to warn you. I only saw Carlos become involved with a couple of other women, but once he did, no one ever saw them again. Not at the club anyway.'

'I've escaped Karen. My friend Lucy, and her husband Tom, whom I met in Phuket, were going to help me get away from him. We had it all planned but the day it was due to happen, the tsunami struck. It provided a different opportunity. I can't go into how we achieved it, but I'm Lucy today because I had to give you a name to use. A name that if any of your staff are questioned about means that Lucy was here, not someone called Kelly. For your own protection, I won't tell you what name I'm using now. But if Carlos turns up again you can tell him that Lucy and her daughter came to see you to give you the news about Kelly. I want him to think I'm dead. You can tell him Kelly mentioned you in her last moments as they were clinging to a tree together – because you were one of her only friends from the past.'

'You think he'd fall for that?'

'I don't know, but unless you can think of something else … Carlos has been hassling Lucy for information. He hasn't spotted me as I've been in hiding. I was worried he might become suspicious though and look up some of my old friends. I'm really sorry if he has caused you any problems.'

'I wasn't happy to see him as you can imagine. I

didn't even know he knew where I was or what I was doing. I've since taken some precautions in case he turns up again. I've hired some *protection*, you might call it. I suspect over the years you've been with Carlos, you will have gleaned that he is a dangerous man – to put it mildly. There were rumours going around the club that he'd buried a few people in concrete on some of his building sites.'

'That wouldn't surprise me. He's a first-class bastard. Look I'm sorry to turn up like this, but I can't keep living off Lucy's money, I need access to my own money. I wanted to collect the savings account book I left with you together with some of my other personal things. Do you still have them?'

'Of course I do. But they're not here. They're at home. Much as I'd love to catch up at length with you, we can't take the chance of spending time together. Carlos instructed me to get in touch with him if you or your friend Lucy turned up here. So we need to get this dealt with quickly. I'll get my protector, Jim, to accompany me home to collect everything. Do you have your own car? Did you learn to drive?'

'Not when I was with Carlos. He'd never grant me that kind of independence. I've only learned recently. I've borrowed Lucy's car and I'm parked down the street.'

'Well, take the next right, and immediately turn right again. You'll be in a lane running along the back of this street. Halfway along you will see a driveway and a few cars there with 'Marshall's Estates', written on them. I'll come out in a minute with Jim and turn into the lane.

You follow us. So, this is your friend Lucy's daughter I assume?' she asked looking at Clara properly for the first time. Clara had remained silent throughout our conversation. I'd noticed her frowning a couple of times as I glanced down at her so I knew she was listening to every word we said. I hoped she hadn't understood our conversation.

'Yes, this is Clara. I'm looking after her today.'

'Okay. See you in a few minutes.'

I hugged Karen and left with Clara, returning to the car. I followed her instructions, waiting until her vehicle pulled out into the laneway, then set off after it.

A few minutes later we pulled up outside a modern two-storey detached house. She signalled for us to follow her inside while Jim remained in her car. I'd only been inside a few minutes, admiring the comfort and luxury of the house when Karen came hurrying down the stairs carrying the small bag I'd left with her.

'Everything is in there just as you left it with me all those years ago. Except that once a year I deposited thirty dollars in your account close to Christmas. If you don't use accounts for a certain number of years, any money in it goes to the government. The thirty dollar deposits kept it ticking over. I'd hate to see your hard-earned money go to the government.'

'That was very good of you Karen. Thank you. I must owe you a lot of money,' I said getting my purse out. I thought it was so good of her to keep my account going. I had no idea I could have lost my money.

'Forget it. I don't want it back. Look, I'm really sorry we can't pick up our friendship Kelly, but you understand why, don't you?'

'Only too well. And congratulations. You've done really well for yourself Karen. You deserve everything you've achieved. I really admire you. How's Bobby by the way?'

'He's ten now and doing very well at school.' Her eyes lit up momentarily and then she grimaced, looking towards the front door. 'Sorry, look, I've no time for small talk. I have to get back to the office. Now it's *your* time to build a new life for yourself. Find something that you can succeed in, far away from Carlos and Melbourne.'

'I have a plan, don't worry. Listen before I go, do you know if the credit union I have my savings in has a branch here in Shepparton?'

'Yes, they do. In the Shopping Mall. Now I really have to go. Please don't call me again.'

I was shocked at Karen's brusque business tone and felt a little hurt. She clearly didn't want anything to do with me, so I couldn't come near her again. Not that I blamed her for wanting to sever ties with me. Carlos would frighten anyone off.

'Thank you again, Karen. Take Care.' I embraced her and I could see she was close to tears when we pulled apart. So she wasn't totally hard-hearted. I quickly wiped tears from my own eyes, picked up Clara and left without looking back.

I found the shopping mall and turned into the underground car park. After checking out the mall directory I located the credit union. There was a bit of a queue and Clara said she needed a 'wee-wee' so I took her off to find the toilets. As we had been working hard on toilet training, I needed to respond to any requests from Clara to use the 'big toilet'.

When I eventually reached the counter at the credit union I told them I'd been living with my wealthy boyfriend for some years which is why I hadn't used the account. I also explained my lack of ID from losing everything in the tsunami. They matched my signature to the one on record and thankfully let me withdraw my money.

With the accumulated interest over the six years, I had just over three thousand dollars in the account. I left feeling rich! This was largely my own hard-earned savings from the days when I was free.

There was a Michelle's in the mall where we stopped to have an early lunch. I ordered sausage rolls, lamingtons and chocolate milkshakes. It was good to indulge occasionally. After that, we strolled around the shops for a while and I tried on different cardigans. I was partial to cardigans and I hadn't found any in Lucy's wardrobe; only jumpers. She had loads of smart jackets she must have worn to work, but I needed more casual wear. After much browsing I purchased three cardigans from different stores. The weather was starting to turn colder and I needed something I could just throw on. I also bought another new pay-as-you-go sim card, with $40 credit, thinking I ought to ditch the one I used for contacting Karen.

We made another quick visit to the toilet before leaving in case I needed to change Clara. She was dry and obligingly peed as soon as I held her over the loo. Her toilet training was going well. I was tempted to dispense with the nappies altogether and put her into normal pants.

On the way out of Shepparton, Clara spotted a park on the other side of the road and kept shouting 'park', 'park'. I pulled over, did a U-turn and drove back. She hadn't had a run around at all today, so taking some time out for her was only fair. She was likely to sleep on the way back if she tired herself out with physical activity.

Clara liked to pretend she was a horse so she galloped around me making silly noises while I sat on the grass laughing. A little boy, who I guessed might be a year or so older than Clara, came over to join her and they both giggled and galloped between me and the boy's mother. The boy finally stopped and pointed at the enclosure of baby swings and slides, asking Clara if she wanted to have a go on them. Clara shouted 'yes', jumping up and down, looking from me to the boy. I hesitated. I wanted to get on the road before the traffic became too heavy, but Clara was so excited I finally nodded and joined them.

The boy's mother was keen to engage me in conversation and seemed disappointed when I told her we were only visiting Shepparton. She confessed that she'd only moved to the area a month before and knew very few people. We pushed the kids on the swings for a while until the boy, becoming bored, shouted that he wanted to go on the slides. Clara cried out 'me too.'

The little boy climbed up first. Once he reached the

top he shouted, 'Wave Mummy!' His mother obediently complied. When it was Clara's turn, she mimicked the boy and said 'Wave Mummy!' to me. I was touched. It was the first time she'd called me 'mummy'. I waved at her, my eyes brimming with tears, not realising that wave would be my undoing.

35
'Lucy'

Llandudno, March 2010

Gwyneth and Howell announced today that they've decided to sell the hotel. Howell would be 63 this year, Gwyneth 61. They wanted to retire and buy a small house in the town. They planned to spend six months of the year at their house in Spain and six months in the UK. They asked me if I would be interested in buying the hotel. I wasn't. I discussed other options with them. When I talked about how much the hotel and restaurant tied you down, they pointed out that the business I was considering would be a year-round tie. They reminded me that they had three months off each year over in Spain, (which Clara and I had also enjoyed some years before she started school) but it was the daily grind for the other nine months that did me in. If I had a delicatessen/café business, like the one I'd fantasised about for years, it might tie me down, but I would have the evenings to myself with Clara. If I made enough money then I could pay someone to manage it and enable me to spend even more time with Clara during her school holidays. At the hotel, I only had late afternoons and early evening time with her and any holidays during our three-month break. It was often Howell or Gwyneth who put Clara to bed as I was tied up with the restaurant. I also believed that having a business where I worked through the day might create more opportunities for me to develop a healthier social life.

Working at the hotel and looking after Clara had restricted my opportunities to form friendships. On the one hand, this initially suited me, as I was afraid of developing close ties with all that I was hiding. But it was a somewhat lonely existence; a loneliness I realised, that stretched back to the loss of my family. I'd had friends in the schools I'd attended, but these were friendships that seldom extended much beyond the school gates. A foster child was not encouraged to bring friends home. Friends would have never been welcome at the Hill's house either (nor would I have wanted anyone to come there). They wouldn't allow me to attend the occasional birthday party I was invited to, particularly after my attempt to report them. I thought I must 'deserve' the life I was living with the Hills looking back to that last enjoyable night I'd had with my close friend Kylie while my family perished. I argued against that logically in my mind, but I sometimes wondered if, perhaps, I'd unconsciously sabotaged possibilities ever since. I'd convinced myself that during those first few years in Melbourne I was 'in hiding', and so had to be very careful who I mixed with. Even after I moved into

Karen's house, I just worked hard and seldom socialised, except occasionally with my housemates. Karen was the closest thing I had to a friend, but really she was just a 'ship passing in the night.'

During my years with Carlos, I became accustomed to greater isolation. I realised that I was continuing the pattern here in Llandudno. Whilst I'd accepted invitations to the odd party and dinners, these were few and far between. I'd formed no real close ties. Anna, the Polish woman I worked with was the closest friend I had, but she was now married and we seldom socialised outside work these days. Once the hotel was sold I would have more time and could make an effort to have a social life.

It wasn't a particularly good time for selling. The UK was still in the throes of the recession that hit the country in 2008 and property prices were still down. It gave me the opportunity to purchase a large double fronted empty shop with a two-storey maisonette above it (also empty), for a song. Right in the centre of town. It was just off the High St, but an ideal location for my planned business venture. It had previously been a hardware shop and no one had lived in the floors above for many years. There was a garden of sorts at the back, with rear lane access for parking, similar to the hotel. I approached my bank (which was also Gwyneth and Howell's bank) with a viable business plan, asking about borrowing. I had a substantial deposit and the capital to fit the shop out. They told me they were not giving out mortgages until after the election, when they knew which way the wind would be blowing. The manager told me to come back at that time. He assured me that in different circumstances he would have been willing to lend me the money as he knew I'd built up the successful restaurant business. He told me the directive to freeze business loans had come down from head office and was out of his hands.

I was devastated. The election was only a few months away but I was worried that the property I had my eye on would be sold during that time.

Contrary to the market position, Howell and Gwyneth sold their hotel in a matter of weeks from making the decision. It hadn't even gone on the market. They were about to look into appointing an agent when a local couple approached them and said they were interested in buying it. Word had spread on the town grapevine. The couple were cash buyers who'd recently returned from successful careers abroad. They wanted to run a business in their home town. Here was a ready-made, successful business that appealed to them (good luck with that).

Howell then insisted that they would lend me the balance I needed to buy the property I wanted. He reminded me that they'd obtained a decent selling price partly due to my success with the restaurant. Realising I could now fulfil my dreams I accepted and set about starting the process of my purchase.

My chain-free purchase completed without hitches and Clara and I moved into the rather grotty accommodation above the shop. I not only had the shop to kit out, but the flat to renovate as well. My priority was the shop though, and two months later I opened for business, just in time for the high tourist season.

Anna, who now spoke perfect English came to work with me at the deli. She had continued working at the hotel while the new couple settled in, (I also worked with them part-time to this end) but was happy to leave there to work with me for a better wage.

We must've done something right as the Deli Kitchen, as I called it, was a success from day one, picking up local and tourist trade. We didn't open until 10 am (so I could see Clara off to school myself) and closed at 5 pm.

It seemed wonderful to have so much time to myself – even though I worked at home for a few hours a couple of evenings a week. After Clara went to bed, I used those evenings dealing with stock, and updating the accounts. I usually baked early each morning before taking Clara to school. Howell or Gwyneth collected Clara after school most days and took her to their new bungalow until I could pick her up later. When they were in Spain I would have to make other arrangements, but it was looking like I had reliable staff who I could leave in the Deli, so collecting Clara wouldn't be a problem.

The flat, which needed a total renovation, took a further few months to complete while Clara and I camped out. Some days the dust was so bad I asked Howell and Gwyneth to have Clara overnight, concerned it would damage her lungs. Those days I would go into the deli early to bake there as we no longer had a usable kitchen.

About the only thing I didn't have to do to the flat was replace the roof. It merely required a few replacement slates, otherwise, it was in good condition.

Clara and I travelled to Chester and Liverpool shopping for new furniture and accessories. Gwyneth and Howell had lent us some fold up beds to camp out on during the renovations. The mattresses on these were not exactly comfortable, so it was wonderful when we finally had our own comfy beds installed.

Clara was almost seven years old by then. I hadn't been able to give her much attention at the hotel but strived to make up for this with the increased time we now spent together. Over the years she'd become used to adults busily working around her, but she always had the attention of one of us to see to her needs. She called me 'mum' now, announcing that as she was a *big* girl she couldn't call me 'mummy' anymore. That was just for little girls.

Clara was a lovely kid and I had no regrets about my mother role. Her only shortcoming, if you could call it that, was she had a great sense of right and wrong. Much like me. She couldn't have inherited it from me but I know the real Lucy had been like it too – from my short acquaintance with her and from reading her diaries. I think it was a 'Libra' thing; our birth signs. Clara would become righteously outspoken if she perceived an injustice. It had got her into a spot of bother more than once at school. This materialised into a calm, assertive verbal statement to the 'guilty' party rather than any form of violence. Once or twice I'd had to collect her with a black eye or split lip with an assurance from the school that the aggressor had been suspended. I told Clara that people didn't like to be preached to. Sometimes it was better to keep quiet rather than publicly point out that someone was in the wrong. They *knew* they were in the wrong most of the time and didn't *always* need reminding. I told her she should choose with care which battles she took on.

I'd learned to keep quiet when I was with Carlos as speaking out was too dangerous. I had a stubborn side to my personality; I wouldn't apologise or beg and plead with him – which infuriated him further during moments of violence. Instead I withdrew, tucking away the 'real' Kelly, keeping thoughts or comments to myself in order to survive. When there was only me to consider I let things slide past, but when I had Clara to consider and I'd experienced a taste of 'freedom', it was an entirely different matter.

36
Franco

Shepparton, Victoria, March 2005

I was on my way back from a public toilet when Lucy Jones and her daughter turned up at the estate agents we'd been watching. Craig placed a call through to Carlos who jumped in his car and raced up to join us. If it had been me who'd spotted her I wouldn't have made the call. I thought this woman had suffered enough. Carlos seemed obsessed with the idea that Lucy Jones was helping Kelly. He'd wanted to track Lucy down after she went walkabout from her flat. According to Carlos, the woman who owned the estate agents was one of Lucy's close friends.

Craig stayed at the estate agents while I followed the poor woman. God it was tedious work. After she collected a bag from her friend's house she went to a shopping centre and I had to spend hours keeping tabs on her there, with Carlos phoning constantly to see where we were.

By the time Carlos finally arrived the woman and her

kid were in a park. I persuaded him to send Craig back to Melbourne. I was worried about what Carlos planned to do and the last thing I needed was for that young thug, who would do anything for Carlos, to be around. He agreed and Craig turned up in a cab to collect the car we'd been using.

'So, what's the plan?' I asked Carlos once Craig had driven off.

'We'll wait here for Lucy to come back to her car. Then I'm going to have a nice long chat with her.'

Lucy was across at the swings with another woman and her little boy. That meant we could be here for god knows how long. I closed my eyes and leant back in the seat, hoping to catch forty winks while we waited, but my rest was disturbed when Carlos shouted, 'What the fuck?'

'What's wrong?' I asked him.

'That's not Lucy. That's *Kelly*! Hadn't you noticed you bloody idiot?'

'What?' I didn't appreciate him calling me an idiot.

'The woman you've been following. It's Kelly.'

'No,' I said. 'It can't be.'

'It bloody well is. I just watched her waving at the kid and no one waves like her. I should know, I've been watching her fucking wave for years!'

He knew it was Kelly because of the way she waved? That didn't seem realistic to me.

'I haven't seen her up close, as I was keeping my distance from her, but she didn't look anything like Kelly to me. And she had a kid with her. I assumed she was the woman called Lucy. Craig confirmed that was her name.'

'I don't care what name she gave to the estate agents. That is Kelly. And it's Kelly who knew Karen, the sheila you've been watching. Karen is Honey. You know, the one that used to dance at the club.'

Now I was really confused. The woman at the estate agent was *Honey*?

'Christ, I had no idea. I never knew Honey's real name. And I haven't seen her for five years. She looks so different.'

If I'd known that was who we were watching, there was no way I would have been willing to come up here.

'I visited Karen a few weeks back and I told her to get in touch with me if Kelly or Lucy ever turned up. So I'll be having a little chat with her as soon as I've finished dealing with Kelly. She's had plenty of time to ring me since she saw Kelly and hasn't.'

He went to open the car door and I put a restraining arm out to stop him.

'You can't just charge in there,' I said. 'Let's sit in the car for a minute and talk it through. If that's Kelly, then you need to decide rationally what —'

'I know what I'm going to do Franco. I'm going to kill her.'

'I said you need to be *rational*.'

'Fuck rational. No sheila does that to me! You should know that.'

'Look, it's one thing to rough them up a bit, but murder? You can't. She's got a kid with her.'

'So what? That's Lucy and Tom's kid. We'll dump the kid back at Lucy's place later. I'll be wanting a quiet word with Lucy as well. She's clearly been hiding Kelly somewhere.'

He reached under his seat and pulled out a gun and a silencer attachment which he fixed to his weapon.

'Whoa, you can't use that,' I told him.

'Watch me,' he said.

I could see Kelly or whoever she was making her way back to the car when she stopped, then picked up the little girl and ran. She must have worked out it was Carlos's car parked in front of hers.

Carlos jumped out of the car, started running after her and aimed some shots at her until I caught up with him and knocked the gun out of his hand.

'You'll bring the cops down on us using that, for god's sake.'

He took off after her by foot then.

I raced back to the car, did a U-turn and followed them. I knew what he'd do to her and I had to stop him. I'd seen them turn into an alleyway and just hoped I would get there in time.

37
Kelly

Shepparton, March 2005

As we headed back across the park in Shepparton, Clara was jabbering away, communicating as though we were having a proper conversation. I identified enough words amongst the gabble to understand she'd enjoyed herself.

'So you had fun then, did you kiddo?' I had to stop calling her kiddo, it was becoming a habit I found difficult to break.

'Yes,' she shrieked. I bent down and tickled her and she folded up in laughter. As I stood up and reached out for her hand, I looked out into the street. Parked in front of the Hyundai I could see a flashy sports car with blacked out windows. It wasn't the car that I had last known Carlos to drive, but it was the type of car he would drive. I froze; terrified. I was convinced it *was* Carlos. I lifted Clara and ran. Away from the car towards buildings – and, with any luck, safety. Clara was still giggling when I first lifted her, but she must have sensed my fear as she soon started to cry. As I looked back I saw two men climbing out of the car. It was only a quick glimpse but I was sure one of them was Carlos.

Soon after I heard what sounded like a 'ping' and saw pieces of bark flying off a tree in front of me. He was shooting at me! He was going to kill both of us! My sunglasses fell off, but I didn't stop to pick them up. I spotted a wide alleyway ahead and turned into it. Hopefully, there would be somewhere to hide, or someone who could help me. It looked like the type of laneway that ran at the back of Karen's office. But there were high fences or gates either side, with none open. I looked at one or two of the gates as I ran past but could see they were locked. It wasn't until I'd got almost to the end of the alley that I realised there was no way out. I stopped and turned. Carlos was just entering it, so the only way out for me was to get past him and that was going to be impossible if he was carrying a gun. I couldn't believe it had come to this.

Clara was still crying and looked confused and frightened. I held her for a second, then put her on the tarmac behind me, re-assuring her in soft tones that everything would be alright. Then I turned and faced Carlos. Anger coursed through me. For years this man had kept me virtually under lock and key. Now he wanted to kill me. The arrogant prick. I wasn't having it. Clara needed protecting. God knows what he'd do to her if he killed me.

He walked closer and said, 'Kelly' in a tone that was familiar and was always a precursor to violence in the past. I stood my ground just looking at him. Clara kept crying and I turned for a moment to calm her again. I was worried her crying would anger him further, knowing he couldn't stand the sound of young children crying. Many a time in the past when we were out somewhere he'd drag me off if there was some child persistently crying. It seemed to enrage him. Miraculously, Clara quietened and I could sense her standing still.

'I told you what would happen if you tried to leave me again Kelly.'

I nodded, not saying a word, just looking over my shoulder to make sure Clara was okay. I was trying to work out how he knew it was me. I was quite a distance away from him when I spotted the car and I knew he was short-sighted. With my short hair and sunglasses, how come he knew it was me? Had he been hanging around the town? Had Karen betrayed me?

'You know what gave you away? How I knew it was you, Kelly? Not like those clowns who work for me. They both thought you were Lucy. But I knew, because I know all your irritating little habits so well.'

I didn't know what he was talking about so remained quiet and he laughed. 'It was your wave. You always did that bloody stupid wave, as though you were the Queen.'

The way I waved! Such a stupid, silly little thing that gave me away!

Carlos said his men thought I was Lucy. Had they been following me or had they been watching Karen? And where was the other man I saw with Carlos?

He came at me and I launched into an attack, aiming

for his groin first where he doubled over in pain. He hadn't expected that. I swiftly followed that with further kicks. To his head and body. Not ones I'd learned in self-defence, most of my learning went out the window – just frantic kicks that might put him out of action and give us a chance to escape. He fell back, hitting his head on a piece of brick that was lying in the middle of the alley and seemed to lose consciousness. Had I killed him? I paused for a second and could see his chest moving. So not dead. Now was our chance to get out of here. But to where? Would the other man I'd seen him with be waiting near my car to grab me? I had the answer to that as I picked up Clara. The sports car I'd seen was turning into the alley. It drove right up to us and stopped. The sun was in my eyes so I couldn't see who was sitting in the driver's seat. I felt my heart rate increase as the door opened. A tall well-built man I recognised stepped out of the car and I felt relieved but resigned to the fact that I was now trapped unless …

'Franco,' I said.

Although most people found Franco intimidating, I'd always felt comfortable and safe with him, but many a time he made it clear that escape was not an option.

He walked over and looked down at Carlos before speaking.

'Hello, Kelly. I have to say I'm surprised to see you here. I joined Carlos in Phuket and we searched everywhere for any trace of you without success.'

I didn't speak but was busy calculating the possibility of whether Franco would let us go. He'd had a kind of sneer on his face as he looked down at Carlos.

'I hadn't realised it was you I'd been following today. I thought you were some woman called Lucy. You look quite different. How did you manage it?'

'That doesn't matter Franco. What matters is this little girl. I'm all she has. You have to let us go.' I spoke with an assertiveness that masked my fear. If Franco wasn't prepared to let us go, I stood no chance. But of all the guards Carlos had watching over me, Franco was the nicest. He was a family man, so he understood about children.

'What do you mean, you're all she has? She has a mother doesn't she?'

I didn't want to tell him I was supposed to be Lucy. He would then know my identity, but he was going to figure it out anyway.

'Look, Franco, you have to trust me when I tell you she has no-one but me.'

His confused expression seemed to clear; I think he'd worked it out.

'Was that a shot he fired at me while I was running?' I asked.

'Yes, the bloody idiot – in broad daylight. I took the gun off him.'

'You know he wants to kill me, don't you Franco?'

'I've gathered that since he realised you were Kelly. He came up here thinking he was going to be talking to someone called Lucy. Don't worry I won't let that happen. But you need to get out of here, quick smart. And get right away – out of Melbourne and Victoria altogether.'

'Yes, I will.' He was going to let us go. Was it too

good to be true?

'What happened to him?' he said nodding at Carlos.

'When he came at me I kicked him in his most delicate place. When he started to double over I kicked him again. He stepped back losing his balance, then fell and hit his head on that small piece of brick.'

Franco nodded. Now I had to know whether it was safe to go back to the house in Mt. Martha. I also wanted to know if Karen betrayed us.

'How did he find us?'

'Carlos has had a couple of us watching Karen's workplace since he came up here the other week. Come *on* Kelly. You need to go.'

So Karen hadn't betrayed us and they didn't know about Mt. Martha.

'What about Carlos?'

'Don't worry, I'll take care of Carlos. Now get going before he comes round. I didn't know you had it in you Kelly. Good for you. Leave. *Now!*' he shouted.

I didn't need telling again. I ran. Back to the car, strapped Clara in, did a U-turn and took off. I was shaking, making it difficult to control the gear stick. I crunched the gears constantly until I was out of town, heading back on the highway.

With a head start on them, I thought I might have time to call at the flat. I wanted to collect some things now I had to change my plans.

The traffic was heavy as I made my way across Melbourne and back to the flat. I packed up the things I needed and then ran upstairs to see Kim. Laurie answered the door, inviting me in. I said I wouldn't come in as Clara was downstairs alone and I couldn't leave her for more than a minute. I explained that I had given notice and was moving out in a few weeks, that I had found somewhere else to go. Kim appeared at the door then. She'd overheard what I'd said.

'So where are you moving to?' she asked.

'It's probably better that I don't tell you that. In case that Carlos comes around again. He might use persuasive measures to make you reveal my whereabouts.'

'He's already been around again. But I didn't know where you were. Where *have* you been Lucy? You missed Freddie's second birthday last week,' Kim said with a sullen look on her face.

'I'm sorry. We've been all over the place. Look, none of that matters. What matters is that Carlos doesn't know where we are. I've been through enough without having the likes of him stalking me.'

'The police take stalking seriously,' Laurie said. 'You could call the police and report him.'

'I don't think so. Not at this point anyway. It's best just to move.' I couldn't stand here all day listening to this. 'Look, I've—'

'So, will we ever see you again?' Kim asked.

'Of course. It's only until this guy calms down and accepts his girlfriend is dead and that I'm not going to be her replacement,' I lied. I doubted I would ever see them again.

'You think that's what he wants?' Kim asked with a horrified look on her face. 'God, he's the last person you'd want to become involved with. I don't know how anyone could be involved with him.'

'Quite. Look I'd better go, I can't leave Clara any longer.'

'I'm coming down to say goodbye,' Kim insisted. She followed me down, picking up Clara and giving her tight hugs as we walked out to the car.

'I'll miss her Lucy. She's such a lovely little girl,' Kim sobbed after buckling Clara into her car seat.

'I know. Goodbye Kim. I'll be in touch as soon as I can. Thanks again for everything.' I embraced her then and I felt her first stiffen, then relax and hug me back. I hadn't always liked Kim, but she had a good heart and both Lucy and I owed her a lot.

I checked there were no potential surveillance vehicles on the road before driving off. I'd collected more documentation and files that I was going to need. Plus more kitchen pots, utensils, the toaster and the hands-free telephone set. I'd bought some new kitchen items since we'd been at the Mt. Martha house, but we were existing with very basic equipment and I was limited in the cooking I could do. Our diet needed greater variation.

The landline was due to be connected while we were in Shepparton. When we returned to the house I plugged in the hands-free set I'd collected. It was working! The reception on my mobile phone wasn't great and I wanted to make sure I had reliable connections in case I had to phone the emergency services. I also wanted to contact Tom's parents. On the drive back from Shepparton I decided I needed to take Franco's advice and leave Melbourne, but why not leave Australia altogether? I could exchange the tickets I'd found at the flat and travel to Wales to see Tom's parents. I had to find out about a passport for Clara though. Did I need visas for the UK? I wasn't even sure where you applied for passports. Carlos had dealt with mine, having my passport photograph taken at the penthouse and providing me with forms to complete. I would ask at Australia Post. They were bound to know.

Clara was grizzly that night and her sleep fractured. It was unlike her not to sleep through, but she woke several times crying out, wanting to be held. The incident at Shepparton must have disturbed her. I didn't sleep at all myself, jumping at every little sound I heard outside and checking to make sure it wasn't Carlos.

I phoned the removal company the next day and asked them if they could bring the date forward for the move. With our things going into storage I would just have to put up with discomfort and minimal living a bit longer.

38
Franco

I told Kelly I'd take care of Carlos, so I had to work out a plan quick smart.

I'd always felt sorry for Kelly. I knew she desperately wanted to get away from Carlos. If I'd been single, I would've helped her. But it wasn't worth jeopardising my life – or the life of my wife and three children to assist her in any way.

From our searches in Phuket, the conclusion Nico and I came to was that she was dead. At least then she'd be free from Carlos, who is a crazy psychopath.

I'd refused to go with them to Phuket over Christmas because being with my family was more important to me. I'm one of Carlos's few employees who will stand up to him. His older brother Nico and I were old schoolmates. Since leaving school I worked with Nico in the family business before transferring over to work with Carlos. Nico was a straight businessman based solely in construction and property development. He was tough, but a decent man. Not like Carlos. Nico asked me to go and work with Carlos seven years ago, not long after he took over the club. He was concerned that Carlos was becoming a bit of a loose cannon and needed someone steady to keep him in line. That was an understatement. He is an unpleasant, vicious bastard. Especially with his women. The one before Kelly was hospitalised after he'd given her a 'seeing to'. Of course, being terrified of Carlos, she never pressed charges and just claimed she'd had a bad fall down the stairs. Carlos was bored with her so he dropped her then and took up with Kelly a few months later. Kelly was only a kid, young and impressionable.

Kelly had been dealt a bad hand in life. When I escorted her shopping or to one of her lunches, she told me about the loss of all her family in a house fire. And how she'd been shoved from one foster placement to another until an unpleasant couple adopted her. She wouldn't talk about her time with the couple, but I gathered it wasn't a great experience for her.

I always thought it was wrong of Carlos to get involved with her. She was too young and vulnerable. She'd tried to escape a couple of times and I saw the price she paid for that. Not while I was around – I would have stopped him. I don't approve of bashing women. Kelly had injuries that should have been treated in a hospital – but Carlos had a doctor in his pay so she was treated at the penthouse apartment instead.

I looked down at Carlos after Kelly had driven off, thinking it was a shame it hadn't been fatal, but then that would have caused problems for her. He was still out for the count and I could see he had a wound on his head.

I bundled a still unconscious Carlos into the car. I had to think fast. My things were still back at the hotel so I drove back, collected my belongings and checked out. But not before crushing and grinding down some sleeping pills and tipping them into what remained of a half bottle of brandy I'd opened last night.

The sleeping tablets were actually Carlos's. When I'd mentioned I was having trouble sleeping recently, he'd handed me a bottle with five 20mg tablets in them. He claimed I should try them as they really knocked you out. He'd been on them since Phuket and told me he had plenty more. I'd only taken one tablet since then – in Shepparton three nights ago. I didn't like the heavy head it left me with in the morning, so I hadn't taken any more.

Carlos was starting to come around when I returned to the car, clutching his head in pain. I drove off, heading back towards Melbourne.

'What happened?' he asked confused.

'It looked like you fell and hit your head on a brick,' I told him. 'Here, have some brandy, you'll need it.' He took a good swig and then handed it back to me.

'No, you keep it,' I said. 'Finish it. It will help ease the pain.' He took more swigs, emptying the bottle. Good.

'Where have you put Kelly?'

'I haven't put Kelly anywhere. When I arrived at the alleyway there was no-one there but you, lying unconscious.'

'Whaddya mean? She couldn't have got away that fast.'

'I'm telling you she was gone. By the time I got you

into the car, reversed back out and headed back to the park, the car she'd been using was also gone. She must have got out of the alleyway before I drove up.'

'Shit! Turn around then and go back to that bitch's place.'

'What bitch are you talking about?'

'Karen! Honey! Kelly's probably gone back there.'

'I doubt it very much, boss. She wouldn't be that stupid. She'd be well on her way back to Melbourne by now. That's where we ought to be heading.'

I kept driving, glancing at him to see if the tablets had begun to have any effect yet.

'Turn around Franco, we nee ...to ch...check.'

I could hear he was beginning to have trouble with his words. 'Are you alright boss, you don't sound too good?'

'I don ... don't fee...' He was unable to finish the sentence before slumping unconscious in the seat.

We were caught up in peak hour traffic when we arrived back in Melbourne. It was late evening by the time I turned into Lucy's street and parked the car outside her block of flats. Carlos had had me watching the flat a couple of weeks back so I knew exactly where it was.

I sat there in the car for a while contemplating what I was about to do until I saw a few people returning to the block. I drove off after I noticed a man stop and look at the car. It was important that Carlos's car was seen that evening at the flats. With the blacked out side windows and the dark evening, they wouldn't be able to see me clearly.

39
Kim

'Kim, what kind of car does that man Carlos drive?'
Laurie asked me when he returned from the supermarket.
He'd popped out to buy something I'd forgotten when I
did the shopping.

'I don't know. It's some kind of flashy sports car I
think. It has blacked out windows.'

'That's what I thought. There's a car like that sitting
outside in the street. He's back.'

'Oh God, it's a good thing Lucy didn't hang around
for long then.'

'I think we'd better call the police.'

'No, don't Laurie. He'll be furious if you do that.
Don't forget I'm at home all day while you're at work. I
don't want him coming around here bothering me again
or having a go at me because you called the police.'

'But if we call the police, they might put a stop to it.'

'Unlikely. How are they going to do that? They
wouldn't put someone on guard outside day and night,
would they? Don't call them Laurie. It's too dangerous.'

'Well, I'm going outside to talk to him then. This has

to stop. Lucy's been driven out of her home because of him. Now you're worried about going out.'

'I'd rather you didn't go out there. What if he attacks you?'

'I'll take my cricket bat with me if you're that worried.'

Laurie disappeared into the hall and grabbed his cricket bat from the cupboard. He pocketed his keys and shut the door after him. I looked out of the living-room window but couldn't see anything. I ran into Freddie's room and looked out of his window but again I couldn't see Laurie or Carlos's car.

Some minutes later I heard the key in the door and took a sharp breath in, terrified it was Carlos. The tread of footsteps clunked down the hall. It sounded like Laurie, and I peeped out of Freddie's room to see the cupboard door open. I couldn't see who was standing on the other side of it. The door closed and I breathed a sigh of relief when I saw it was Laurie.

'So did you speak to him then?' I asked.

'No, he'd gone. Maybe he's come to his senses.'

'I suspect he'll be back though.'

'I'm worried about you Kim. You've been nervous about going out since his last visit. You claim you keep forgetting to go to the shops, or when you do, you forget to buy everything we need.'

'I've been busy with Freddie, and I'm missing Clara. That's all.'

'No, that's not all there is to it. Is it? You haven't gone further than Janine's or the local supermarket in the past few weeks.'

He approached me then, took me in his arms, walked

me into our bedroom and shut the door.

'What's really going on Kim?'

I burst into tears and told him that Carlos had threatened me when I saw him last.

'Why didn't you tell me?'

'I was terrified of what you might do and that something would happen to you. And I've been terrified that some harm might come to me or Freddie.'

'Oh, Kim, don't you see, this is why we must call the police.'

'That frightens me even more. I can't handle it. I think we ought to move as well.'

'Running away is not the answer. We can't let men like him bully us out of our home. You like this neighbourhood. You have friends here. Freddie has friends here.'

'Lucy ran.'

'Yes, but that's different. It was her he was after. This place is cheap compared to many we looked at. And the low cost enables us to save money each month so that we can eventually buy our own place.'

'I can't see us ever being able to afford our own place until I return to work and we have more income. Anyway we're trying for another baby, aren't we?'

'Yes, of course. But you need to stop worrying about that man. Everything will be alright. Let's go and make some dinner now I have our crucial missing ingredient.'

40
Franco

It was completely dark by the time I pulled into the deserted industrial estate down near the river. It was a spot where Carlos had held meetings with business associates in the past. He would remain asleep for some hours yet, so I decided to return to the club and set up an 'alibi' for myself. I moved him into the driver's seat, threw his empty bottle of tablets onto the passenger's side, after wiping it down and placing his hands all over it. Then I grabbed my bag and set off on foot to look for a cab.

The club wasn't open yet, but some of the staff were busy stocking the bar in preparation for the evening. Craig was sitting at the bar knocking back beers with whiskey chasers.

'You should be taking it easy Craig,' I said placing a hand on his shoulder, 'The boss might want you later.'

'I assumed I had the rest of the night off,' he replied. 'Where is he? What did he do with the chic with the small tits he wanted to speak to?'

Argh! The way these young men spoke about women

really made me cringe. And I knew Craig considered any woman who was under 34DD to have small breasts.

'Oh, he went running after her and slipped and hit his head. Knocked himself out the silly sod. I was busy checking he was alright, so the woman got away.'

'I bet he was mad after all that surveillance.'

'Yeah, he was. I'm a bit worried about him. I drove his car back while he swilled the last of my brandy. Once we hit Melbourne he insisted we stop and he took over the driving. He dropped me off, so he could head off to her place again. He told me to go home so I've come to collect my car.'

'Well if he told you to go home, then that means he won't want me either. I'll head off as well.'

'Suit yourself, but don't say I didn't warn you if he calls you demanding your presence for some job.'

'You really think he might?' he asked concerned.

'I'd stick around for a bit if I were you. In case.' I didn't want Craig out on the streets. It was better to keep him at the club.

'Righto. I will if you think that's best.'

Carlos owns a large garage near the club which can fit about 30 vehicles. Roughly half the spaces were for staff or 'work' vehicles and the rest Carlos let out to local residents. I collected my car and drove back towards the industrial estate. I knew there were no cameras in the vicinity. That was why we used it as a meeting place.

After putting on some surgical gloves, I took some plastic sheeting out of the boot and opened it out to make holes for my eyes and mouth. There were always gloves and sheeting in there in case Carlos needed me to clean up after 'jobs' for him. I wanted to protect my clothing from what I was about to do. After pulling the plastic over my head, I grabbed a bottle of water, two cloths I had in the boot and retrieved the other unopened half bottle of brandy I had in my bag. I wiped them free of all prints.

Carlos was still dead to the world. I tipped his head back, forced his mouth open and poured some of the brandy in. Most of it dribbled down his shirt. He stirred a little and moaned. I then walked over to the perimeter wall and emptied the rest of the bottle, before returning to the car. I placed his right hand around it and then threw the bottle on the ground. I pulled his gun out from under the seat, gave it a good wipe down and then put his hands all over it, before positioning it carefully in his right hand and curling his fingers around the trigger. I put a thin cloth over his hand so that I was able to gain a good grip on his trigger finger.

Holding the gun up against his head with my right hand, I used my left hand, to splash water from the bottle over his face. I wanted him to be conscious in his last moment. I slapped him lightly a few times. When I could see he was coming around I dropped the bottle on to the passenger seat. He seemed disorientated and tried to turn his head, but I held it in place.

'You're a crazy bastard Carlos and the way you treated Kelly is shameful. Who the fuck do you think you are? Deciding you were going to kill her, just because she didn't want to be with you. And planning to have one of your *quiet words* with Karen. That was never going to happen on my watch. This is a goodbye present from

Kelly.'

He sensed what was about to happen and tried to pull the gun away from his head with his free hand, but it was too late. Standing clear as much as I could I pulled the trigger and he slumped back into the seat.

I let his arm drop and the gun slipped onto his lap. I checked for a pulse. He was gone. And so was half his head. Which was lying partially on the passenger seat of the car, his lap and on the ground near where I was standing. Very little had hit the plastic sheeting I was wearing and the bit that had I shook off onto the ground. There were still a couple of things to complete. I went around to the passenger door and placed his left hand on the water bottle to leave fingerprints on that as well, dropping it on the seat. I grabbed the drugged empty brandy bottle to take with me. Leaving the driver's door open, I turned and walked away. With any luck, it would be some days before Carlos was found. By then perhaps rats would have had a good nibble at him.

The ground was asphalted so there would be no visible footprints. With a torch from my car, I checked to make sure though. Lastly, I removed the used plastic sheeting, bundled it into a carrier bag with the empty bottle, jumped in the car and drove off.

I'd roughed up few blokes in my time working for Carlos but normally I didn't have to go that far. Just my sheer size and being threatened by Carlos caused them to cave in and spill the beans. Carlos was the first person I'd ever killed.

I'd fantasised about killing Carlos for years, but wasn't sure I'd ever be able to do it. Now that I'd actually done it, I thought it had been relatively simple and hadn't affected me. But when I stopped on the way home to buy another bottle of brandy and dispose of the plastic carrier bag in the car park, I suddenly felt ill and puked up in the bin. My hand was shaking when I returned to my car, so I opened the brandy bottle and took a swig.

In my head I reasoned the world would be a better place without sickos like Carlos in it, to justify my actions. But I *knew* that murder was never justified – I just couldn't see another way out of the problem. I couldn't grass on Carlos and he had too many coppers in his pay anyway. I'd just have to live with it for the rest of my life. I knew for a fact that *he'd* killed a number of people over the years. I'd witnessed him killing one bloke and heard about others he'd killed from colleagues.

After returning home I rang his brother Nico, relating some of the events of the past few days. I didn't tell him that it was Kelly we'd spotted that day. I stuck to the story of it being Lucy.

Whilst Nico had little feeling for his younger brother, he wouldn't be happy about the manner of his death – if he knew the truth.

'I can't work for the bloke anymore Nico. Seven years I've had of this mindless bloody stuff. When I agreed to it, I thought it would be a short term thing. I can't do it anymore, no matter how much he pays me.'

It was true – I had had enough of Carlos and was on the verge of resigning. I was not really cut out to be a hoodlum's thug (despite my actions earlier tonight) and, as much as I liked Kelly, I thought babysitting Carlos's women was a pointless and mindless task.

Who keeps women imprisoned like that? Certainly not someone who loved them. Carlos disgusted me and I felt as though I'd become contaminated since working with him; being party to anything he did. It was beginning to impact on my family life. My work with Nico had been nothing like that. I'd organised things for him and visited building sites to determine progress with contractors. A world away from my duties with Carlos.

'He's become obsessed with this poor woman,' I told Nico. 'He's just constantly hounding her. After he dropped me off he was heading over to her place again. After drinking almost half a bottle of brandy. He's crazy. You need to have a word with him. Get him to stop this madness. Anyway, I'm finished with him.'

He agreed that the events in Phuket seemed to have sent Carlos off the rails even more than usual. He said he understood about me not being able to work for Carlos anymore and generously offered me my old job back. I accepted.

41
Kim

Four days after Laurie had seen Carlos parked outside our flats I was over at Janine's when I spotted the headlines in her paper. 'MELBOURNE PROPERTY TYCOON COMMITS SUICIDE AFTER LOSING HIS GIRLFRIEND IN BOXING DAY TSUNAMI'

I almost dropped my cup of tea in shock when I read it. It was Carlos! There was a picture of him with his glamorous girlfriend who had died in Phuket. I scanned the story. His name was Carlo Mosta (aka Carlos) and his body had been found yesterday in a disused industrial estate where he'd blown his brains out with a gun after consuming alcohol and drugs. The article said he'd been dead for some days. I wondered if he'd done it straight after Laurie had seen him outside our flats.

I was pleased he was dead, and felt the tension and fear I'd been holding in my body for weeks ease. It was a relief to know he wouldn't be bothering us again.

Perhaps now Lucy would return to her flat and I could spend time with Clara again. Freddie really missed her. He kept calling for 'Lara' and 'Lu-lu' when we passed their flat door. I wondered if Lucy knew about his death.

When our buzzer went tonight I was shocked to hear a man announce over the intercom that he was a detective wanting to speak to Laurence Seymour. Laurie went down and was talking to them at the entrance doorway, but a few minutes later they came up to the flat. They introduced themselves as two detectives who were investigating Carlo Mosta's death.

'Why have you come to see us?' I asked them.

'I phoned the police to make a complaint Kim. The day after I saw that man Carlos outside our block. I gave them his rego number. I had to tell them about his threatening behaviour.'

Laurie had failed to mention to me that he'd contacted the police, and I kept sending him scowls. The detectives wanted to know everything about the man's visits. Between us, Laurie and I explained about Tom's death in Phuket and how Lucy and this Carlos's girlfriend had been together when the tsunami struck. How Lucy said he'd hassled her in the hospital in Phuket and then started stalking her flat when she returned. That she was so frightened of him she'd taken off on a holiday and had now moved somewhere else. No longer afraid of Carlos, I gave them the full details of his threatening behaviour the last time I'd seen him.

They asked us when we last saw Lucy. We told them we'd seen Lucy earlier the same evening Laurie had seen Carlos parked outside the block. They confirmed the dates and times with us, then hit us with their next bombshell.

'Can you tell us what you were both doing that night?' one of the detectives asked.

'We were here – all night,' Laurie assured them. I nodded to confirm what he'd said.

'Do you have any way of proving that?'

'No,' Laurie said shaking his head.

'You did talk to your cousin on the landline about 9pm,' I reminded Laurie. 'You could check that, couldn't you?' I asked the detectives.

One of them noted all the information down that Laurie gave them.

'Do you think he died that night? The papers said it was a suicide,' I asked the detective who'd introduced himself as Detective Sergeant Jackson. 'From your questions, it seems you're suggesting it wasn't.'

'We're just covering all bases,' he replied. Not, I noticed, answering my question about when Carlos died. 'We have to investigate all violent deaths when there are no witnesses. Do you have you any idea where Lucy Jones has moved to?'

'No. She didn't want to tell us in case that man turned up and attempted to put pressure on us. She has a removal company collecting her stuff soon. They'll be able to tell you her new address but I don't know the name of the company she's using.'

'Okay, well thanks for your help. It's not likely, but we may wish to speak to you again.'

'How could you?' I challenged Laurie after the detectives had gone. 'You could have put Freddie or me in danger by contacting the police!'

'I decided I had to make an official complaint after what you told me. His behaviour was not acceptable. If anything else had happened they'd want to know why we hadn't complained.'

'Because we were afraid to? Duh!'

'Well, it's no longer a problem now is it?'

'No, except they were questioning our whereabouts after you'd seen him that night. As though *we* were suspects.'

'I don't think they thought that. They were just eliminating us from their enquiries. As the detective said, they had to cover all bases.'

'I hope that's all it was.'

42
Kelly

Two weeks have passed now since my encounter with Carlos. The day after I'd seen him I traded in the Hyundai and bought a second hand larger Holden of similar vintage while I was still able to provide the flat as my legal address for registration. As Carlos had seen the Hyundai, I was worried that he might be able to trace me to Mt. Martha – imagining his spies in the police out all over Melbourne looking for me. I knew it was crazy to be spending money on a car if I was going to leave the country, but our safety was paramount.

The removal company packed up and cleared the flat. Everything was stored for eight days before it was delivered to our 'new' house. It's great to have a bed to sleep in once more, rather than roughing it on the floor. I'd moved my bedroll in next to Clara's cot after my close encounter with Carlos and hadn't slept well since – always with one ear listening out for the sound of approaching footsteps. Having a bed again, meant it would be easier for me to jump in and out of it and I wouldn't have such a stiff back of a morning.

With the arrival of the furniture Clara decided she wanted to sleep in her little bed, rather than her old cot. She'd made a fuss about going into her proper cot on the first night it was installed in her room and kept pointing to the single bed saying 'No, bed.' So I caved in, packed the cot up and put it in the shed along with the foldaway one.

I still haven't phoned Tom's parents since my last call to them but have been moving forward with potential plans. I'd applied for a passport for Clara through Australia Post. I'd contacted the British Embassy in Canberra about a work visa. There were financial requirements I had to fulfil – but that wasn't an issue. What might be an issue was whether we would be welcome at Tom's parents.

A letting agent I contacted came and assessed the property for potential rental. He told me I needed to replace the stove and have the hot water system checked. So I ordered a new gas stove that ran off bottles and had an electrician in to check everything. I told the agent I would be in touch if I wanted to let it.

I finally telephoned Tom's parents a few nights ago, which was their morning, and had a chat about travelling over to Wales to stay with them. They'd just returned from a holiday, Tom's father told me. He said they were looking forward to seeing us. I told him we would come over as soon as we obtained visas. Tom's father gave me their address and said I was to put it on my application to the British Embassy and make sure I told them they were family. I said I would.

With my 'office' now set up at home, I printed off visa application forms from the British Embassy. I had to wait for Clara's passport before applying, but our plan was now set in motion.

As I was preparing our breakfast this morning I heard the sound of car wheels crunching down the drive. I ran into my bedroom and peered through the shutters. Two men stepped out of a car and approached the door. I didn't recognise them and they didn't look like the type of men that Carlos would hire. They knocked on the front door and I hesitated. Should I answer it? They could see the car outside so would assume someone was home. We could have gone out for an early walk though, couldn't we? I decided not to answer. But Clara, who had been playing in the living room destroyed that notion in seconds. She ran to the door shouting, 'door, door.' *Yes, thank you, Clara.* I then had no choice but to open it.

They flashed badges at me, introducing themselves. They were detectives from the Melbourne Police. Oh God, had Carlos been to see them claiming I'd assaulted him? Had he told them I was still alive? Were these some of his 'friendly' police? I'd seen one or two at Carlos's penthouse and didn't recognise these men. But knowing Carlos, he had many more on his books.

'Lucy Jones?' one of them asked.

I nodded.

'I'm Detective Sergeant Jackson and this is Detective Constable Connelly. We'd like to ask you some questions about Carlo Mosta,' he said.

I stood looking at them while Clara clung to my legs. She peeped around me and said 'hello', which was not like her at all, particularly since my run in with Carlos. They were instantly distracted.

'Hello to you too,' the same detective answered, smiling at Clara. He then turned to me asking, 'Is this your little girl?' *Was this a trick question?*

I nodded again.

'May we come in? I'm sure it would be more comfortable asking you these questions sitting down somewhere. Contrary to common belief, we don't bite.' the detective said.

'Of course. Sorry, come in.' I led them through to the sitting room and indicated the couch.

'Is that a kettle I see about to boil on the stove? I wouldn't turn down a cup of coffee,' the younger one said as they sat down.

I turned and looked at the old kettle as though it was a foreign object and could see, from the steam pouring out and the sound it was making, it was about to reach whistling point. I hadn't found the electric kettle yet – it was still in a box somewhere in the sunroom.

'Sorry,' I said, 'please excuse my bad manners. I'm not used to the police being on my doorstep first thing in the morning. How did you find me? I haven't given anyone this address yet.'

'No, please excuse my *colleague's* manners,' the one who'd introduced himself as Jackson said. 'We traced you through the removal firm you used. And we understand why you hadn't given your address to anyone. That's partly why we're here.'

What did he mean by that? Who had they been talking to? I needed to stall him to give me time to sort my story out. In case.

'How would you like your coffees?' I asked. 'Or you could have tea? I have both.'

'Two coffees with milk and two sugars would be great,' Connelly said.

I busied myself in the kitchen making their coffees and a tea for me. I also prepared a bowl of cereal and fruit for Clara. If she didn't have her food soon she would start pestering me, with her cheerful single word questions of 'seal?' (Clara's word for cereal) or 'toast?'

I plonked Clara in her low chair near the sunroom, giving her the cereal, fruit and a drink. When she finished she could safely climb out of there herself. The younger detective came over to help carry the coffees back.

'Are you aware that Carlo Mosta is dead?' Detective Jackson asked just as I was about to swallow a mouthful of tea. I almost choked as the tea stuck in my throat and then regurgitated spraying from my mouth in shock.

'Sorry I didn't mean to startle you.'

I rushed over and grabbed a tissue from the box on the worktop, hastily wiping my mouth and t-shirt, before sitting down again. *He's dead? How? When?*

'No. I wasn't aware he was dead. When did this happen?'

'It's been in all the papers and on the news,' Detective Connelly said.

'I've been busy with house improvements and settling in. I haven't read a paper in weeks and I haven't got the television up and running yet. The aerial doesn't seem to be working.' Much to Clara's disappointment – although I had set up the occasional DVD for her to watch.

Detective Jackson continued, 'His body was found in an industrial area near the river almost two weeks ago now. He'd been sitting in his car, dead, for some days.'

'Didn't anyone on the industrial estate notice his car there – or the fact that he was dead?' I asked.

'No. It was parked in a yard amongst a disused complex of old warehouses.'

'Oh,' was all I could say in response.

'When was the last time you saw him?' Jackson asked.

'He kept coming around to our flat in Yarraville,' I started (avoiding a direct answer to his question), 'bothering me about his girlfriend Kelly. He did the same to me when I was in the hospital in Phuket. I was with his girlfriend when the tsunami struck.'

'What did happen to her?' Detective Connelly asked.

'Who, Kelly?'

'Yes.'

'The last I saw of her she was being swept out towards the sea when the first wave was receding,' I lied. 'We'd been clinging to a tree together but when the water was surging back, some large obstacle, which was being carried along with the water, knocked against us. She lost her grip on the tree. I know she was never found.'

'Must have been a pretty horrific experience for you,' he said shuddering.

'Yes, it was, as it was for thousands of others.'

'Do you think she died, or just grabbed an opportunity

to escape? From what we've heard, Mosta's girlfriend was desperate to get away from him,' Detective Connelly continued.

I looked at him before carefully answering. 'I wouldn't know. I was badly injured and then, as soon as I could, I made my way back to Melbourne.'

'Why did you move out of the flat?' Detective Jackson asked deflecting attention away from tsunami events.

'I was afraid for our safety. That man was prowling around outside our flat one night, banging on windows, trying to open them, calling out my name. I was too scared to answer. He sounded drunk, angry and aggressive. I moved here the next day, camping out here for the first few weeks.'

Jackson nodded. 'You already owned this house?'

'Yes, Tom and I – that's my husband who died in the tsunami, bought this house and land almost two years ago. We were planning to demolish and build a new house. Then our son Christopher, Clara's twin brother, died, and all our plans were put on hold. After Tom died, I couldn't face the idea of building anymore, so I've just painted out the old house and had some bits and pieces done.'

'You've done a good job of it. It's looking great,' Connelly said looking around him. 'I really like those shutters you have on some of the windows. And this colourful rug really brightens the living-room up.'

Really?

Detective Jackson cleared his throat and glared at the other one as if to say, *will you shut up!* 'I'm sorry for all your losses. So... the last time you saw Mr. Mosta was at your flat?' he asked. He seemed determined to have an answer. I wondered how much he knew. If he'd questioned Franco and the other guy who had been in Shepparton with him, then they might have told him about events of that day. But what version? I decided to be honest. Well partially honest anyway.

'No. I saw him in Shepparton. I don't understand why, but he'd been staking out a real estate office there. One of Kelly's old friends – a woman called Karen. I was on a road trip and saw a sign to Shepparton and decided to see if I could find this Karen. Kelly talked about her while we chatted at the pool when *he* wasn't around. She said Karen was the only friend she'd had in Melbourne before getting involved with that man. They lived in the same house and worked together. I wondered if she knew about Kelly and I wanted to tell her that Kelly had never forgotten her.'

'Yes, we've talked to Karen Marshall and she told us much the same thing. Apparently, he had some crazy idea that his girlfriend was still alive and you were hiding her. He'd been up there threatening Ms. Marshall.'

'She mentioned that. That's why I didn't hang around her place. After I left her, I went shopping, then stopped so Clara could play in a park. On my way back to the car, I spotted him. He was shouting at me and looked like he was waving a gun around. I just picked up Clara and ran. I think he shot at me while I was running.'

'He shot at you?' Connelly asked looking shocked.

'I think so. Maybe just to get me to stop. He came after us and threatened me, so I kicked him. He stepped back and then tripped knocking himself out. One of his men turned up a few minutes later and told me to leave before he came around. I didn't need telling twice. The man was wild and crazy.'

'So what day was this?'

'It was a Tuesday. A few weeks back. Around the 22nd March.' The young one was frantically scribbling in a notepad now while Jackson led the questioning.

'That is the last day anyone saw him. So you didn't see him again?'

'No. I called into our flat on the way back to collect a few things as we didn't have much stuff here with us. I spoke to Kim and Laurie, my neighbours, telling them I'd given notice on the flat. After saying goodbye to them I returned here.'

'And Mr. Mosta didn't know about this house?'

'No. I had the removal company put our things in store for more than a week, rather than coming here with everything straight away, just in case he was hanging around and followed them.'

'Yes, the removal company told us why you hadn't wanted your things brought here the day they moved them out of the flat. Must have been a hefty additional expense?'

'Yes, it was, but it was the safest option, given everything that'd happened. So, that day I saw him in Shepparton was the last time anyone saw him? Do you think he died that day? He didn't die as a result of falling and hitting his head in Shepparton, did he?'

'No, he didn't. Ordinarily, I wouldn't be able to tell you how he died, but as it was splashed all over the papers last week, I can tell you he died from a self-inflicted gunshot wound to the head.'

My eyes widened in surprise and I involuntarily let out a 'Jeesus'. It was not something I could imagine Carlos doing to himself. In fact, I was pretty sure he hadn't done it to himself. After collecting myself I asked Detective Jackson why he'd come to question me.

'It's just routine,' he replied. 'We've followed his last known movements and phone calls. You were the last loose end. But it has taken us some time to track you down as you haven't made this your official address. You still have everything registered at your old flat.'

I stiffened when he said this. 'I know, I keep forgetting to deal with it. There's been so much to do here. I was also a bit worried about that man finding out my address somehow if I made it official.'

'Well, I would suggest you sort it as soon as possible. Did you know, by the way, that he went to your old flat again that night? He dropped off one of his employees in the city and then drove straight to your flat. Your neighbour, Laurence Seymour, spotted his car outside the block that night.'

'No I wasn't aware of that. I haven't seen Kim or Laurie since that evening. I was quite shaken up by what happened in Shepparton so I haven't been out much since.'

'Well, you needn't worry about going out and about again now. Seeing as he's dead,' Detective Jackson added in a reassuring tone.

'Are you sure it was him? If he blew a hole in his head, were you able to identify him?'

'Yes, we're sure it was him.' He stood up and the

younger detective also scrambled to his feet, after gulping down the last of his coffee. 'Look we won't take up any more of your time. You've confirmed everything we've already been told. We can finish our report now.'

'Right. So you won't need me to come in and make a formal statement or anything?'

'No. It's fine.'

'Don't you think she should—' Connelly started before Jackson cut him off and glared at him.

'No. We're not treating his death as a crime,' he said turning back to me. 'If it was, then we would need you to give a statement. I'd heard of the man and his reputation, but had never come across him.'

'Sounds like he was a bit of a psycho really,' Connelly added. 'Maybe he did the world a favour shooting himself.' He received another glare from Detective Jackson who ushered him out of the house.

Or maybe someone else did the world a favour.

'We'll be in touch if the situation changes,' Jackson said as he was leaving.

I certainly hoped I wouldn't see them again. Carlos was dead! I couldn't help smiling when I shut the door. It meant I was free! I'd wished him dead many a time and now he finally was. I immediately questioned what sort of person that made me, being happy about his death? *A relieved one.*

I didn't have to worry about going to the UK now. But then again, there were a few loose ends here in Victoria which could cause me problems. One was Franco. He would realise that when I discovered Carlos was dead, I would suspect him of being responsible. He'd said he'd take care of Carlos. That must have been what he meant. Who else could it have been? I didn't think he would, but I wondered whether Franco would worry about my knowledge that he was the killer. More importantly, there was the issue of Lucy's sister Eva. What if she decided she wanted a reconciliation? Without any other family, Eva might decide she wanted to see Lucy again. Staying here was too great a risk. We could always spend a short time in the UK and then, after returning to Australia, settle in one of the other cities. Like Brisbane, Adelaide or Perth. I hadn't been to any of those cities and as far as I knew Lucy and Eva had always lived in Victoria.

These were all pipe dreams though. My immediate priority was to leave Australia.

43
Kelly

Following the police visit, I altered all our documentation to the Mt. Martha address. I also went to see the agent I'd previously spoken about leasing the house. Now we had all the furniture in the house I didn't want the hassle of moving it back into storage. Would he be willing to let it furnished? He told me that wasn't their practice because most people were looking for unfurnished properties. After a great deal of wrangling, we came to an agreement. I had to find my own tenant who was willing to take the house furnished. I also had to complete my own inventory. If I found someone suitable his agency would manage the rest of the process for me.

Frustrated with the agent's attitude, I drove to the nearby suburb of Frankston. At the local newspaper office, I placed an advertisement for the house. I thought it was probably best to attract someone who already lived not too far away, or who knew the area. I couldn't understand why the agency wasn't willing to take the house on, fully kitted out. I supposed it was dealing with irritating little matters like whether there were still six teaspoons left in the drawer at the end of a tenancy. I wasn't bothered about that. I just wanted someone who would appreciate the property and look after the grounds.

The advertisement attracted calls from many interested parties. When I questioned them, I rejected most. There was only one who I thought might be suitable. A widower with two young boys who had recently returned from California. He was staying with his sister and her family in Frankston. I arranged for him to visit the following day.

'Luke Lundell,' he confirmed shaking my hand when I met him outside the house. My full name is Lukas, spelt 'L-U-K-A-S, my grandfather was Swedish, but everyone calls me Luke.'

'I thought all Swedes were blonde-haired and blue-eyed?' I said with a silly grin on my face. Luke had brown hair and he was rather gorgeous.

'My grandfather was, but he married a dark-haired beauty, and my parents were both brunettes,' he said, with a smile that didn't quite reach his dark blue eyes. He told me one of his boys was aged 4 and a half and the other almost 3. They seemed excited – after jumping out of the car they began running wildly about the yard whooping and yelling. He watched them for a minute, his eyes scanning the grounds before turning back to me.

This time the smile lit up his eyes. 'This is a great place!' he exclaimed. 'I could really do something with this.'

'Sorry?'

'I'm a landscape gardener by profession. I can see that it was once a garden that someone loved and cherished, but that it hasn't had much attention for some years.'

'Oh yes. My husband and I bought it a few years ago. It was already somewhat wild then. We planned to re-build the house, but other events intervened. I'm afraid it has been a little neglected. I've left some parts wild, but I had all the weeds and overgrown grass surrounding the house cleared so that I could keep on top of it. I've been a little too busy to give it much attention. Would you like to see the house?' The fact that he liked the grounds and was a landscape gardener was promising.

Clara had followed me outside and was now running after the boys. I didn't allow Clara to run around outside on her own. I didn't think those boys were old enough to be unsupervised either.

'Clara,' I called and turned to Luke suggesting he call his boys in.

After we'd settled the children with drinks and a range of activities in the sunroom, Luke explained that his wife had died of cancer five months back. They were living in California at the time – where she was from. He told me that he was originally from Victoria, had grown up in Frankston and still had most of his family in the area. When his wife died, he decided to return to Australia and he'd only been back a few weeks.

'Clara and I are leaving for the UK as soon as possible,' I told him. 'I've only recently settled all our stuff in here and I didn't want to move it back into storage. The agent wouldn't advertise it furnished and equipped which is why I put my own advertisement in the paper.'

He looked at me, nodding enthusiastically.

'I don't have a lot of money at the moment. What little I have I need to invest in a vehicle and some equipment. So, renting a place that provides everything would be ideal for me. My wife's treatment ate up all our savings.'

'You had to pay for her hospital treatment?' I asked astonished.

'Yes, unfortunately, the health insurance we had didn't cover the bulk of it. Our property was a rental so we had no large assets to sell. The money we'd been saving to buy our own house has now largely gone.' I could hear his voice begin to falter.

'I'm sorry. It must have been difficult for you, especially with two young boys.'

He nodded, but didn't speak for a moment and I watched as he swallowed.

'It was difficult. Bloody difficult. I didn't particularly get on with Sarah's family, so after she passed, I decided to return home.'

'So what do you think of the house?' I asked him.

He looked around the open plan space of the living room, kitchen/diner as though seeing it for the first time. 'You've done a good job of renovating it. I like it. The sunroom provides the extra space I'd like to have as a play area for the boys. Especially in the winter. And the land is just brilliant. Lots of space for energetic boys to run around and for me to tend to. I'd have to buy another single bed, otherwise, it's perfect for us. How long do you think you might be away?'

'I'm not sure. It all depends on how things work out with my in-laws. At least a year, maybe longer.'

'Would you be willing to lease it for at least a year?'

'I'd be willing to lease it for two years if you wanted. If Clara and I return to Australia, we'll be moving to another state. Melbourne holds too many sad memories for me.' I told him about Christopher and Tom's death, looking suitably sad.

'What about your family?'

'They're all dead. Except for one sister,' I remembered to add at the last minute. I keep forgetting that I am supposed to have a sister. 'We don't speak.'

'Oh,' he said sounding surprised. 'I'm sorry for your losses. I understand some of what you might be feeling. I felt the same about the house in California. Too many memories. But, if you return to Australia, you'd be wanting to sell this place then surely?'

'No. Probably not. I'd like to hang on to it. For some years at least and decide what to do with it further down the line.' I shifted uncomfortably on the couch, hoping me wouldn't ask me any probing questions.

'Okay, I would like to lease it. Preferably for two years. That would give me time to become established with a new business. The rent you're asking is very reasonable.'

'It's more important for me to find a good, reliable tenant than to make money. A local agent agreed that if I found someone suitable they would deal with everything. The deposit, references, the lease agreement and management. Are you able to pay one month's deposit and do you have references?'

'Yeah, no worries.'

'I'll give you the agent's details. You're welcome to leave your sons here while you go to see them if you want.'

He grimaced and shook his head. 'Thanks, but the boys can be a bit of a handful at times. I'll drop them back to my sister's then pop over to see the agent. When will you be ready to lease it?'

'Clara's passport arrived yesterday. I have to apply for visas now, but I'm tempted to drive to Canberra and wait there until they're issued. I've still got some things to pack that I'm shipping over. That should take about another week or so to organise. So maybe two weeks. Three at the most. Would that suit you?'

'Yeah, that'd be great. The sooner the better. The boys are in my sister's spare room and I'm camping out on the couch. I'd better get going and sort this business out with the agent.'

I gave him the agent's name and address and checked I had the right mobile phone number for him. He also gave me his sister's landline number. We shook hands and he called his boys, who were sitting over Clara's wooden puzzle. She was between them and they were showing her where the pieces went – although she was quite capable of placing them herself. Her face lit up with a big smile, she clapped her hands and said 'yes,' each time they placed a part correctly. It was a cute scene. Like caring older brothers. So they could be quiet.

Two hours later Luke turned into the drive again. This time without the boys. Clara and I were outside at the time, Clara attempting to peddle around on the tiny tricycle I'd bought her.

'Thought I'd call back up to tell you that I have been to the agents and everything is sorted. I've also paid the deposit,' he said.

'That's grand,' I said. What was I doing? – I sounded like my father! He'd say 'that's grand' all the time when I was little. I'd never said it. Now it had just popped out of my mouth – with an Irish accent! I cleared my throat with embarrassment and said, 'I phoned and told them to expect you.'

While he'd been gone I'd been considering his situation.

'Luke, you said earlier you had to buy a vehicle. Is this car not yours?' I asked him pointing at the Mazda he'd arrived in.

'No it's my sister's. I'll need to buy a truck or van for work. Really I could do with two vehicles. One for work and one for personal use with the boys, but I can't afford both.'

'I could leave you my car when we fly out,' I said pointing to the Holden. 'I've decided I *will* drive to Canberra to sort out the visas and then return with the car. If you drive us to the airport when we return, you can have the car as part of the deal. We'd have to transfer ownership though.'

'You mean *have* it, like for *free*?'

'Yes. It would be a hassle for me to try to sell it before we leave and better to leave it with you. This place is a bit isolated. You need a car. It would give you time to find a suitable work vehicle. I imagine from what you've said that you'll be looking at second-hand ones. You'll need another car to drive around in while you're looking. You're welcome to mine.'

His face lit up with a beaming smile. 'That's so generous Lucy. Are you sure?'

'Yes of course, as I said, as long as you drive us to the airport when we leave.'

'Righto. You're on!' he said reaching out to shake my hand.

It's easy to give things away – especially when they're not really yours. But I'd decided Luke could do with a helping hand to become re-established. He seemed a really nice guy and was the perfect tenant. I shuddered to think of the damage those young tearaways of his might inflict on the house. But I was sure Luke would be responsible enough to repair any damage they did.

44
Kelly

My time in Canberra was prolonged after I discovered that I could obtain a British passport for Clara. I could also apply for 'British citizenship by descent' for her. Obtaining the British passport necessitated providing further photographs of her and documentation of Tom's place of birth. I'd brought all Tom's documents, including Tom and Lucy's marriage certificate with me. I thought it was wise to have the two passports for Clara after I discovered this. If I wanted to leave Clara in Wales with her grandparents, one of the options that Lucy suggested, it would be better if she had British citizenship.

We stayed in a cheap motel while we were in Canberra. To pass the time we visited various sights and explored the surrounding countryside. I sent Kim and Laurie a postcard from Canberra saying we were 'living' there for a while – without giving them an address.

One rainy day I found an interesting delicatessen that also had a café attached to it. Clara and I spent hours in there sampling the range of food on offer. Some things were excellent and others, rather tasteless. I thought they could have expanded the range of goods on offer and sat fantasising about how I would do it better. If only I had the opportunity.

With everything in Canberra taking so long, I contacted Luke and agreed that he and the boys could move into the house before our return. I'd already given a set of keys to the agent and only needed to ring them to finalise details. I told Luke we would find a hotel or motel for our final nights in Melbourne, but he insisted that we should come and stay at the house. He offered to sleep on the couch and said the boys could double up in the new bed he'd bought, leaving Clara's bed free. At first, I didn't feel comfortable with this, but when I thought about it, it made sense. We still had things at the house to pack in the large suitcase and any hand luggage we'd be taking with us. Luke had been up to the house a couple of times since we'd first met and I did feel relaxed in his company. In any other situation, I suspect we would have drifted towards a relationship with each other. There seemed to be a mutual attraction between us. However, circumstances were not appropriate. He was still grieving for his wife. He thought I was still grieving for my husband, but actually, I was overjoyed to be single and free from Carlos. I was not entirely free though with the care and responsibility of Clara. I'd made the promise to Lucy and intended to keep it as far as it was possible.

On the first night of our return to the house, the sleeping

arrangements went as Luke had suggested. But on the second night, several drinks down the line, we ended up on the couch in each other's arms. One thing led to another and we had a wonderful night of passion. At 3 am he nudged me awake and suggested that I grab a few hours of more comfortable sleep back in my bed. I had a long flight to face later that day. It wasn't particularly comfortable on the couch and I suspect he didn't want his sons to walk in seeing us entwined together.

Luke was only the second man I had willingly slept with. And my first one night stand. It's not how I'd always viewed a one night stand. Acquaintances I'd had in the past always talked about a one night stand as someone they picked up at a party or in a bar. But it would be our only night together. It was liberating to have this encounter with Luke and be able to walk away the next day. It was a new experience for me.

Luke seemed happy once we were up breakfasting, exhibiting no signs of guilt. We smiled over toast and coffee without saying much as the kids were around.

At the airport Luke gave me a huge hug and whispered, 'thank you for a wonderful night,' in my ear. He then stepped back and in a louder voice said, 'Have a good trip – I hope everything works out well for you, and thanks for everything Lucy.'

I wished him good luck and then, taking Clara's hand we turned and walked through the departure gate.

45
'Lucy'

Llandudno, April 2018

A certain Mr. Lukas Lundell was nestled firmly in my brain after my *dramatic discovery*. He kept flitting around between my thoughts and feelings. One moment terrified. Next excited, nervous or confused. What was I going to do?

Luke, who had rented the house back in Mt. Martha all those years ago had contacted me last December with his annual Christmas wishes. He was coming to the UK in March, to be 'best man' for one of his oldest friends, who was marrying his fiancé in Birmingham. He'd wanted to know if I would like to be his 'plus one'. I thought about it for a while and thought why not? We would just be friends.

There had been no one in my life since a short spring fling a few years before with a Swedish man who was travelling around the UK. I'd met him in the Deli Kitchen and we were instantly attracted to each other. After our first night of passion, he'd extended his stay in Llandudno for a further three glorious lustful nights.

Clara was in Spain at the time, with her grandparents and one of her school chums. I didn't think the affair would harm anyone, and I certainly didn't regret it. But Luke was a different story.

Luke had been in touch with me by email many times over the years, suggesting and requesting various things to do with the property. I'd given Luke permission to build a log cabin on the grounds a few years before – a hangout for his teenage sons. He'd also asked me a few times if I would consider selling him the house and grounds. He always offered a fair price, but each time I turned him down. It wasn't mine to sell. It was Clara's and when she was older, she could do what she wanted with the place. Mains water and sewerage were now connected to the Mt. Martha property. It had been a costly, but worthwhile process.

Luke had been engaged back in 2009, but things had gone sour before they could set a date for the wedding. He hadn't liked her attitude towards the boys. He'd broken it off, saying the boys were his priority. I knew exactly what he meant. Clara, although not my child through birth, was still my daughter. I would choose her any day over a man.

Clara and I had an easy, fun relationship most of the time. Friends and acquaintances told me things would change when she hit puberty. They warned me she'd stop being so amenable, there'd be long periods of moody silence or she'd become argumentative. I had seen some minor changes. She'd become a little feisty – at predictable times of the month. Sometimes I received the silent shrug treatment that I'd seen most of her friends give their mothers. She coasted at school, no longer the model student. Homework was rushed, but she passed tests and assessments with ease so I wasn't too worried.

Another change in Clara was the way she spoke these days. For the past year, Clara and her friends kept adding 'like' to almost everything they said. It drove me mad sometimes. I'd been reassured it was a teenage thing and would pass in time.

I'd organised for Clara to stay with a school friend while I went off to Birmingham to meet up with Luke. The moment I saw him I knew the old spark was still there. He'd officially booked us separate rooms in the hotel, but it became obvious as the first night wore on (the night before the wedding) that we would end up together.

That first morning after our night of passion, he'd turned to me and said, 'You do still have the coil fitted don't you?' *Coil? Oh my God, we'd not given a thought to contraception!*

'Oh God, Luke. No. I had that out years ago. I didn't think.' *Shit!*

'Me neither. I'm sorry, I just assumed. I should have checked with you.'

'I should have thought of it as well. Oh well, I doubt anything will happen at my age.'

'Well if it does, you'll have to come back to Australia and settle down with me.'

He sounded quite serious. I turned and gave him a

sceptical look and he added 'I'm only kidding. Although I would be very happy if you were living back in Australia. We'll have to take precautions from now on.'

'From now on?' I asked propping myself up on the pillows.

'Yes, there's the wedding reception tonight, (by then it was 2am) and we're booked in again tomorrow as well.'

'Oh, I was planning to go home the morning after the wedding.'

'I'd like you to stay on,' he said reaching out and touching my cheek. 'I've paid for the room for another night. Can't you make arrangements for Clara to stay with her friend for an extra night?'

'I suppose so. We'll see.' I remained cautious. While my night with Luke had been wonderful, earlier in the evening he'd asked me probing questions about why I wanted to hang on to the Mt. Martha property for Clara when she might never return there. I'd argued it was Clara's inheritance. He brought the subject up again this morning.

'Couldn't you buy an investment property like I did, if you want something to hand over to Clara? It doesn't have to be the Mt. Martha property you leave her does it?' he'd asked. I knew he really loved it there and wanted the property, but I couldn't explain to him that it wasn't mine to sell.

I wasn't convinced staying on in Birmingham would be sensible. After a bout of passionate persuasion, I agreed on condition he stopped trying to persuade me to sell the property.

I found the loving intimacy I shared with Luke addictive. The way he tucked my hair behind my ear; the way he ran his fingers gently down the side of my face. How he held my hand when we were out anywhere. Lying in bed with his arm wrapped around my shoulder, my head resting against his body. These were only a few of the ways he expressed his feelings towards me. I'd never experienced this kind of relaxed intimacy before. What I'd initially mistaken for love with Carlos had merely been lust.

While I was in Birmingham and Luke was otherwise engaged with his friend, I'd finally sought out a jeweller's and had Carlos's rings valued. I'd kept them hidden for years. The valuation of the diamond white gold ring was £28,000. The other, a decorative white gold with a couple of tiny diamond studs was £2500. I knew the larger diamond one was valuable, but the figure I was given surprised me. I then traipsed around looking for a jeweller who purchased second-hand rings. I finally found one but he was only prepared to offer £9,000 for both rings without evidence of provenance. I suspected he would sell them for at least double that, but I decided to take the money. The jeweller wrote me a receipt and a cheque, which I promptly banked in my savings account.

With savings in the bank I had a comfortable cushion to tide me over if I chose to have the baby. But I had no idea how to move forward on the matter.

Now, as well as the dilemma of what to do about my pregnancy, I had Eva's presence to deal with. I just prayed she'd set off for Paris soon and leave us in peace.

46
Eva

I dozed on the trip back from Snowdonia. It had been a long day and not as boring as I thought. The sun had been out, the wind had dropped, but it was still brisk. All that fresh air was exhausting. I dozed off thinking about Lucy, trying to work out how she could know details of our childhood if it wasn't her. I still wasn't convinced she was Lucy. Even though we didn't get on that well – especially after Noel's death, Lucy was my twin. Twins have a connection, unlike other siblings. I just didn't feel *any* connection with her.

I snapped out of my doze with sudden clarity, realising how she'd done it. Lucy's diaries! If Lucy had kept them, she would have had access to them and studied them to read about our lives. So who was she? According to that man Carlos, Lucy had been swept away in the tsunami with his girlfriend. He'd shown me a photograph of his girlfriend and her picture had been in the paper with him after he'd been found dead. I often wondered if he had discovered anything about her. That woman had had a Eurasian look about her, but 'Lucy' here didn't look anything like her either, from my memory of the picture in the paper. But, in the photograph he'd shown me and the newspaper one standing next to him, the woman looked like she'd was wearing a lot of make-up. Too much make-up. Scrape that off and she might look more like the woman I'd been talking to.

Another thing I remembered Carlos telling me was that he had spoken to Lucy through the bathroom door in the Phuket hospital. So he hadn't actually *seen* Lucy after the tsunami. But surely he would have recognised his girlfriend's voice if it had been her? What was her name? I racked my brains for the answer, taking myself back to the trip in the car with that horrible man. Kelly! That was it. Kelly something the paper had said. But if she was Kelly, why was she here in Llandudno with Clara? Why would a total stranger be masquerading as the mother of my niece? It didn't make any sense.

The money. It had to be the money. Lucy still had our parents and grandparents' inheritance. As far as I knew Lucy and Tom only ever rented property and had never owned a place of their own. This 'Lucy' took the money. Money that should have been *mine* if Lucy was dead. Lucy probably died in the tsunami, like Tom. Instead of *Kelly* missing, it was probably Lucy who was never found. But how could she fool everyone like that? How could she possibly do it?

My UK phone had a roving internet connection but there was no reception. It wasn't until we were almost back in Llandudno that it clicked in. I searched for the newspaper article about Carlos's death. I couldn't remember his surname, but I just put his first name, death and year in, and up it popped. An article in *The Age*. His real name was Carlo, but he was known as Carlos. There was the photograph I'd seen. I enlarged it on my screen. It didn't look like 'Lucy' but without all that makeup it could be her. Maybe. I would confront her about it in the morning. See what she had to say for herself. If she was this Kelly, she had no right to have Clara or that business, because she would have used *my* money to pay for it.

It was 10.30 am before I made my way to 'Lucy's' business the following day. I asked for her in the Deli but was told she was at home. I rang the bell and Clara answered in her school uniform.

'I would have thought you'd be at school by now,' I said following her up the stairs.

'I had a dentist appointment this morning. I'm leaving for school shortly.'

'Morning,' I said cheerily to 'Lucy' when I entered the kitchen.

'How was yesterday?' she asked me. 'Did you have a good day at Snowden?'

'Yes, it was enjoyable. But exhausting. We didn't arrive back until late. I then had to collect my luggage from the old hotel and drag it down to the new hotel. I was absolutely shattered by the time I checked in. It was too late to eat then, so I just collapsed into bed, not waking until seven thirty this morning when I ate a *huge* breakfast – something I don't do as a rule.'

'Coffee?' she asked.

'Yes, thanks.'

I watched as she prepared the coffee, studying her features. Maybe with make-up she could have looked like 'Kelly.' I would have to test her reaction.

Clara had disappeared and re-appeared with her school bag.

'I'm off mum. Bye.' She leaned over and kissed her 'mother' on the cheek. It made me sick to see her showing this woman affection.

'Bye. See you this afternoon.'

'Yep.'

Clara clattered down the stairs and 'Lucy' said she would be back in a minute. She went through to the living room and I followed her without her noticing. She was standing at the window with the shutters open waving at Clara. *Gotcha* I thought watching her. Now I was convinced I was right.

I retreated to the kitchen and she soon returned but before sitting down excused herself and rushed off to the bathroom.

'So how are you today *Lucy*?' I asked her when she finally came back into the kitchen looking quite pale.

'Actually, I'm feeling a little off colour this morning.' she murmured.

'You don't look too good this morning *Lucy*, or should I say *Kelly*.'

'What?' she asked. 'Why did you call me Kelly?'

'I've been doing a little research. You remember Carlos, don't you? From Phuket?'

'Vaguely. Why?'

'Well, I pulled the article about his death up on my phone last night. And guess what? You resemble his girlfriend Kelly more than my sister Lucy.'

'That's just crazy.'

'Is it? Lucy had money she inherited from our parents and grandparents. Did she tell you about it? Is that why you have been pretending to be her? To get your hands on her money? Money that should have been *mine* if Lucy was dead.'

'No, you have it all wrong. And if I was dead, it would be Clara who inherited the money, not *you*.'

'Clara would have been a toddler at the time. If both her parents were dead, it was *me* the money would have gone to as Lucy's next of kin. I doubt either Tom or Lucy would have had wills. The courts would have awarded me the money seeing as it came from my parents and grandparents.'

'No that wouldn't have happened. If I'd died in Phuket maybe some of the money would have gone to you for Clara's care. But any court would have awarded most, or all the money, to Clara to be held in trust. And what would you have done with Clara if I'd died? Shoved her into care I imagine? You never wanted kids and *you* wouldn't have brought her up.'

'That's neither here nor there. You know what finally clinched it for me this morning?'

'What are you talking about? What did you mean by "you know what finally clinched it for me this morning"?'

'It was the wave you gave Clara. I watched you waving to her from the living room window. Lucy would never wave like that. She always looked like an excited, silly little girl when she waved. Short rapid small movements of her hand. To and fro, to and fro. You did slow hand movements as though you were some kind of bloody royalty.'

Her eyes bulged in surprise.

'That's just preposterous Eva,' she finally said. 'Look I'm really not up for this. I'd like you to leave.'

'I will, but I tell you what, I want you to take a DNA test. I'm sure that will prove I'm right.'

'Oh Eva, you're crazy. Please go. And get a life of your own for God's sake! Leave us alone.'

'I'm going, but I'll be back. If you don't agree to my demand for a DNA test, I am going to go to the police with my suspicions. And you have stolen *my* life.'

'Your life? What? How do you figure that?'

'Because you've stolen *my* money,' I said as I turned and began walking down the stairs.

'Not everything is about money,' she called down after me. 'It is a shame you never worked that one out. And I'd be careful about going to the police if I were you. I might tell them about Noel's death.'

47
'Lucy'

It was unbelievable. Supposedly undone by a wave. Again. *Seriously?* Noting how others waved? I should have learned my lesson with Carlos. But with him long gone, it would never have occurred to me that it was an issue. Now Eva had worked out, or had strong suspicions, about who I really was and she was demanding a DNA test. I couldn't do a DNA test!

Eva thought it was all about money. Of course, for her, it was. I threw the comment about Noel's death down to her, hoping she would reconsider the situation.

I'd been sick with my pregnancy several times again this morning and now this. It was all too much. I put my head in my hands and broke down sobbing.

A few minutes later I felt arms enfolding me. At first, I thought I was dreaming until Clara said, 'Mum.' I looked up to she had a concerned look on her face.

'What are you doing here, I thought you'd gone to school?' *Had she heard what Eva said?*

'I did set off, but then, like, some instinct led me back. I didn't trust Eva,' she said, taking a seat beside me.

'I didn't hear you come in.'

'No, I was quiet. I took my shoes off at the door and crept up the stairs.'

'How much did you hear?'

'Like, pretty much everything. You were in the bathroom when I dumped my bag in my room and crept back down.'

'Oh.'

'Mum, who are these people she was talking about? Who are Kelly and Carlos? And wasn't Noel your younger brother?'

What should I do? Lie to her? Keep up the façade? I just didn't have the energy for it and if Eva returned I wouldn't get away with it for long.

'You're too young Clara. I was going to tell you everything when you were 18. Not now. You're only fourteen and a half.'

'Like, fourteen and a half going on 40 you always say. Tell me. You need to tell me, like, *everything*. Is she right?'

'A little. Not entirely. She's way off course on many things.'

Clara looked shocked, but reached out and took my hand.

'So tell me.'

'We'd better phone your school first to say you won't be in. This will be a long session.'

I told her everything. About my wonderful childhood until the death of my family. The foster years, the abusive adoption years and all that entailed. The escape to Melbourne. My waitressing years, then dancing at the Club. The hideous years with Carlos and the violence. Then Phuket. Meeting Lucy and Tom. The close friendship that developed. Everything Lucy told me about their lives including her deep depression following Christopher's death. Lucy's insistence that she wanted to help me because she believed I had helped her recover. The plan we formed for my escape, foiled by the tsunami. Witnessing Tom's death. Our terrifying experience after the wave struck.

'When we were clinging to that tree Clara, your mother made me promise her that I would return to Melbourne if she didn't make it. She wanted me to look after you, while pretending to be her, and then possibly take you to your grandparents in Wales. She didn't want Eva to have you. She was very clear about that.' I didn't tell Clara that at the time I'd thought her mother was referring to a pet dog. I left that bit out. I thought she might have felt insulted.

Clara sat in silence when I stopped talking. She had a shocked expression on her face. I had no idea how she was going to react to all this, so I was surprised at her next question.

'Why do you think she made you promise that? She'd only known you a short time,' Clara asked in a quiet voice.

'I'm not sure. She knew I had wanted children with Carlos in the early days. I guess she thought if I made it, I would care for you better than Eva.'

'And she probably would've been right about that,' Clara said. 'That selfish bitch wouldn't have wanted me.'

I chose not to take her to task for referring to Eva in that manner.

'Your mother was afraid she wasn't going to survive and thought I might because I was a strong swimmer. It wasn't about being a strong or weak swimmer, Clara. The power of the water and the devastation caused by it cancelled out those factors. To tell you the truth, I thought we were both going to die. But I gave her that promise because I believed it might help her. She was struggling emotionally and we both had serious injuries. When I survived I'd hoped that she had as well. I hoped we could leave Phuket together with your grandfather's help.'

'So at the hospital, they thought you were Lucy because you had her passport on you?' I noticed that Clara kept referring to her mother as 'Lucy'.

'Yes, I tried to tell them I wasn't Lucy, but with my injuries, I could barely speak. Not only because of my injuries – I was also doped up on painkillers. Then when I heard Carlos asking about me I kept quiet out of fear. Later I tried to tell a man from the embassy but he wouldn't listen to me. He became impatient with my poor speech. In the end, I was afraid to say anything and I was worried that I'd be charged with a crime. I was also terrified they'd contact Carlos.'

'They probably would have.'

'That's what I thought. As the days went on I was worried about getting back to you in Melbourne. So I kept quiet. Then when your grandfather showed up thinking I was your mother, I went along with it. I felt so alone and your grandfather seemed like a saviour to me.'

'He'd, like, never met Lucy had he?'

'No, and because we had a 'similar' look, he just assumed I was her. Don't forget my face was badly smashed up. I wasn't a pretty sight. He's such a lovely trusting man, it wouldn't have occurred to him that I wasn't Lucy.'

'No, he wouldn't. And, like, you know he adores you.'

'Yes, I know. And I adore him. I've always felt terrible about deceiving him like that though. But because I brought *you* to them it assuaged my guilt somewhat.'

'Well *you*, like, also helped them at the hotel all those years. Taid said you worked for a long time with no wages. So, like, did this Carlos come looking for you again?'

I summarised events with Carlos ending with the day at Shepparton. 'He died later that day and I don't think he killed himself. I think the man who was with him that day killed him. I decided to take his advice and leave the country. Also, as I said earlier, one of the options I promised your mother was to take you to your grandparents.'

'It was never about the money, was it? That's, like, why you haven't sold the house in Mt. Martha – you keep saying it's mine. I understand why now.'

'There's also a large sum of money in the bank that belonged to your parents which has increased over the years with rent Luke paid. That will be yours as well,' I told her.

She nodded. 'You, like, could have sold it and spent

that money. You told me that Luke wanted to buy it.'

'Yes he did, but it wasn't my property to sell.'

'So apart from making a promise to my real mother, why else did you stay with me? Why not, like, leave me with Nani and Taid – one of the options Lucy suggested, and go off to have your own life? You've, like, been tied down with me instead.'

'Do you really believe that? No, you haven't tied me down, Clara. I *wanted* to be with you. I fell for you the moment I laid eyes on you. And I waited for months to see if your mother returned. When it became obvious that she wasn't coming back, I couldn't leave you. Even when I brought you over here. You had become my life.'

I hesitated at this point not sure whether to be completely honest. Clara was taking all this too calmly. I half expected her to blow up at me in anger.

'I *did* consider the option of leaving you once I knew your grandparents were good people, but I just couldn't do it. Then Nani had her accident and it was no longer an option.'

Clara nodded as though she understood. She wouldn't have remembered her grandmother's accident. Over the years she's witnessed how much Gwyneth has suffered and knew it was due to her accident.

We spent another hour or two talking in more detail about various things I'd revealed. After showing her the picture of my family, Clara suddenly asked, 'Why did you mention Noel's death like that to Eva? Why would you threaten to bring his death up with the police?'

'I was trying to warn her off going to the police. The police here wouldn't be able to do anything about it.'

'How was Eva involved in Noel's death?'

Should I tell her? And would Clara confront Eva about it if I did?

'Your mother had suspicions about Eva being responsible for his death.' I explained Lucy's thinking to Clara, without giving her too many of the details.

'Right,' she said and fell into silence. I could see she was thinking over everything she'd learned. After a few minutes she said, 'I can, like, see why my mother wouldn't want Eva to have me if she thought that. But why didn't you pass me on to her?'

'Put you into Eva's care? Never, Clara. I'd made a promise and from what your mother told me during our chats, Eva hated kids. I was terrified she'd put *you* into care. After what happened to me, I didn't want that for you.'

'I can understand, like, why you wouldn't. So how did you, like, know about all the things from Eva and Lucy's childhood? You know – when she questioned you the other day.'

'I read your mother's diaries. They were all at the flat. She'd been writing them since she was nine and stopped after Christopher died.'

'Where are they now?'

'Locked in a trunk in the shed at Mt. Martha. You could read them all one day if you want.'

We fell into silence again. Clara was frowning and I couldn't help but say, 'I hope you've never doubted my love for you.'

'No, I've always known that you loved and cared for me.'

'You're not angry?' I almost wanted her to be angry. To show some sort *emotion*.

'Why would I be angry? You, like, saved me from a potentially unpleasant childhood. And kept my inheritance intact. Not that I care that much about the inheritance.'

'I thought when I started telling you, you'd be angry at me for 'lying' to you all these years.'

'You had no choice.'

'There's always a choice.'

'But you made the best choice for both of us. More, like, for me I'd say.'

'No, both of us.'

'You, like, need to know, although you might not be my birth mother, you *are* my mother. You have *always* been my mother for as long as I can remember. So I will, like, always think of you as my mother, no matter what happens.'

It was such a relief to hear Clara say this. I had always planned to tell her the truth once she reached maturity. But I always dreaded the prospect, believing it might end up with her rejecting me altogether. I was worried that she was taking everything I'd told her too calmly. It didn't seem natural.

'Thank you Clara, and hearing you say that reinforces my belief that I did the right thing all those years ago. But please remember you can't tell anyone about this. And I mean *anyone*. None of your friends or Nani and Taid. It has to remain between us.'

'Yeah, I know.'

I reached out and gave her a huge hug.

'Okay, mushy stuff over,' she said releasing me, 'Now I think I need some time alone in my room.'

I made myself another coffee and sat in the kitchen, wondering if Clara was up in her room punching pillows. I knew she did that to release her anger – I'd been about to walk in her room to talk her one day after we'd had a minor disagreement (because I wouldn't allow her to catch a train to Chester with her friends without an adult present) and spotted her doing it. She hadn't seen me and I retreated to allow her privacy. She'd come downstairs later with a calmer attitude and apologised for running off in a huff.

Clara had taken everything I'd told her today too calmly, so I hoped she was letting go up there.

Forty minutes later she re-appeared.

'What are we, like, going to do about Eva?' was the first thing she said.

She had a worried expression on her face. 'Are you okay Clara?'

'I'm fine. So Eva?' It looked to me as though Clara was focusing in on one thing. Eva.

'I don't know. She's demanding a DNA test and threatening to go to the police if I don't.'

'Yeah, I heard. I'll meet up with her and talk to her. Like, make her see sense.'

'I don't think that would be wise Clara. You're likely to lose your temper with her. It's not your responsibility to be involved in this anyway. It's between her and me.'

'No Mum, it's between the three of us,' Clara said with a determined look in her eye. 'I'm, like, cool. I

335

know how to be sweet and lovely when the occasion requires. As you well know.'

'Hmm.'

'I'm going to, like, send her a text, asking her to meet me later this afternoon. We can, like, go up to the Great Orme. She hasn't been up there on the tram. Maybe the lovely scenery there will, like, make her more amenable than talking over a coffee indoors somewhere. Also, I don't want anyone to overhear us. I'll, like, pack a picnic afternoon tea,' she said standing. 'It's a lovely day, she won't be able to resist me.'

I was an emotional wreck all afternoon. Once Clara left to meet Eva, I paced back and forth from the living room to the kitchen. Running through all the possible scenarios if the truth came to light. All were unbearable. At one point I had a panic attack. I couldn't breathe, just thinking about the idea of no longer having Clara in my life. I felt as though I was underwater in the tsunami all over again, struggling to surface. I collapsed on the floor clasping my chest, gulping and gasping. When my breathing calmed and resumed to a steady rhythm, I sat reasoning out the situation. Everyone knew I was Lucy who had survived the tsunami. I was an accomplished liar. Hadn't I achieved my greatest lie for the past thirteen years? I could deal with this. Eva could be dismissed as a hysteric. The only problem I could see arising would be if Eva, in her determination to expose me, convinced the police that I should take a DNA test. Then all would be lost. I could only hope with my little mention of Noel, Eva would drop her quest. I doubted it though.

I suspected Eva wanted to get her hands on Lucy and Tom's money. As a lawyer, she was bound to come up with justifiable reasons why Clara should return to Australia with her. One of her arguments would be that Gwyneth and Howell were too old and unwell to take care of Clara. Despite them being blood relatives, I couldn't see Clara and Eva ever becoming bosom buddies. They'd clash disastrously and could end up with one of them killing the other. I'd already witnessed how Clara had reacted to her. The other alternative would be that Eva would shove Clara into care. That lovely young girl could turn into a difficult and troubled teenager encountering abuse like me. I couldn't let that happen. Then there was my baby to consider. He or she would no doubt be taken away from me and placed in care if I was charged. I could spend many years in jail and never know my own child, let alone ever see Clara again.

No. If necessary, Eva had to be stopped somehow. That was the only option. But I didn't want to think about that at the moment so decided to go down to the Deli and distract myself with work.

48
Clara

I was gobsmacked by everything Mum told me today. I think I went into numb shock and engaged with her in robotic detachment. As though we were talking about people who had nothing to do with me. It's going to take some time for me to fully absorb it all. I told mum that I wasn't angry. But I was. Not with her, but with the circumstances that led to this whole thing happening. The death of mum's family and what followed in her life. The death of my parents in the tsunami. And the situation we have now with Eva. After we finished talking I went to my bedroom and pummelled my pillow to release my anger – I didn't want Mum to see me. Releasing my anger usually made me feel energised afterwards, but today I ending up dissolving into tears and burying my head in my pillow.

One of the things that upset me the most was that I'd almost recoiled from her when she went to hug me. I'm so glad that I didn't. What was that about? She was still the same woman who'd hugged me all my life – whose loving arms I'd always felt safe in. Was it because I now knew more about her and was shocked that she was capable of deceiving me and my grandparents for so long? After my tears subsided I lay there thinking about everything.

Mum had never talked much about my father, no matter how much I pleaded with her to do so. She always deferred me to my grandparents. Now I know why – she barely knew him. When I persuaded her to talk about her childhood she always supposedly talked about times she spent on her grandparents' farm. I'm now sure she was drawing on memories from her *real* life with her own family.

Mum had a horrific time after losing her family. That bastard who abused her ought to have been castrated. Later, when I talked to her about how awful it must have been, she said at least her first ten years had been within a chaotic, crazy, loving family. And that had sustained her during all the terrible years that followed. She said she hung onto those memories to prevent herself from becoming too hardened with life. She dug out the photo of her family and showed me. They looked lovely and it must have been great to have so many brothers and sisters. It's such a shame what happened to them.

It was incredibly brave of her to take off to a different city hundreds of miles away where she didn't know anyone and create a new life for herself. I've seen documentaries on kids who have run away as teenagers and they often get into drugs, alcohol or prostitution. So she did well to find a job and a safe place to live – although the hippy house sounded a bit dodgy.

At least mum has given me a caring upbringing, and

now with Taid and Nani, I'm part of a loving family. I don't care what anyone would think if they knew. She *is* my mother. She might not have given birth to me, but she gave me a chance in life. My life would have been very different if she hadn't assumed my mother's identity and come back for me.

Everything mum told me is *huge*. Including two possible *murders*. It's unreal, and as though I'm part of film drama, not real life. In a way it's exciting, but also frightening. I don't know what to do with all the information. I would love to talk it over with someone and tell all my friends about it, but I know I can't. And my grandparents must never know the truth. They think the world of mum. Especially Taid. He'd be heartbroken to think she's lied to him all these years. And Nani – although I know she is very fond of mum, I can remember a time when she wasn't so friendly towards her. Nani has mellowed over the years, but if she knew the truth – she might do something stupid.

Dealing with Eva has to be our priority. She has to leave Llandudno before my grandparents return next month. I have to persuade her that we are not interested in her little games. Mum said she didn't want Eva to know about the property we own in Melbourne or cash that's in the bank back there. In case she tries to take some foolish legal action when she returns to Australia. But I want Eva to know that mum has only spent a fraction of my parent's money – for legitimate reasons, and that she's keeping it safe for me.

I arranged to meet Eva at her hotel. I'd packed a flask

of coffee for her and fruit juice for me. In case she didn't fancy coffee or juice, mum allowed me to take a bottle of white wine she had in the fridge. She'd used a tiny bit of the wine to put in a sauce the night before and said she wouldn't be drinking it so I may as well offer it to Eva, who we'd witnessed was partial to wine. I also packed some of mum's home-made orange cake.

Eva was waiting in the hotel lobby when I arrived. She smiled at me – reminding me a little of a snake. I greeted her with a big grin hoping she wouldn't see through it to notice I was both angry and a little nervous.

It was quite late in the afternoon by now, but she hadn't been available earlier, saying she had some things to take care of. Mum was worried she'd been to see the police.

'So we're off up the mountain are we?' she asked as we set off.

'We don't call it a mountain. It's like, called the Great Orme or Pen y Gogarth in Welsh.'

'Why is that?'

'The name Great Orme is like, supposed to be derived from the Viking or Old Norse word for a sea serpent. It's a limestone *headland*, not a mountain, and is, like, supposed to resemble a sea serpent. I've never been out to sea here so, like, I couldn't tell you if it does. But the Vikings must have thought it looked like that, I suppose, when they, like, named it. We are taking the Great Orme tramway up to the top. It's a funicular tramway and Britain's only cable operated street tramway. We have to, like, change at the halfway point and a second tramway takes us to the top.'

'You sound like a tourist guide, apart from all the 'likes.' she said sarcastically.

'Oh, you're just the same as mum. Whatever! It's the way we, like, talk,' I said attempting to keep calm.

'We? You mean young people?'

'Yes, and we're, like, proud of our tramway in Llandudno. I love going up to the Great Orme. My friends and I often, like, hike up there. You have to pay for the tram.'

'I know. You told me that in your text. Don't worry I'll be paying today.'

'Well, that's only, like, fair as I've brought afternoon tea. I know you don't drink tea though, so I've brought you coffee. Or chilled white wine if you prefer. Or orange juice,' I said, smiling sweetly at her.

'Your *mother* let you bring wine? Isn't she worried you might drink it?'

'No, she knows I, like, wouldn't. Not without her present anyway. She allows me to have the odd glass of red mixed with water or white mixed with lemonade. I can't say I particularly like wine anyway. I brought it as an option for you.'

'I'll look forward to it. And I'd prefer wine to coffee at this time of the day.'

We arrived with a few minutes to spare for the tramway. Eva bought our tickets and we climbed on board. As the tram set off she started making strange noises.

'You're not, like, afraid of heights are you because this becomes quite steep?' I secretly hoped she was afraid of heights – it might give me an advantage with her if she was nervous.

'I'll be alright. I might have to shut my eyes here and there.'

'But you'll, like, miss the wonderful views if you do.'

'Has there ever been an accident on this thing?'

'Yes, but, like, once a long time ago. Don't worry, it's perfectly safe. Hundreds of people travel on it every day.'

'That's what worries me.'

I looked at her as though she was stupid. Actually, I did think she was stupid. I don't know how she could be a lawyer with such warped views on life. Especially about children. She was, gripping the edge of the seat as though worried she might be flung off it by the motion of the tram. In a short time, we arrived at the halfway point and changed trams.

'The second part is easier,' I told her.

'Sure it is. How can it be easier, when we are going *higher?*' Although she said this in her 'know-it-all' arrogant manner, I could tell she was a bit nervous.

'You'll see.'

'Why is it called a tram*way*? Why not just a tram? We have trams in Melbourne, but they're not the same as these. They move *fast*. We could have walked faster than this thing.'

'Yes, you could walk it faster. My friends and I, like, have done it many times. It's very steep though and extra tough on the legs. I thought you'd prefer this. And we do call it a tram as well. It's, like, a bit of a mouthful to say 'tramway' all the time. But it's officially a tramway because trams, like, run on roads, and trains, like, run off the road on special rail*way* lines. This is, like, halfway between a tram and a train, but it's operated by cable.'

'Right. I understand everything perfectly now,' she said in a sarcastic tone which I ignored.

I was tempted to say 'I can't help it if you're so stupid' but I kept my mouth shut. I noticed she was more relaxed on the second leg of the trip and was busy looking around as we ascended. 'See, I told you it was easier,' I said as we climbed out. 'Come on, I know a great spot where we can sit.'

She followed me across the Orme, past the café and down towards the limestone cliff edge.

'That's close enough to the edge!' she shouted.

'Look it's perfectly safe. Like, it doesn't even drop straight down. There's, like, a few ledges down there. Anyway, we're not going to sit on the edge, just near it. It's where you get the best views.'

'If you say so.'

I spread the rug I'd packed and unloaded all our goodies. 'So will it be wine or coffee for you?'

'Wine please.'

I unscrewed the cap and filled the large plastic wine glass I'd brought. She reached out for it and then immediately took a sip.

'Oh, still well chilled. It's lovely. Thank you. So tell me what's it's been like growing up here. Your *mother* brought you here when you were still very young. Why did she leave Australia so quickly after recovering from her injuries?'

'She wanted to bring me over to see my grandparents. Mum and Dad had, like, planned to come for a visit that year in the summer anyway. We were only going to stay, like, for few months, but Nani had an accident and was in hospital for quite a while so mum, like, agreed to stay on to help Taid.'

'You call your grandfather 'tide' like in the sea tides?'

'It sounds similar but has a different spelling. Yes, that's the Welsh word for grandfather.'

'It's a strange sounding language. I've heard people speaking it around the town.'

I shrugged. It didn't sound strange to me. 'Only because you can't, like, speak it,' I said.

'Does your *mother* speak it?'

'A little. She's not fluent like me. I've, like, learnt it at school since I was five and my grandparents spoke to me in Welsh before that.'

Eva sat with a sneer on her face. 'I don't see the point of Welsh,' she said, before leaning over to grab the bottle of wine. I couldn't believe she had finished her first glass so fast. 'I mean, you live in the UK. Why bother speaking a different language to the rest of the country?'

I watched as she poured herself another large glass, before answering. 'Although Wales is part of the UK, it is also, like, a separate nation within the UK. We have England, Wales, Scotland and Northern Ireland. In Scotland they, like, have their own language as well – Gaelic. It's, like, a cultural issue. But we're all taught English at school of course.'

'So you like living in Llandudno do you? It's so *provincial*. You're Australian really.'

'No, I'm part Welsh, part Australian, with Vietnamese and Chinese backgrounds,' I said. 'So, *Aunt* Eva, tell me a bit about *your* life growing up in Australia.'

She launched into what it had been like growing up in Melbourne. Then spoke about her grandparents' property out in the country. I thought it was an opportune moment to mention her brother. As she hadn't.

'You had a younger brother as well didn't you? Noel?'

She frowned and quickly skimmed over him.

'Yes, he drowned when he was six. Anyway, you should have grown up in Australia as well.'

'What, like Noel?' I couldn't resist having another little dig. She waved her arm angrily.

'No. Like your *real* mother and me. Because *she* is not your mother. I believe your mother died in the tsunami along with your father.'

I stared at her, not sure how to answer. 'If that was true, why didn't they, like, find her?' I said finally.

'Lots of bodies weren't found.'

'Look Eva, she is my mother and, like, nothing you say or do is going to alter that. Have some cake.' She ignored my offering and gulped down more wine. Then poured herself yet another large glass, emptying the bottle.

'So your *mother* has told you that I don't believe she's my sister Lucy?'

'I, like, heard everything you said to her. I came back this morning. I didn't go to school because I, like, knew you were going to say things to upset her. And you did. I'd like you to stop doing that. It's nonsense.'

'I don't think it is. She is a criminal. She has stolen *you* and all the *family* money my sister inherited.'

Her manner was so arrogant. I wanted to slap her

face.

'That's, like, not true. My parents bought land with an old house on it. They were going to demolish the house and build their, like, forever home. After my brother Christopher died it was, like, all put on hold. The old house on the land wasn't habitable. Mum renovated it and we moved there for a while before we travelled overseas. She's been renting it out since we moved over here and, like, all the money from it is being held in trust for me until I'm twenty-one.'

'I didn't know your parents bought a property. Where is it?'

'None of your business.'

'It *is* my business. When my sister died that property should have come to me.'

'No Eva, it wouldn't have. It would have come to *me* if both my parents had died and it would have been, like, held in trust. But mum didn't die anyway. She didn't want to sell the place because of all the dreams she and my dad had for it. And, like, she wants me to have it anyway. She has built a successful business and home here.'

'Yes, on *my* sister's money.'

'No, on her own hard work, savings and borrowing.'

'So, you're taking her side, even though we can prove she's not my sister? A simple DNA test will settle the matter once and for all.'

She gulped down more of the wine, leaving only a tiny bit left in her glass. She'd drunk almost a whole bottle in just a really short time. Was Eva what they called an alcoholic, I wondered. I'd watched her guzzle loads of wine at our house the other night and when she took us out for a meal. She hiccupped and looked at me with a satisfied grin on her face. It's a good thing I hadn't brought another bottle as I'm sure she would've soon started on that.

'We're not, like, going to take your stupid DNA test and I really wish you'd stop saying that about mum. She *is* Lucy Jones and I don't understand why you keep saying otherwise.'

'Because she's a fraudster. And a thief. She wanted to get away from her controlling boyfriend and saw an opportunity to do so when the tsunami hit.'

'She's, like, not a fraudster. Stop saying that. She is my mother.' I stood up then and started pacing around trying to control my anger.

'Look yooo were onlee tiny at the time. How wool... you know?' Eva seemed a bit drunk now having drained the last of the wine from her glass. I could hear she was starting to slur her words. She stood up and approached me.

'So *if* my mother *had* died in the tsunami what would you have done with me? Would you have brought me up?'

'Oh, I couldn' have dealt with a young chile. I have an important job you know.' She hiccupped again. 'I couldn... ave done that as well as deal with the needs of a whiny 'lill kid. I would have fos... fost'd you out ...til you were ol nuff. At the age you are now you'd prob'ly be alright. I'll ta...tay you back to Melbourne with me. I could jus 'bout cope with you and I wouldn nee babysitters. You're big 'nuff to loo... after yerself.'

'I'm not going anywhere with you Eva. I am, like, staying here with my mother and grandparents.'

'You're grandpees are too ol' to be lookin' afer you an *she* is *not* your mo...mother.'

'Stop saying that you bitch!' I went for her then and shoved her. In her drunken state, she lost her footing and stumbled back precariously close to the edge. *Oh shit*. She was swaying and looking at me strangely. I moved towards her intending to pull her back onto safer ground but she stepped back further as though she was afraid of me and slipped, disappearing from view. I let out a cry and rushed over. She was sitting down on the next ledge looking confused.

'Stay where you are, I'm coming down to get you,' I shouted to her. I looked around to see if there was anyone I could call out to, to help us. I could see some people a distance away heading towards the tram. Otherwise, there was no-one about. The Café looked like it was closed now.

'No!' she cried. 'Don' you come anyshwhere near me. I'll may ... may my own way back up.'

Eva sounded panicked and frightened. 'You've had a bit too much to drink Eva. I'll come down for you. I know a safe way back up. I've been down there with my friends, like, loads of times.'

'I said NO! I don' trus' you. You'd be likely to push... sh me over the edge.'

She was scared of *me*. I would have laughed except it wasn't really a laughing matter. 'Don't be ridiculous. You only fell down there because you stepped back yourself in your drunken state. You've, like, had too much wine.'

'I'm fine. Pish off Clara. I don' want you 'roun. You've made me verra ang... angra now. I'll be going to the poleesh 'bout this.'

'Ha! And say what?' The stupid woman thought she could report me. She'd stepped over the edge herself. I felt my anger starting to rise again. 'Will you tell them we, like, had an argument and you stumbled in your drunken state then stepped back over the edge. They'll, like, just laugh at you, do a blood test and see you've consumed too much alcohol. They might, like, even lock you up for being so drunk. And don't forget to mention Noel,' I added.

'I'll jus' stay here for a bit then. Watch the sun...set.'

'Suit yourself. I'm, like, not hanging around. The last tram will be going soon. I'll leave your handbag up here shall I?'

'Yes.'

'Fine. Whatever. I'm going.'

I took one of the tram tickets out of her bag. Her one would be useless if she didn't come back up soon. I knew I should sit and wait for her, but stuff her. If she didn't want my help that was her problem. I packed the basket and set off.

I decided to mention her to the tram people though. There was only a few more trams after the one I was going to catch. I told one of the staff at the tram station what had happened (not that I had pushed her first). I suggested someone go over and help her to climb up as she was quite drunk.

He said he would.

I caught the tram down and walked home. I'd had my juice but realised we hadn't eaten the cake. I knew Mum would still be in the Deli kitchen cleaning up.

'How did your afternoon tea go?' she asked when I arrived. I shrugged.

'Not so well then, judging by the look on your face,' she said.

Mum would only worry if I told her what had happened. 'Eva was, like, her usual bitchy self,' I remarked stuffing a piece of the uneaten cake from the picnic in my mouth.

'Is she still demanding a DNA test?'

I nodded and after swallowing the cake said, 'Yes, but I told her, like, we wouldn't do it.'

'What did she say?'

'Not a lot. I'm going upstairs. What's for dinner?'

'I told you earlier I made a Chicken pie last night for tonight's meal. Stop changing the subject. What did she say?'

'She called you a fraudster and a thief.'

Mum sighed and looked worried. 'She's not going to give up is she?'

'Nope. Doesn't mean we have to do what she says though. We can, like, stand our ground.'

'Has she gone back to her hotel now? Or do you think she's gone to the police?'

'No, she's still up there. Says she's going to, like, sit up there watching the sunset. She wouldn't come back down with me. She's sitting on one of the ledges over past the café.'

'Why is she sitting there? You didn't take her down to

the ledge did you?' she asked, her face looking worried.

Mum knew my friends and I climbed down the edge of the cliff and she'd never been happy about it.

'No.'

'But you got into an argument with her, didn't you?'

'Yes,' I said in a quiet voice nodding. I didn't want to talk about it.

'Did anyone see you after you left her there?' she asked frowning.

'Yes, I reported her to one of the tram employees. He said he'd go and speak to her.'

One of the Deli staff came into the kitchen then so mum and I stopped talking. It was a good opportunity to escape.

'I'm going upstairs. I've got homework to do. See you later.'

Mum followed me out into the eating section and told me she would be a while as she still had lots to do. As she shut the door behind me I could see she looked very worried.

49
Eva

Why did they keep mentioning Noel? For goodness sake. He died *years* ago. There was nothing they could prove. Not after so long and with Lucy gone. The real Lucy that is. If Lucy had written something in one of her dairies it couldn't be much. I'd checked her diaries for weeks after Noel's death. There was nothing incriminating. I checked for the next few years on the anniversary of his death. Still nothing. Lucy might have *said* something to that woman. But that would be inadmissible. Only hearsay. She had *nothing*. It was all a bluff. Anyway I hadn't killed him. He'd conveniently drowned himself. What no one knew was that I'd stopped trying to resuscitate him after Lucy went for help.

I'd been looking forward to today's picnic. It had been Clara's suggestion and I saw it as an opportunity for a little aunt-niece bonding. And to put her straight about her so-called mother.

I would have preferred to walk up here today rather than take that stupid 'tramway' as Clara refers to it. I thought Clara was being a bit obtuse, but once we settled on the grass everything was better. She wanted to hear all about our upbringing which was nice. When I introduced the topic of her phoney mother, she became all defensive again. But she is just a silly child. She has fallen for all the lies her so-called mother has told her. She admitted that she'd overheard me challenging that woman. I expected it to be quite a shock for her to discover that the woman she has known as her mother, isn't actually her mother. But Clara wouldn't have it. She kept saying that woman was her mother, that she was Lucy.

And God, that irritating habit she has of saying 'like'. I really don't think I could tolerate hearing that day in day out! She'll have to stop doing that when she comes back to Melbourne with me.

When Clara got up and started pacing about. I could see she was becoming angry. I felt uncomfortable sitting, so stood up and went to join her. I don't know what I said that upset her so much but she charged at me, pushing me backwards. I suddenly felt very weird, my world was tilting a little and I stumbled. Then when I saw her coming at me again I stepped back. Into thin air. It was so fast I was confused at first. Looking around me I could see I was on a large flat ledge. Was the silly bitch trying to kill me? She offered to come down and help me, but I didn't believe her – or trust her. I was so angry I told her I was going to go to the police – but her remarks about me having too much to drink might destroy my credibility.

I knew I had begun slurring my words a bit. I

wondered if she'd drugged my drink or something. I'm capable of drinking large quantities of wine without it affecting me. But then again, I seldom drink during the day without eating. I hadn't had any lunch after my huge breakfast. And I'd already had several vodkas in the hotel's bar with some peanuts before meeting up with Clara – while thinking about DNA tests.

I sat there admiring the view for a while when I heard a voice calling 'Eva?' I looked up to see a man in a uniform standing at the top. How did he know my name? Was he a friend of Clara's?

'I'll come down and help you up,' he said.

'I'm fine,' I told him. 'I don't need any help thank you.'

'You shouldn't really be down there. Didn't you notice the signs?'

I didn't answer him.

'Have you been drinking?' he asked me.

'I had a glass or two of wine earlier, but I'm fine,' I repeated. 'I wanted to watch the sunset.' I was no longer slurring my words but I had to enunciate everything with care so he wouldn't think I was drunk.

'The last tram will be leaving shortly.'

'It's alright, I plan to walk down anyway.' I needed to sober myself up before I went to the police. It would be quicker anyway than those stupid trams.

'Can you throw my bag down to me though?' I wanted my phone.

'I don't think that's a good idea. Having something to carry as you make your way up will make it more difficult for you. I'll leave it up here for you. And you should make your way down before it gets dark.'

'I know.'

'Well ... if you're sure you're alright, I'll—'

'I'm sure,' I said cutting him off. He was beginning to irritate me.

He didn't speak again and disappeared. Had I been foolish not to accept his help? He seemed genuine. I sat there for some time after he left. I didn't know what the time was as my phone was in my bag. It must be getting late though as I was starting to feel a bit cold and the sun was beginning to sink on the horizon. It was a beautiful sunset. Blues, pinks and oranges. I sat mesmerised by it for a time before realising I had to climb up before the skies darkened too much. It would take me a while to walk down to the town and I only had the torch on my phone.

I stood up too quickly and felt dizzy. Too many glasses of wine? Or was it due to drugs? I'd have to be careful. Once my head cleared I began making my way up. It was tricky and I kept sliding back and would have to start again. For some reason, I thought it was funny and laughed. I started up again, slower this time, checking my footholds were secure. I was looking down as I almost reached the top when I felt something press hard against my head and chest forcing me backwards. I went tumbling back down, landing uncomfortably on the ledge again with my right foot tucked under me at an awkward angle. Was it sprained? That was going make my climb trickier. Had someone pushed me? Looking up I couldn't see anyone, but the light was fading fast now. I tried to stand up, being careful with my foot. I didn't immediately realise that I was very close to the edge of a long drop. My feet weren't gripping solid ground and I began to slide. *Fuck.* In desperation, I clawed at grass, but none would hold my weight. Clumps tore free of their precarious hold. I couldn't stop giggling and didn't dare look down. Then I started slamming into hard rock knocking the breath out of me. The pain was unbearable. I tried to cry out, but the sound coming from me was feeble – I was too winded to scream. My descent increased in speed, the pain greater each time another piece of rock tore at my skin until suddenly I was flying. I'd always wondered what it would be like to fall from a great height. Before I could analyse how it felt, I collided with a large slab of stone and stopped. My brain told me to get up, but I was unable to move. The remarkable thing was there was no longer any pain. I couldn't feel a thing. I was so tired I just wanted to go to sleep.

50
'Lucy'

I barely slept the night of Clara and Eva's picnic. I kept expecting the police to knock on my door at any moment. But no one came and I finally drifted off for a few hours. Clara came in to wake me at 8.20 and said she was leaving soon.

'Did you, like, have another bad night?' she asked. She knew I hadn't slept well since Eva's unexpected appearance in our lives.

'Mm.' I managed to reply half drowsy with sleep, nodding.

I staggered out of bed and shuffled into the bathroom. My body ached and felt so stiff. I made a mental note to start exercising more. I threw water over my face and stumbled, in a half drunk-like stupor, into the kitchen before collapsing into a chair.

'Take the day off mum, you look dreadful.'

'I can't. One of the regular staff is off sick, another one is away on holiday. I need to do some baking and go in to help out. I'm worried the police will turn up if Eva went to see them.'

'I'm sure she'll, like, be quite hungover today. She drank all the wine on her own in a very short space of time.'

'So she was drunk?'

'Yes. Like staggering around and starting to slur her words, talking in a stupid childish way.'

'You didn't mention this yesterday.'

'You've seen how she, like, drinks. I think she's an alcoholic. I, like, offered to help her, but she refused. She said she didn't trust me.'

'What did she mean by that?' I stood then, concerned.

'I don't know, you'll have to ask her! The woman is a stupid cow. Threatening to go to the police and all sorts. Look, I have to go, otherwise, I'll be, like, late. See you later.'

Clara clattered down the stairs then before I had a chance to say another word. Worried, I turned to the cupboards, collecting the ingredients I'd need for my baking. While the scones were baking I sent Eva a text asking if she could come to see me after the lunch rush, at about 3 pm. As I'd hoped, she didn't reply. I checked the recycling box we kept glass in and spotted the empty bottle of wine Clara had taken on the picnic.

We heard nothing from Eva, or anyone else, that day or the next. It was the following morning that the police finally knocked on our door. I'd been on tenterhooks the whole time, guessing they would turn up eventually. Clara had already left for school. It was one of the local detectives who was a regular at the Deli, accompanied by a uniformed constable. Here we go, I thought.

'Could you confirm that a Miss Eva Harrington is your sister, Mrs. Jones?' he asked me formally.

He'd said *sister*, not 'supposed sister'. That sounded promising. With any luck, she hadn't been to see them before the picnic. 'Yes,' I replied giving nothing away.

'Would you mind if we came in for a few minutes, we'd like to ask you some questions?' the detective asked.

'Sure, no problem,' I said, trying to remain calm. I stood aside while they walked past me and up the stairs. I closed the door and followed them. 'I have to check on the scones, do you mind coming into the kitchen for a minute?'

'Ah, the famous scones,' the detective commented. 'So you bake them here at home?'

'Yes, I have all the required health regulations in place if that is what you are wondering.'

'No, not at all. I always wondered who made them. They're so delicious.'

'Thank you, but I'm sure you didn't come here to talk about my scones,' I said all business-like, placing the two large trays of scones on top of the cooker after removing them from the oven. I just wanted to get this over with. I waited to hear what they would say next.

'Do you mind if we sit at the table?'

'No, that's fine.' We all sat down and I waited for the questioning that might lead to the end of my life as I knew it.

'When did you last see you sister?'

'Three mornings ago. She came around about 10 am, had a coffee with me and then left. My daughter met her for a picnic tea later the same day. We haven't heard from her since.'

'You didn't find that strange?' he asked with a quizzical look on his face.

'We'd had a falling out that morning. I sent her a text the following morning asking if she would meet me that afternoon, but she didn't reply. I thought she was still angry with me.'

'Yes, we've picked up that message.'

'When you say you've "picked up that message", what do you mean by that?'

'Her phone was handed in two days ago along with her handbag, which only came to us yesterday afternoon. The battery in the phone was flat. After we plugged it in we found your message. We have to tell you that the woman we believe to be your sister has been found dead. Of course, a formal identification will have to be made.'

'*What?*' I shouted. 'Where, when?' I opened my mouth in shock.

'Her body was found early this morning at the foot of one of the limestone cliffs off the Great Orme. Her handbag was found two days ago and handed in by a member of the public to the tramway station at Great Orme. They thought one of the people up there that day had wandered off without it. Staff put it aside thinking the person would come enquiring later. One of the staff went up to the spot where the bag was found and looked over but couldn't see anything, so thought there wasn't an issue. It was forgotten about. When a different member of staff came on duty the following morning he recognised the bag from an incident two days prior. He contacted us and gave a statement. The hotel your sister had been staying at had also reported her missing. She hadn't returned to her room and was due to check out yesterday. All her luggage was still at the hotel and her bed hadn't been slept in. They didn't know who her contact was in Llandudno but they were able to inform us where she'd been staying before moving to them. Our enquiries at that hotel this morning led us to you.'

'Oh God. My daughter told me Eva drank a whole bottle of wine very quickly and seemed a bit drunk. Do you think she fell?'

'Yes. All the evidence points to that. Your daughter reported your sister had slipped onto a ledge to an employee at the tram station. She told him your sister had refused her help to climb back up. He then went to speak to her.'

'So, this employee saw Eva? Why didn't he help her?'

'She refused the tramway employee's help. She didn't appear to be drunk, according to the man who spoke to her. After encountering your sister he left a message with his supervisor who, he hadn't realised, was away for a few days with his phone switched off. He'd also intended to report the situation to the police as he'd had minor concerns for her safety. But he forgot in his rush to go off duty and catch a ride on the last tram. It was his son's 18th birthday and they had a big night planned. She'd told him she was fine and that she planned to walk down. And for most people climbing back up would have been easy enough. Young people regularly sit down on that ledge, despite warning signs telling them not to. But we've learned that your sister had had several drinks at the hotel before she met your niece and then if she drank more up at the Orme, climbing back up would have been—'

'I knew my daughter returned alone the other evening and that Eva had remained behind, but I didn't know she had fallen. Oh God Eva, you stupid woman! Bloody stubborn fool.'

'Was she inclined to be pig-headed then?'

'Yes... yes, she was.' *So she was dead.* Eva clearly hadn't been to see them before going on the picnic and had died before she could pay a visit to them later.

'How did you discover where she was?'

'From all the reports we had, it was the logical conclusion. Investigations, early this morning, led to the discovery of her body by a member of the rescue services. We had hoped to find her alive, but injured, and possibly suffering from hyperthermia, but I'm afraid her fall was fatal.'

'Do you think she might have survived if she'd been found sooner?'

'I'm not in a position to answer that. She might have survived the initial fall. For how long I couldn't tell you. The post-mortem will reveal more information but judging by the height of her fall, it's highly unlikely she would have survived in the long term – even if she'd been rescued immediately. Early reports indicate she died several days ago.'

He paused for a moment before asking, 'Can you tell me what you argued about the last morning you saw her?'

'Why do you want to know?' I asked a little defensively.

'It would be helpful to gain a bigger picture of her state of mind. Whether anything you argued about might have caused her to commit suicide.'

'No, definitely not. Eva was not the kind of person who would commit suicide. She had plans to go on to Paris next. When I didn't hear from her I thought she must have already left Llandudno. We hadn't been in touch for many years until she turned up here. She believed I snatched her boyfriend from her – Tom, the man I married. Although it happened a long time ago, she'd never forgiven me. Things between us weren't easy and the old resentment surfaced again that morning.'

'I see.'

I didn't know what else to say, so I stayed silent, waiting to see what they'd say next.

'Could you tell me your whereabouts on that afternoon, between roughly the hours of 5.30 and 7pm?'

'Where I was? Why?' I asked putting on a shocked and innocent expression.

'Just dotting all the 'i's' and crossing all the 't's'

'I was downstairs, working in the Deli.'

'Can anyone corroborate that?'

'Yes, several members of staff were still on duty while we were clearing up for the day. I was still working when Clara returned.'

'Okay, we'll need those staff member's names if you don't mind. And can you confirm what time your daughter arrived home?'

'Yes, she was back here by about 5.30pm. She came

to see me in the Deli, ranted about her aunt for a bit and then went upstairs to do her homework.'

'Did you return to your flat immediately after finishing at the Deli?'

'No, I went around to my in-laws to water their indoor plants. I realised just as I was about to leave the Deli that I hadn't watered them for more than a week.'

'Did anyone see you when you went around there?'

'Yes, the next door neighbour. He was locking his car just as I was about to open the door. I waved to him and called out a hello.'

'Okay, thank you. When could you formally identify her?'

'Sorry?'

'We need you to carry out a formal identification of your sister. I have to warn you though she's not a pretty sight.'

I sighed. It wasn't something I wanted to do, but I knew I would have to. 'I guess I could come with you now. I'll have to deliver these batch of scones to the Deli first and tell the staff I won't be in.'

Identifying Eva was horrible. I'd seen some dead bodies floating about me in Phuket, but I'd never seen the dead body of someone I knew. They showed me her 'good side' through a viewing window. You couldn't help to see that the other side of her head and face were quite badly damaged. I had to race off to the toilets to be sick straight after. They told me there would be an inquest and that my daughter would be asked to provide a statement.

After leaving the morgue I drove to Clara's school, informed them of my sister's death and asked permission to take Clara out of school. I didn't tell them that she had to go to the police to give a statement.

'Dead?' Clara exclaimed when I told her the news. 'The stupid bloody bitch. I, like, told her it could be dangerous. I offered to help her up, but she refused.'

'Why didn't you tell me that she'd *slipped* down onto a ledge, Clara?'

'I didn't want to, like, worry you. I knew Eva had upset you that morning. Then that long conversation we had – like, talking through all that stuff. It must have been hard for you.'

Clara was right about that. I had found it upsetting – but also a sense of relief that most things were out in the open.

'Well, the police want you to give a statement about what happened when you were with Eva at the Great Orme. What are you going to say?'

'I'll, like, tell the truth. Not necessarily the *whole* truth though.'

Clara's statement went well. It corroborated some of the things I'd said. I insisted that I sat in with her while they took it. Clara was good. She told the truth but lied by omission. A girl after my own heart. A survivor. Thank goodness Clara had spoken to the tramway employee. That, and the fact that she'd been chatting to some of her friends while she was supposed to be doing her homework. That put her completely in the clear if, for some reason, they had any suspicions about Eva's death – Clara couldn't be linked to it.

I asked the police when they would release Eva's body. They said the post-mortem would be completed by the following day. Her body could then be collected – depending on the findings. I was confident that everything would be okay and then I'd have to make a decision about what to do with her.

When we returned to the flat I broke the news to Clara about my pregnancy. It was a subject I'd been avoiding, but decided I should tell Clara before anyone else. It had been the two of us for so long, and I was worried she might think that I no longer wanted her if I had the baby. Not if, when. There was no question about it. I wouldn't consider having an abortion. Being pregnant was damned inconvenient. Being a single parent again would be hard, but I'd already done it once in much more complicated circumstances. Clara's eyes bulged in surprise at the news and she tipped her head back shaking it.

'As if, like, my brain hasn't enough to absorb with all the information it's received in the past week. A baby. Wow! Are you, like, going to have it? Are you going to tell Luke? I assume it's his, from your wedding trip to Birmingham? Was it an accident?'

'So many questions Clara. Yes, I plan to have it. Yes, Luke is the father and it *was* an accident. We forgot to take precautions on the first night.'

'Why didn't you, like, take a morning after pill?'

'We didn't think of it. I guess I foolishly believed that I was probably too old to fall pregnant. It's not just young people who make mistakes.'

'You, like, haven't answered the question of whether you are going to tell Luke.'

'I don't know if I'm going to tell Luke. He did talk about us – that is you and me, both returning to Melbourne and living with him and the boys.'

'Would you consider it?'

'Oh Clara. I can't have a serious relationship with a man and not tell him who I really am and how I came to have you in my life. And I don't't' think I could marry someone using a false name.'

'Why not? It's worked so far.'

'I just couldn't do it. Looking after you seemed the right thing to do. And in doing so I was keeping a promise to a woman who was facing death. But being in a serious relationship with someone and not telling them the truth, I couldn't live like that.'

'Is that why you've never, like, had a serious relationship with anyone?'

'Partly. But it's also because I've been very cautious of men after my experiences. You were the priority in my life and I've just never met anyone who I was interested in being involved with. Until Luke. But we live on opposite sides of the world. It's not meant to be.'

'It could be. Just, like, tell him the truth. If he's the right man, he will love you all the more for everything you've done.'

'I could only tell him face to face. It's not something I could do in an email or on the phone. Besides I wouldn't want to write down anything incriminating.'

Clara laughed, then nodded. 'Then let's, like, go on a

trip to Australia.'

'I can't just leave the business like that.'

'You do when we go on holiday to Spain. Why not to Australia? I know, like, I've just had a few weeks off school over Easter, but this is really important Mum. You need to see Luke and I really want to come with you. I'd like to see the house there. Besides, we have an excuse now with Eva dying.'

'I suppose we could. But it's such a long way. I don't think I could face travelling all that way for only two weeks. We'd have to stay at least a week or two longer.' *To give me the courage to face Luke.*

'Oh come on mum! Let's, like, just do it. This whole Eva thing has been awful. It would be good for both of us to get away. I can miss some time off school this year.'

'I'll think about it. We need to have Eva cremated here first and take her ashes back to scatter there. In a memorial garden or something. I'll have to look through her things, find out more information about her and notify people of her death.'

'She said she was on Facebook. We can look her up on there. Can I do it?'

'Yes, alright,' I sighed. I was sure Clara could navigate her way around Facebook with ease. I wouldn't know where to start. I'd fobbed Eva off by saying that I didn't have time for Facebook, but the reality was it was something I'd deliberately avoided. For someone like me, it was potentially dangerous.

'So we can, like, leave for Australia as soon as you can have her cremated?'

'Not necessarily. There might be an inquest. I'm not

sure if we'll be required to attend that. We'll talk some more in the morning. It might not be easy to organise everything at such short notice.'

'I'm sure you *could,* like, make the necessary arrangements quite quickly for work. We could book for early next week if seats are available. With the holidays over it should be easier. I'll go and look online for ticket deals and check out Eva's profile on Facebook.'

Clara disappeared into my study/office where I kept our main computer. I remained sitting at the table considering possibilities.

Clara and I both had current British and Australian passports. I'd obtained British citizenship for Clara when she was still very young and it looked like we were staying in the UK. I'd applied for my British citizenship back in 2013. It had been a costly and lengthy process, but worthwhile. It certainly made our trips to Spain much easier. I'd also renewed our Australian passports.

We could do it – if the cremation could be done quickly.

A quick phone call to a funeral service explaining the situation confirmed that I could have Eva cremated any time if there was no service or other matters involved. I wasn't sure what they meant by 'other matters' and really didn't want to know. I booked in a provisional time and told them I'd confirm this with them when the police released her body. Simple.

But the idea of sitting down with Luke and telling him everything was a different matter. It was terrifying! What if he reacted badly? What if he totally disapproved of my actions and decided I had to be reported? If he was the man I thought he was, then I doubted he would do anything like that. But really, how well did I know him? We'd communicated for years by email, sent Christmas greetings, but I'd really spent very little time with him.

As the father, Luke had a right to know about the baby I was expecting. It was such early days yet though. The idea of seeing him again *was* very tempting. But would that ultimately mean leaving our life in Llandudno behind? I didn't know what Clara would think about that. She seemed very keen to travel to Australia, but live there? That was a conversation we would need to have, if, and when, it was appropriate.

I made snap a decision; we *would* leave for Australia, as soon as possible. I went into the office to pass the good news on to Clara who had discovered, from Eva's Facebook site, where she worked. I also made the dreaded phone call to Gwyneth and Howell in Spain to pass on the news about Eva and her death. They were suitably sympathetic, but I knew that was just for my benefit really. Then I hit them with the news about taking Eva's ashes home to Australia but didn't mention my pregnancy. It seemed a little premature to be doing that. I'd book return tickets and could always tell them when I knew the outcome of our trip.

The police released Eva's body without any further issues arising. They didn't suspect any foul play in Eva's death. The coroner ruled her death an accident. I had her cremated and collected the ashes so we were all set for our journey back to Australia now.

51
Clara

Melbourne, Late April 2018

I'm actually quite happy that Eva is dead and that I'm never going to see her again (although I would never tell mum that). It does seem strange that she's gone forever when she was alive and breathing just a short time ago. The news of her death had shocked me but hadn't surprised me all that much. She had seemed so drunk on that final afternoon I saw her. Her death at least meant that we would have no further threats from her. That stupid woman actually thought I would return to Melbourne with her. I hadn't told mum about that part of my conversation with Eva. It was too much. I didn't tell Mum that I'd pushed Eva either. Nor did I tell the police or anyone else. Not even my best friends. I had a few sleepless nights worrying that someone witnessed me doing it. But if anyone did, no-one came forward. It was a good thing that I covered myself by going to tell the man at the trams about her and that he had gone to help her. Otherwise, the police might have suspected me of doing something to her. I didn't ask Eva to stand and follow me about that afternoon and she chose to drink all that wine and say all those stupid things. And I'd offered to help her climb back up hadn't I? My conscience is clear.

When we went to Eva's apartment, Mum found a copy of her will and we discovered that she'd left everything she owned to me – to inherit on my 25th birthday. At first I said I didn't want anything of hers, but Mum made me see sense. We had gone to Eva's apartment to remove anything personal that I might want to keep. Like family photographs that Mum didn't already have to pass on to me.

Eva's place is really cool and we found out that she has an old flashy sports car parked in the underground car park. I suggested we could use it while we were in Melbourne, but mum said we'd have to wait and see what the lawyer said first. Mum could see I was impressed with the apartment and asked me if I would like to hang onto it. She said it could be rented out once probate had gone through. But I said no. Much as I liked the place, I would never be able to live here. Where *she* had lived.

While we sorted out stuff to do with Eva, mum and I stayed in a hotel in the city. We had to visit the place where Eva worked, to tell them about her death. They mumbled condolences to us and then introduced us to one of the trustees of Eva's estate, who worked in another part of the firm. Mum was named as another trustee. There was apparently a load of legal stuff to sort out. I left it for mum to deal with while I played on my phone contacting all my friends on WhatsApp.

Mum hadn't told Luke we were coming to Melbourne until after we arrived. She finally phoned him last night and we travelled out to the Mt. Martha house today, using Eva's car after the lawyer said it was okay and mum organised insurance. The car was great, but I couldn't persuade mum to drive fast in it. She's always driven within the speed limit to avoid attracting any attention from the police. I understand now why she does that. She has an official British driving licence, but her Australian one has expired she told me. Of course neither licence was in her real name.

On the way to Mt. Martha mum suggested I start reading Lucy's diaries in the cabin while she talked to Luke.

I liked Luke straight away and felt comfortable with both him and the whole place. Luke's boys are at school so I won't see them until later. One of them is seventeen and a half now, the other one just turned sixteen. Their log cabin is great. I can't wait to sleep in there. I've been in the cabin for ages now, reading through the diaries. Mum was right, Lucy seemed like a lovely person. Eva wasn't. How could twins be so different?

When we first arrived and I saw how much land there was, I suggested that we could build several more big log cabins for all of us to live in when we're older. Mum just laughed at me. I also suggested that we scatter Eva's ashes here on the land, but mum didn't like that idea, saying it wasn't appropriate. She wants to have Eva's ashes placed in the same memorial gardens as her parents. We found the documentation at Eva's place showing they have a niche with plaques. We haven't visited the gardens yet, but plan to in the next few days. Mum said she'd like to visit N.S.W. while we're in Australia and look at the crematorium gardens where her family's plaques are. She's never been there. I told her I'd like to do that with her and that I thought it was really important thing for her to do.

Luke and mum have been talking now for a *really* long time. I hope it's going well for her. She deserves to find some happiness with someone. I don't know what that will look like for us in the future, but the idea of a baby brother or sister is great – although I'd prefer a sister. Two older stepbrothers might be fun as well.

52
Kelly

Well, I've had 'the conversation' with Luke now. Telling him everything. Well, *almost* everything. He listened closely as to why my life was 'complicated'. First registering shock on his face and then neutrality so I couldn't tell what he was thinking. But when I finished he said I should immediately revert to my birth name so that we could marry. And that was before I'd told him about the baby. His face lit up with genuine delight when I gave him the baby news.

I explained that I had to continue being Lucy or Clara could be taken away from me. Much as I wanted to be 'Kelly' again, I didn't think it would be possible. Luke came up with a range of ridiculous suggestions and possible options; none of them feasible. He finally accepted the situation, and admitted he would find it difficult to think of me as anything other than Lucy – but still wanted us to marry. There were so many decisions to be made – paramount among them my business in the UK.

I asked him what his boys might think about

everything. He said he'd told them about me. They always knew Clara and I existed, because of the house. When he returned from the UK last month, he told them that if I wouldn't marry him, then he wasn't ever going to marry anyone else ever again.

Apparently, the boys had since encouraged him to return to the UK and try to persuade me to accompany him back to Melbourne. So he assured me they wouldn't be a problem. They're due home any minute now and he is going to talk to them. I asked him not to tell them about my true identity. It worried me that I'd asked Clara to keep everything I'd told her a secret. It's such a huge responsibility to place on a child. I didn't think that Luke should expect the same of his sons. They're still very young.

I've left Luke alone with the boys now. I told him he shouldn't make any snap decisions and take time to talk it through with the boys. Clara and I need to do the same. I made myself a cup of tea and have been wandering about the grounds, admiring how Luke has transformed the place. I made the right decision to let him live here cheaply all those years ago.

It's a relief to be *me* again. For this moment at least. I don't know whether Clara and I will make a permanent move to Melbourne, but I'm confident that no matter what happens we'll be okay – now that Eva is no longer a threat. Eva thought I'd assumed Lucy's identity to get my hands on Lucy's money. She was the kind of person who could never imagine a person doing what I've done over the years for the love of a child. I told Eva's

ashes yesterday that my actions had nothing to do with
money and that her death was necessary. For Clara and
my baby's sake.

Acknowlegements

Thanks to Judy who, as usual, was the first person to read my early draft of *The Wave* as it came off the printer. Thanks for your scribbles over my mistakes and feedback. Thanks to Heather, who read several incarnations, picked up typos and gave her feedback. Thanks to Laura for reading an early version and giving feedback. Thanks to Jackie – a fellow writer (who I've dedicated this book to). She made contact with me from Africa bout *The Wave* and we exchanged many emails on it. Sadly Jackie is no longer with us. Thanks to Bianca in Italy – a professional beta reader whose feedback is always invaluable. A big thank you to Jon who suggested I rethink some of the characters which resulted in me making many changes. Thanks to Liat for your work on the print and digital files and improving my website. Thanks to Bojan from Pixel Studios for your cover work and thanks to all my other friends who have encouraged me to carry on writing and offered feedback on my previous work.

About the Author

L.E. Luttrell was born in Sydney, Australia and spent the first 21 years of her life there before moving to the UK. After working in publishing (in the UK) for a few years she went on to study and trained as a teacher. From the 90s she spent many years working in secondary education, although she's also had numerous other part time jobs. A frustrated architect/builder, L.E. Luttrell has spent much of her adult life moving house and wielding various tools while renovating properties. Although she has written many 'books' now, *The Wave* is only the fourth book she has put out into the wider world. There will be many more to follow.

L.E. Luttrell lives in Merseyside England, but also spends time travelling between there, Wales (UK) and Australia when there is not a Covid crisis.

Follow on   🛑: L.E. Luttrell – Author

          🐦: @LLuttrellauthor

Go to: www.lelutrell.com and sign up the the VIP list to receive a **FREE BOOK**

Lightning Source UK Ltd.
Milton Keynes UK
UKHW040911210921
390925UK00002B/348